Consumed

AN UNLUCKY 13 NOVEL

BAILEY NICOLE

Blurb

Welcome to Black Diamond Resort and Spa…
Growing up in a small town in Georgia,
I never dreamed of starting a band that would blow
up from a viral video or that I'd live in a mansion
on the beach in Miami, Florida.
Since we were seven years old, my best friend Percy
had dreamed big enough for both of us.
He'd always known this would be our future.
But he's been slowly killing me for years, and yet he's
the only reason I'm still alive. He needs me.
He needs me for comfort. He needs me to hold him
and love him. Percy wants to live in my skin,
and even that wouldn't be close enough.
But he doesn't want me the way I want him.
Money. Fame. Medications. Therapy.
None of that could've prevented what transpired
that night, and even though it put me in a mental
health facility, I don't regret it. Not one bit.
Because without him, there is no me.

For those who need a tether to stay alive.

Playlist

"I Need You" by Lynyrd Skynyd

"Upperdrugs" by Highly Suspect

"Serotonia" by Highly Suspect

"Chicago" by Highly Suspect

"Fly" by Highly Suspect

"Mister Asylum" by Highly Suspect

"Lydia" by Highly Suspect

"Pale Blue Eyes" by The Velvet Underground

"Letters To A Dead Friend" by The Plot In You

"Vermillion, Pt. 2" by Slipknot

"Sober" by TOOL

"Bright Eyes" by Art Garfunkel

"The Words ''Best Friend'' Become Redefined" by Chiodos

"Dai the Flu" by Deftones

"Are You Really Okay?" by Sleep Token

Authors Note

Consumed is a standalone, full-length novel in the Unlucky 13 shared world series. This story deals heavily with mental health. A main character has bipolar disorder and borderline personality disorder. A lot of his struggles are written explicitly. This is something I tried to handle with care. I struggle with the same mental illnesses as him, so a lot of it is deeply personal. Having said that, I still had a sensitivity reader assess the story.

I don't want this to be harmful to anyone, so some sensitive topics in this story include:

-Cheating (Not between the MC's)
-Attempted suicide
-Suicidal ideations
-Parental suicide
-Alcoholic parent
-Drug abuse-cocaine
-Alcohol abuse
-Marijuana use
-Violence
-Depression
-Mania
-Panic attacks

Welcome to Black Diamond Recovery Center

Black Diamond Recovery Center was founded in 2001 by father and son, Craig and Dexter Diamond. Wanting a place for those in the public eye to go to seek help with their addiction and mental illness, Black Diamond came to fruition.

We recognize that addiction and mental illness are complex diseases that affect every aspect of a person's life, and we provide comprehensive care that addresses all of our clients' needs. Unlike other recovery facilities, we don't just treat the addiction; we treat the whole person. Our approach is designed to provide support and healing for our clients' physical, emotional, and mental well-being, helping them achieve lasting recovery and a brighter future.

During your stay, you'll enjoy relaxing living quarters, gourmet meals, and luxurious amenities—all carefully curated with your healing and comfort in mind—while still receiving the utmost levels on anonymity.

PART ONE

Beneath The Oak Tree

Epilogue

WINSTON

O ne thing Winston missed about Georgia was the changing of the seasons.

Leaves crunched beneath their shoes as they approached Percy's towering, pale yellow house. When he looked back on his childhood, this was the place he considered home. But when he looked at the treeline to the left, he felt a pull to go see his father. He'd been away for five years now without a single word from him.

Percy's hand landed on Winston's lower back. He hadn't even noticed that he'd stopped walking. "Did you want to go see him first?"

Winston considered it for a moment before nodding. "Yeah. I won't be too long, darlin'."

Percy's soft lips pressed against his, and he immediately felt lighter. "Take all the time you need. We'll be here." He grinned and continued up the path.

Prologue

WINSTON

Winston had been sneaking out of his bedroom window for five years now. His dad knew the worst punishment he could give him was to not let him see Percy, but for someone who got in trouble as often as he did, it wasn't long before he realized he didn't have to stare at the ceiling and suffer through it.

That was what he'd been doing since he'd gotten home from school; just waited for the opportunity to get the hell out of this place. One look at his alarm clock told him it was nine at night, and his dad usually didn't stay up that long, so he hauled himself out of bed. He would be worried about the way the soles of his boots thudded against the floor, but once his dad was asleep, nothing could wake him up.

Winston cracked the bedroom door open and peered into the hallway to check if the old bastard had drunk himself into a coma yet. He found him snoring in the filthy recliner, a beer can in one hand and a lit cigarette in the other. It's the same picture he saw every night, and if Winston were luckier, the cigarette would burn their house to the ground, but he wasn't. It only burned little black holes in the carpet and the recliner. Burned the skin between his dad's calloused fingertips.

There was a half-eaten TV dinner on the coffee table. Mashed potatoes, Salisbury steak, and green beans. A staple in their house. His stomach revolted.

There was no use in wishing things were different. Winston knew that. He really did, but how could he not?

This is all he'd ever known. A drunk father and a ramshackle house in middle-of-fucking-nowhere Georgia.

It was getting harder to see the point.

Percy Lovell.

He was the point and always had been.

It's just that sometimes things got too bleak, and Winston needed to remind himself that he wasn't completely alone in this world. There was someone. The best someone anyone could ever hope to meet in their life, but good fucking luck. Percy was *his*.

Winston stepped back into the room and shrugged on a hoodie. Then, he grabbed the most valuable thing he owned—an acoustic guitar. It was a Christmas gift from the Lovell's two years ago, and he still remembered the way tears had threatened to spill over when he'd seen it. But he'd held them back. He always did. Even now.

After a lifetime of this, it bothered him that he still felt so much. It still stabbed at him from the inside, wanting so badly to explode outward and let the knives fly at everyone and everything in his vicinity. And sometimes he wanted them to plunge deeper. Pierce his heart, shred his lungs, and turn it all black.

He had to hope that someday he'd make it out of here, away from this town. Winston didn't know where he'd go, but he figured he'd just follow Percy wherever he went.

He flicked the lock on the door and slid the old window open, layer upon layer of paint crumbled to the sill, gently lowered the guitar to the dew-dropped grass, and hopped out with a lot less care.

It was autumn. The air was crisper and cooler than the usual Southern fare, and crickets chirped loudly from all directions as he trekked across the yard. Behind a junk car his dad had been holding onto for years was a tree line thick enough to allow privacy. He bet the Lovell's were thankful for it, so they didn't have to see the eyesore that was Winston's house from their stark white wraparound porch.

Damp leaves crunched underfoot, and branches caught and tugged on his hoodie until he made it through to the other side, clutching the guitar to his chest to keep it from harm's way.

Percy's house never failed to make envy claw inside Winston's chest. Two stories tall with pale yellow siding. That porch and the garden Mrs. Lovell kept beautiful all year round. There wasn't a single blade of grass taller than it should be. No junk in the yard—not a cigarette nor a beer can.

He reckoned this was how a home was supposed to be.

"Juney!"

The sound of his best friend's voice snapped him out of it.

Lately, he'd been finding it harder and harder to not get lost in his sadness.

Lately, he found himself wallowing without realizing it.

It was consuming him.

Winston knew it was getting worse because even the sight

of Percy didn't make him feel warmer. There was a bone-deep chill he couldn't shake.

He slogged his way over to the live oak tree toward the back of the house. Each step felt less sure, and by the time he reached Percy, he could've collapsed, but he lowered himself to the ground as smoothly as possible.

The silence that stretched between them wasn't the easy kind.

Winston leaned back. Rough tree bark bit into his pointy spine, a reminder that he needed to eat more, but if it were that easy, he wouldn't be this rail-thin at fifteen when everyone else in their class was starting to fill out. Eating wasn't a thought that crossed his mind more than once a day, and sometimes, not at all. But when it did and he gave in, food felt like cardboard in his mouth and tasted just as bad. When he forced it down, it made him nauseous. Even if he did have a hankering for something, they probably didn't have it in their kitchen. They barely had anything other than roaches.

"Will you play me something, Juney?" Percy asked, barely above a whisper. He was the only one who called Winston that, and it always melted something inside of him.

Winston's middle name was June, after his mom's first name. His dad preferred that he didn't say much at all, but if there was a word that was forbidden, it was that one. The last he heard of it was a year after she died when he got up the courage to ask his dad what had happened. His dad had anger-creased eyes, but they hadn't always looked that way.

He told him, *June had problems even Jesus couldn't fix, try as he might.*

And that was the last of it.

"Juney?"

Winston cleared his throat and rolled his head to the side to meet Percy's round eyes. He knew they were a deep blue color that reminded him of the trip to St. Simon's Island his family brought Winston on a couple of years ago, and he didn't like that he couldn't see them in the darkness.

Percy rested his head on Winston's shoulder, warm and heavy and the only comfort he'd known for a long, long time. He knew he was getting older now, and that maybe it was time to *man up* like his dad had been telling him.

But the last thing Winston would ever do is listen to a single word anyone said unless their name was Percy-mother-fucking-Lovell.

So, he adjusted the guitar, rested it on his thigh, and hugged his arm around the body of it. "What do you want me to play?"

"The Lynyrd Skynyrd song. You know the one—" he snapped his fingers a couple of times, searching for the song's title.

"'I Need You,'" Winston said, and there was a pang in his chest.

Percy nodded eagerly. "Yup. That's the one. You sound just like Ronnie Van Zant when you sing it. It's my favorite."

He swallowed around the lump in his throat as he turned his eyes up to the black sky. He didn't know why that one hurt so bad, but it just did.

His fingertips found the right chords on the fretboard, and he strummed.

This song was an easier one to play. Mr. Seymore, the music teacher at their high school, taught him how to play the guitar. Sometimes they worked on specific songs together like this one, but other times, Winston figured it out by ear.

He opened his mouth to sing. His voice was rough at first, too quiet. There was something about singing that made him feel a little too vulnerable, so he only did it around Percy.

As the song progressed, he grew more confident. The lyrics were about needing someone more than air. About feeling so lonely and wondering if you can even make it. They were about missing someone you love.

And he didn't understand why or how he could miss someone who was sitting right next to him, whose hair brushed along his jaw, and whose body pressed against the side of his.

They couldn't be much closer, and somehow, it wasn't enough.

He didn't think it'd ever be enough, but he would always take whatever he could get with Percy.

He belted out the last few lines, just like Van Zant, but not as well as him regardless of what Percy believed.

"You're so good. I don't know how you do it, but I hope you never stop. You could make something out of yourself with a voice like that."

Winston shook his head, eyes pinging around the yard to catch on the lightning bugs hovering around. "Wish I could dream as big as you, Percy."

Percy sat up abruptly and used his fingers to turn Winston's head to the side, so he'd meet his gaze. Winston's hand tightened around the fretboard.

"Hey, what else do you have to do around here? There's plenty of time for dreamin'."

"Oh yeah? What do you dream of?"

Percy brought one leg up and crossed it. That was fine and all, but his thigh rested on Winston's now. Winston hadn't expected to sweat tonight considering the cool temperature, but he'd be damned if a sweat didn't break out on the nape of his neck and the palms of his hands.

"The beach," he said. "I dream of us living by the beach someday."

Us.

He wondered how long it'd be before that changed. Someday, he would fall in love, and *us* won't mean Percy and Juney anymore.

It was only a matter of time.

The thought of Percy resting his head on someone else's shoulder felt like a kick in the gut that forced all of the air from his lungs. It was a pain like he'd never felt, and it hadn't even happened yet.

His eyes burned, and he looked back up at the sky.

Lately, these thoughts have consumed him like many others. He knew he was on borrowed time, and at any moment it'd run out. It left him in a constant state of anxiety. Things with Percy had been perfect. Always perfect. Nothing in life could be that perfect forever. It just didn't happen.

"You really think we can do that?" he croaked.

Percy moved the guitar from Winston's lap and grabbed his arm. He hugged it close to his chest, resting his cheek on Winston's shoulder. "Of course, we can, Juney. We will."

Something about Percy's closeness and his soft, reassuring words, and the way he said *Juney,* made Winston's heart race. It was a full-on assault, and he knew that Percy wanted it to hurt. It wasn't his fault. None of it was.

Despite the pain, Winston drew him closer and made him hold tighter because it was worth it. He had to take what he could get and deal with the damage later if he ever even made it that far. Most days, he didn't think he would.

"That's my hoodie you're wearin'," Percy said through a yawn.

"Do you want it back?"

"Nope. Looks good on you, Junes."

He said it so offhandedly like he couldn't ever see a world where it was anything more than that. Like it didn't tear Winston up inside.

But once again, it wasn't Percy's fault.

They sat there like that for what felt like hours before begrudgingly parting when Mrs. Lovell called for him to come back in for the night.

When they stood up and waved bye to each other, he didn't know why it felt like the last time. He guessed it'd been feeling that way more often than not. He watched Percy until the front door closed behind him before heading back to his own house.

He climbed through the window and put the guitar in his closet. He worried that his dad would break it in a fit of rage someday, and that was about as hidden as it could get.

Winston kicked off his boots and made his way into the bathroom. The orange light flickered as he paused at the mirror.

His cheeks were gaunt, and the fringe of his hair was just long enough to shroud his eyes. It was supposed to be a good thing, but it wasn't enough. He white-knuckled the grimy porcelain sink as he looked into those eyes. They were just like his mother's. He'd never forget hers because they were right there on his face.

The longer he stood there, the more he felt like he wasn't looking at himself anymore. He didn't feel real. And maybe he wasn't, or at the very least, maybe he shouldn't be.

His father's tired, flinty eyes flashed in his mind.

His best friend's endless ocean eyes did too.

All of it brought him pain.

The levee broke all at once, and hot tears burned tracks

down his face. He couldn't remember the last time that had happened. His chin trembled, and his blood ran cold, but his jaw was set with determination.

He swung open the medicine cabinet and grabbed his dad's bottle of pain pills. Through blurry eyes, he twisted off the cap and poured them all out onto his palm.

He didn't know how many it'd take, but it was all he had, and his brain was static. Void of anything. So, Winston swallowed the handful of pills, gagging and coughing around them. He fit his mouth beneath the faucet and washed them down.

His breaths were ragged as he swung open the door.

He'd thought about this before. Imagined that he wouldn't care about anything, thought the idea of the end would be enough to make it not hurt anymore, but when he looked at his dad's sleeping form, something lanced through his chest.

Winston rushed into his room and locked the door.

Blood roared in his ears. He didn't know what to do. His skin was getting warmer and warmer, something vibrated beneath it. A numbness was spreading throughout him, and he knew it'd be over soon.

He tugged at his hair, ripping at his scalp, and could barely feel it.

Through the haze, he knew he had to do something.

He rummaged through his backpack and pulled out a notebook and pen. It took forever, longer than it should've.

Winston gripped the pen between trembling, frozen fingers and wrote.

*Dad, maybe you can move on now that you won't
have to look at her anymore.*
Mom, hopefully, I'll see you soon.
Percy,

He tried to make his fingers move, but his hand was a lead weight. Drool rolled down his chin and splattered on the page.

Winston's eyes rolled back into his head and enveloped him in darkness.

One

WINSTON

THREE YEARS LATER

"Still can't believe the Mr. and Mrs. let you run off to Florida with a delinquent like me," Winston said. Wind billowed through the cab of Percy's Jeep, so he spoke louder than he usually would've. Having no A/C in the sunshine state was something akin to hell, and they still had a couple more hours to go.

"They know I've got a good head on my shoulders, and you're not a delinquent."

"My stints in juvie say otherwise."

A small smile tilted his lips, making his round cheekbones even more pronounced, and his lips... *God*, his fucking lips.

Winston's eyes slid back to the road. He'd never stopped wanting Percy. These days, it was more of a whisper in the back of his mind, but sometimes, like now, it was a screaming, pounding, clawing thing. It blared like a siren and made sure he couldn't ever forget.

"A few juvie stints does not a delinquent make." He'd bet money Percy rolled his eyes. "Regardless, they still love you like their own son."

Winston pursed his lips and let out a barely discernible scoff.

"We just graduated last week. We're eighteen. We're *adults* now, Juney."

Sometimes he felt like Percy was too naive. Maybe he was tainting him bit by bit, but this was Percy's idea to begin with. He wanted to go to college down here. Wanted to live by the beach, and he wouldn't take no for an answer.

If you don't come, I'll just have to stay here forever.

That's what Percy had told him, and it'd made Winston sick to his stomach. Still did. Because Winston knew he'd never be able to let Percy rot away in their hometown—unrequited love be damned. Percy was meant to have everything he ever wanted in life.

"We're barely legal," he said, shaking his head. "We wouldn't have been able to make this happen if not for your parents paying for an apartment for us."

"We would've figured it out," Percy said with entirely too much confidence.

Winston found that hard to believe, but he kept it to himself. Percy had always been a dreamer.

After another hour of driving down I-95, they made it to their destination. It was half past eight when they drove through downtown. It was nothing like St. Simons, that was for sure. So many people crowded the sidewalk on either side, holding drinks, rowdy as can be. It seemed like there were more people here than in their entire town.

Back home, Winston stuck out like a sore thumb with his leather jacket and ripped-up jeans. Sleeveless shirts that showed off shitty tattoos and a single ring through his lip. Students drove to school in their parent's tractor for fuck's sake, but it looked like he'd fit in just fine here.

They kept following Percy's GPS. "Junes, turn right at the next light," he said, pointing his finger to the right so there was no mistake. He'd taken the navigation job very seriously throughout this road trip.

It was unbearably cute, and Winston doubted he'd ever think anyone else was cute like Percy was. He white-knuckled the steering wheel, crushing the peeling leather to his palm.

Winston's ex, Logan—who he broke up with a day before this trip—did an alright job of sating the constant desire he had for Percy. There weren't many gay guys back home, and none of them were out. He supposed Logan probably did have real feelings for him, but he'd made it clear from the beginning that their arrangement would never be anything serious. It didn't matter that they hooked up for the last two years.

And he really, truly, did not give a single fuck about how awful or heartless that made him because he knew he had a *devastatingly* big heart, but every part of it was reserved for his best friend.

"Oh! Right up there! The last house on the right," Percy said, practically bouncing in his seat.

But as they turned onto the street, there were people everywhere. Parked cars lined the entire road, and there was a swarm gathered in the front yard of the apartment directly across from theirs.

"Well, I'll be damned," Percy breathed. "A real life house party? Not just a bunch of douches in their trucks at some vacant cow pasture?"

Winston huffed a laugh. They had the same train of thought as usual.

He drove slowly since some of the stragglers were stumbling around in the middle of the street, and the strong, earthy smell of weed filled the cabin.

"Is that a cop?" someone yelled.

They must be drunk or high off their ass because they were in a Jeep that didn't even slightly resemble a police car.

By the time they made it to their apartment, Winston's stomach was twisting. Parading down the street kind of felt like walking through the hallway at school while everyone stared at you. Their whispers didn't meet your ears, and you wondered if there was something on your face, or maybe your shirt had a stain on it.

Yeah, that's exactly how it felt.

Percy leaned over, grabbed his hand, and squeezed it. His eyes twinkled in the soft, orange glow of the street lamp. "I'm so happy you came with me."

"I know."

Percy lifted Winston's hand to his cheek and leaned into the touch. The gesture was so soft, and there was a certain level of innocence to it. The twisting feeling Winston had in his stomach melted into something warm. He wondered for the millionth time if Percy really thought this was how best friends were with each other.

"I know I've told you so many times already, but it's just— I've always dreamed of this, and I was so worried that you wouldn't want to leave because of Logan." Percy frowned, but his frowns always looked more like pouts.

Percy had never warmed up to him. Logan was in the closet, but they'd all hung out together a few times.

The only reason he brought Logan around was that he was

tired of spending his free time with someone other than his best friend, so he figured he could kill two birds with one stone. He quickly realized that wouldn't work when, in a surprising turn of events, Percy was almost... possessive of him. It was like the mere sight of Logan put a sour taste in his mouth, and he'd never seen him be so rude to someone *ever*. Percy was the definition of Southern charm and well-mannered as all get out.

He moved his hand around to the back of Percy's neck and threaded his fingers through the long hair at his nape. Winston couldn't believe Percy would even think that. "Logan never even stood a chance, and you know that."

"You're right. No one will ever come before me," he said. His hands tightened where they were hanging on to Winston's forearm.

He ran his tongue behind his bottom lip and tightened his fingers in Percy's hair, just enough for it to get his attention. "Say that again. Didn't hear you the first time."

Percy smirked, looking pleased with himself. "No one will *ever* come before me, Juney."

Winston's dick twitched.

Torturing himself like this was bittersweet, so he tugged him closer and leaned in to whisper in his ear. "And what about me, huh? What about when you get a girlfriend? A wife?" He sounded a little unstable. A little threatening. He knew there wouldn't be a right answer.

Percy pulled Winston's other arm, forcing Winston to hold him closer as if it weren't enough.

The ice in his veins started to thaw.

He talked into his shoulder. "I'm never going to get married—don't want to, and don't care if my parents expect me to. Not that it even matters when you're the most important person to me. If my future girlfriend has a problem with you, then I'll break it off without a second thought. They will come and go, but you and I will stay. Always."

He almost wanted to laugh, wanted to shake his head in dismay. Percy genuinely thought women would be okay with the type of relationship they had.

They lived in each other's fucking *skin*.

Winston was codependent because he was in love with him and had been forever. But what excuse did Percy have for his codependency? They were both complicit in that way—there couldn't be one without the other.

Neither of them knew what being alone felt like, but he figured it would hollow his very core. Turn him to nothing. What could possibly be left without Percy?

"I mean it," He reiterated, ditching the soft note his voice took on when they were together.

Winston tried to mask his disbelief. It wouldn't do him any good and would only hurt Percy's feelings, so he said, "Okay." Then swung open the door, which flew out dramatically. "Why did you want this shit-box again?"

Percy gave him a droll look. "Number one, I think everyone should buy used cars so fewer new cars get manufactured. And the other, more important reason is that I want us to drive on the beach in it. Always imagined it that way."

His stomach flipped, and he looked away with a scoff. "So your beach dream is more important than carbon emissions? Got it."

"Duh."

He slammed the door shut behind him since that was the only way it'd stay closed and smiled to himself.

The first thing he did was grab his guitar from the back seat. He looked at the sticker-covered thing with love. Probably the only thing he loved. And he never counted Percy because what he felt for him was indescribable. You couldn't put a word or a name to something like that.

He also grabbed his duffle bag as Percy wrangled his two suitcases from the back. "I'll get one if you give me a minute."

"Shut up, Juney."

He snorted and looked past his friend's shoulder at the raucous house party. They were really fucking doing it up. People everywhere he looked were upending beer and liquor. Almost everyone had a joint or cigarette in hand.

Percy rounded the Jeep, approaching the front door of their first apartment. He reckoned a lot of best friends grow up and become roommates. This was normal even if it felt fucking absurd that he should be allowed to live under the same roof as someone he frequently imagined impaled on his dick. It was disgusting—the things he wanted to do to him, seeing as how Percy was straight and his best friend who he trusted unconditionally. But this was his biggest secret—the only secret—between them.

There was a padlock on the door that required a code to unlock, and of course, Percy remembered it. Then he was slowly pushing the door open with Winston at his heels. Freezing cold air breezed out, carrying the scent of lemon cleaning solution that he could already taste in the back of his throat.

The tile floors were sparkling clean, the walls freshly painted and there was only the necessary amount of furniture. A couch, coffee table. The space was *very* small.

"This is all the space we need, really," Percy said, echoing his thoughts.

He hummed in agreement. As long as they had separate rooms—and they did—the small living area didn't matter. He

walked toward the hallway, but Percy yanked his wrist back.
"Shoes off," he demanded.

Winston rolled his eyes but dropped his duffel and tugged his combat boots off while Percy slipped his socked feet out of his Birkenstock sandals. Those were the only pairs of shoes either of them owned, and they'd been wearing them for years.

"Okay. Let's go look at the rooms," Percy said, barely holding back his excitement.

He followed after him and was met with two rooms the size of shoeboxes, but damn. He'd take this over the house he had back in Georgia any day, and Percy didn't seem upset about the massive downgrade from his childhood home either. His grin was so big it pushed his round cheeks up so high that Winston could only see a sliver of his blue eyes. He loved how smiling transformed Percy's entire face.

There was a beat of silence. They finally made it, but what were they supposed to do now?

"Well," Percy said. "Let's break in the apartment with some bong rips."

Winston smirked. Percy 'Goodie Two Shoes' Lovell loved smoking weed just as much as Winston loved his guitar, and he thought Percy would've ended up being a pothead even if he hadn't introduced it to him.

But make no mistake, Percy might've been a stoner, but he wasn't a degenerate or a burnout or anything like that. He graduated top of their class, never missed a day of school, and never had a single detention or suspension. Straight A's and all.

"I'm so tired though. Could you go get the stuff from my smaller suitcase? It's wrapped up in my black hoodie." He flopped down on the couch in a mock display of exhaustion.

Winston rolled his eyes. "That's *my* hoodie, by the way."

"Whatever you say, Junes."

Winston used to wear Percy's clothes, but eventually, he got too tall and wide to fit in them, so now Percy wears his. He got a small amount of satisfaction from reminding him of that fact.

He carefully extricated the thick, blown-glass bong. It was swirled black and green and was so ornate it could pass as a decoration. He snatched the tin that all his weed was kept in and brought it out to the coffee table. He took the bong and carefully filled it with a little water from the faucet.

"Oh, Eleanor. Come to Daddy," Percy said airily.

Winston groaned. "Please don't ever say that shit again."

"You're just jealous."

Winston watched as Percy quickly packed a bowl and brought the bong to his lips.

Yeah. Maybe he was jealous of Eleanor.

Percy cleared all the milky smoke with practiced ease and handed it to him. Winston was bringing the lighter to the bowl when there was a knock at the door. Percy quickly stood up to open it, but he was faster. He nudged Percy back to the couch and opened the door.

A sweaty, red-faced man stood on their porch. He looked to be in his mid-thirties. Significantly older than their eighteen.

"Hey, neighbor. I'm Danny. Live right over there where the party is." He pointed across the street as if it weren't obvious.

"Nice to meet you." He considered telling him their names but decided against it for no real reason.

Danny's brows lifted comically. "That's a southern accent if I ever heard one."

He felt Percy's presence next to him before he could respond. "That's right. We hail from Georgia."

Okay, so Percy was high.

Winston pinched the bridge of his nose, but Danny

laughed boisterously. He noticed Danny eyeing the inside of the apartment, his gaze locked on the bong. "Well, you guys seem like cool people. Wanna come party?"

He heard Percy draw a breath to answer, but Winston cut him short. "Not tonight, man. We had a long drive."

"Feel free to hang out whenever. We do this every weekend." Then he turned around and melted into the crowd of people.

"Would it kill you to be a little friendly?" Percy asked as Winston closed the door and locked the deadbolt and slid the chain into place.

"Perhaps. Haven't really tried it out though, so can't be certain."

Percy shoved his shoulder. "Liar. You're nice to me."

He shrugged and grabbed the bong from the table to finally take his hit. "You don't count," he said on an exhale.

"Well, we could've gone over for a little bit. Looks like a good time."

Winston considered it for a moment, and all he saw were red flags. Hard drugs and a ton of hot girls were two things he wanted Percy to have nothing to do with.

His best friend never showed much interest in girls back home, but he knew it'd be different out here. Living across the street from the local party house didn't help his odds.

He sighed. "Some other day. You were *so* tired just a few minutes ago."

Percy's shoulders sagged. "Yeah, you're right. Wow, since when are you the responsible one?"

The thing is that he had always been known to make spontaneous decisions and do dangerous things, but he also never dragged Percy into them. He always wanted him to be safe no matter what, and so what if he sheltered him a bit? He wanted

Percy to stay the same. Didn't want to diminish his dreamer spirit.

If Percy weren't here, he would've been at that party a long time ago. Danny wouldn't have even had to invite him. He'd be drunk off his ass and looking for a good time.

He stretched his arms above his head, easing the stiffness from the drive, before yanking his shirt off altogether. He didn't miss the way Percy's eyes widened. They always did— well, there was always some kind of reaction from him, and it never failed to stroke his ego just right.

"It ain't fair that you get to look like that, and I look like this," he complained, gesturing at his fucking perfectly lithe body.

"We've been over this before."

He rolled his eyes. "Yeah, yeah. But you're just being a good friend."

Winston wouldn't hear it any longer. He crossed his arms over his chest. "Take your shirt off," he ordered.

Percy looked up at the popcorn ceiling like he'd rather die. It wasn't like he'd never been shirtless around him before. They spent a lot of time swimming in the lake and tubing down the stream, but while Winston almost always had his shirt off, Percy held onto his for dear life.

His cheeks colored as he reached for the hem of his t-shirt and pulled it over his head.

Winston tried his best to keep his expression empty, but he gritted his teeth. For lack of a better word, Percy was a twink. Well, he would've been if he weren't straight, but he would never tell him that.

He grabbed Percy's wrist and ran his finger over the top of his hand. "You're really vascular. These veins standing out, they're hot."

His brows furrowed. "There's barely anything there in comparison to yours."

Winston glared at him and dropped his wrist. He brought his hands up to his shoulders, tracing his thumbs over his prominent collarbones all the way up the column of his throat. Percy's Adam's apple bobbed, and it reminded him that this was so fucked up. He could feel heat rushing to his dick as he took advantage of his best-fucking-friend. Because that's what this was, right?

He tugged his lip ring between his teeth. "This is all perfect," he said, trying his hardest to keep the rough edge from his voice.

"It's called being scrawny," Percy muttered.

For a split second, Winston wanted to seize his neck and force him to shut up. He couldn't stand hearing the way he talked about himself. Instead, he simply said, "There's nothing wrong with being scrawny, but you're not. You're toned with muscle. They might not be ripping through your skin, but they are there."

It wasn't his proudest moment, but he slowly trailed the palm of his hand from Percy's clavicle down to his tense stomach. "Muscle," he reiterated.

He took a step back, and it almost physically pained him to remove his hands from Percy's body. It always did.

But this time, Percy stepped forward and pressed his soft hand to Winston's abdomen, and it *burned*. His nostrils flared and his body stilled. He hadn't been expecting it.

"You have a literal six-pack," he said, brows pinched. "Pec's." He wrapped his hands around his bicep. "And look at these arms. Inhuman. Godly."

Winston willed his dick to stop it and tried to calm his breathing, but Percy was fucking groping him.

Groping.

His skin was on fire, and he realized that Percy's hands on him felt even better than his hands on Percy. Maybe because it was unthinkable. He knew this petting was completely innocent, but fuck. It was a wonder he didn't grab Percy and bend him over the couch right this very moment.

Percy looked up at him and his eyes widened before he pulled away. "Shit, I'm sorry. I know you don't really like being touched."

"It's fine," he said, turning around and quickly heading toward the hallway. "You don't count."

He said that a lot because Percy would always be his exception.

Percy grabbed his shoulder to stop him but pulled it back like he'd been burned. "Sorry."

He spun on him, and Percy stumbled back a step. Winston gripped his dainty wrist and brought his hand to his shoulder. Trailed it across his chest, his side, his stomach. It took everything in him to not bring it to his crotch. "See, Percy? Touch me. I've never cared. Nothing has changed."

Percy floundered for a second, his hand still pressed to his abdomen. "Well... you looked like you wanted to murder me."

Guess he hadn't done a good job schooling his expression. "I'm just tired and frustrated with you putting yourself down. Comparing yourself to me."

He could tell Percy still didn't accept the fact that there was nothing wrong with him, but he didn't give him a chance to voice it. "Good night," he said and went into his new bedroom. He'd been dying to get these jeans off, so he quickly undid the button and shoved them to the floor. He tugged at his briefs, readjusting them.

When he turned around, Percy was still standing there, frozen in the doorway.

"Shit, sorry," he said, and Winston was getting sick of hearing him apologize for nothing, but he hurried away and shut himself in his room before he could say anything.

The bed was way more comfortable than the one he'd slept on all his life. He crossed his arms behind his head and stared through the doorway, which he left open so he could hear if anyone tried to break in. It was maybe a bit paranoid of him, but so be it.

He wondered why Percy had looked so scandalized. They'd seen each other without pants on before. Sure, they didn't make a habit of it, but it was a normal thing especially since they'd had gym class together. Maybe Percy was just feeling off, or maybe it was his fault. Things usually were.

He was just starting to sink into sleep when he heard the door across the hallway open. It jolted him wide awake.

Percy's shadowy form moved closer to him until he was right next to the bed, wringing his fingers anxiously. "It's kind of weird sleeping in a new house, isn't it?" He asked.

Winston blinked up at him a couple of times. "I don't know," he said, voice rough with sleep.

"Well... I just. Okay, so. It's," Percy groaned and rubbed at his eyes, struggling to get the words out. "Could I sleep in your bed, Junes? I'm a little freaked out in there."

It was last year when he'd told Percy that they couldn't sleep in the same bed anymore. He said it was because they were getting too big for Percy's bed, and he needed more space to sleep, but that wasn't the real reason. He was all for the slow torture of being around his best friend all the time, but the sleeping situation was dangerous. It was getting to the point that he couldn't make it through the night without getting a hard-on, and Percy slept too close to him. He had no personal space, and he couldn't get any sleep because his cock ached all fucking night and he couldn't do anything about it.

The bed he was laying in right now was twin-sized because it was all the room could afford to fit.

"It's fine. I'll just go back to my room. Shouldn't be scared anyway," Percy said, sounding sad and resigned. Not that he would've told him no before, but he definitely wasn't going to now.

"Lay down, Percy."

"Are you su—"

"Percy."

"Okay, fine. If you insist." He could hear the smile in his voice.

Percy scooted in right next to him. Lying on their backs, they were shoulder to shoulder, but Percy shifted to his side and grabbed Winston's arm. He hugged it and buried his face against his shoulder like he always had.

This.

This was the problem.

Maybe if Percy faced the other way or didn't touch him, this wouldn't be such a big deal. What made it even harder was that sometimes, Percy's leg would end up hooked around his, just like he was hooked around his arm.

Ever since they were kids, Percy had done this, and not only when they were in bed. He never asked him why, not even when they got older, and he still hadn't stopped. It's like he was his baby blanket or his childhood stuffed animal or some shit like that.

It was the hottest thing on the fucking planet.

It wasn't long before Percy hooked his leg around his thigh. His voice took on that soft note as he said, "It's been so long."

He ached. *Fuck*, he ached so bad. How was anyone expected to resist something like this?

"I know," he said.

Percy squeezed him tighter, and his heart thudded against his ribs.

"I know you want your space and stuff now, so I won't make a habit of this. Just tonight. Being in a new bed in a new house in an entirely different state. I'm just overwhelmed is all, and you always center me," he said, somehow managing to sound softer and needier than ever.

He should feel grateful that Percy still needed him like this. He was always waiting for the day when he'd stop. He always thought it'd be because of a girlfriend, but Percy hadn't ever ended up dating anyone.

As much as he couldn't take it, he never wanted it to end.

He swallowed roughly. "I'll always be here. You know that." And because he hated himself, he said, "Until you get a girlfriend, that is."

Percy's head tilted to look at him, and even in the dark, Winston could tell that he was glaring. "What does that have to do with anything?" He retorted.

Sometimes, he didn't understand Percy at all. "Well, when you have a partner this is kind of... this is what you do. You go to them for comfort."

"I know. I'm not stupid, Juney."

"Never said you were, but you've never dated, so it's normal to not know what to expect." That was kind of bullshit. But he was just trying to make Percy feel better.

Percy huffed. "The *only* reason I'll ever stop is if you want me to."

Winston had to make sure he was understanding correctly,

cause surely that couldn't be true. "So, you're saying that even if you had a girlfriend, you'd still need me like this?"

"Of course."

"What about a wife?"

He sighed exasperatedly. "Yes, Junes. This is different, okay? No one else could give me this."

Winston wanted to scream. Wanted to drink a bottle of vodka and punch someone in the face. He wanted to take a bat to someone's brand-new car.

But he inhaled slowly and deeply.

Percy let go of his arm and did something he'd never done before. He cuddled him. Full-fledged cuddle. He moved closer, wrapped his arm around Winston's middle, and rested his head on his chest. Percy's entire body was glued to his side, and the only thing he could do with his arm was wrap it around Percy and hold him.

Percy hummed and tightened his hold, even the leg he had wrapped around his thigh was closer and he could feel... The only thing separating Percy's dick from his thigh was his very, very thin briefs.

Winston could feel it.

Percy's dick on his thigh.

His brain short-circuited and his heart was in his throat, but worst of all, his cock was harder than it had ever been in his fucking life.

He could feel Percy's mouth against his skin when he whispered, "I missed you so much."

It was so twisted. All of it.

But the possessive streak inside of him wouldn't quit, so he tightened his arm around Percy. It brought him even closer, and in a backward way, he wished they'd done this sooner. The warm weight of Percy on top of him was better than anything he'd ever felt.

Percy hiked his leg up higher on his thigh and Winston froze. All the blood drained from his face. Percy's thigh had landed right at the base of his hard cock.

But he wasn't flinching away with disgust or surprise or anything. He just settled in, shifting his body around to get comfortable, which meant rocking his junk against Winston's thigh.

Winston shot his free hand down to Percy's hip, stilling them for his sanity.

"You know I don't care about that right? You don't have to act weird about it," Percy mumbled.

"Act weird about... what?" He asked, really needing him to be more specific.

"This," Percy said as he rubbed his thigh against Winston's aching cock, just once. "It's not the first time you've popped a boner in bed with me."

Winston gaped. "Not the first time? And you- you're okay with it?"

"Did you seriously not know?"

"Percy, what the fuck?"

Percy lifted his head to shoot him another dirty look. "Yeah, you got them all the time. It's a natural reaction to this kind of closeness, especially with puberty and all that. I know you can't help it."

Puberty.

That's all he thought it was. Winston almost sighed with relief.

"If it's any consolation, I got them sometimes too."

Winston was having trouble processing this.

He...

Percy...

Fuck.

How was he supposed to handle this? He couldn't trust his judgment right now. Not one bit.

Percy relaxed again and buried his face into his neck. "You're still being weird," he complained.

He cleared his throat. "I'm not."

"You're stiff as a board, Juney." Something about the soft way he said *Juney* made his cock twitch, and he knew Percy felt it. He had to. "You're the gay one, and you're this squeamish over some boners?"

Winston's nostrils flared. "Well, usually when this happens, I get to fuck the guy who's wrapped around me. So this is a bit different," he bit out.

The room fell silent.

He tried moving from Percy's hold, but he stopped him. "Wait. Where are you going?" He hurriedly asked.

"Need to go handle this," he said, grabbing his junk. Maybe if he was blatant about it, he could scare Percy off.

Even in the dark, he could see the ridiculously sad pout on his best friend's face. "Did I say something wrong? I'm sorry," Percy paused, considering his next words. "How many guys have you... have you done that with?"

A crease formed between his brows. "Done what? Fucked?"

Percy nodded against his shoulder.

"Why do you want to know that?" Winston asked.

Percy answered his question with another question. "More than ten?"

He scoffed despite himself. "There weren't even ten guys who swung that way in that entire town."

The sigh Percy let out sounded relieved, and he couldn't

figure out why he'd be relieved over something like that. Did he not want his best friend to sleep around or something? No. He didn't think Percy was judgemental like that.

"But you'll find more here, I'm sure," he said.

"That's the plan, yeah. I clearly have a working dick that's in desperate need of attention."

Percy's arm and leg tightened around him. "No."

Winston couldn't have heard that right. "No?" he repeated.

"We just got here, you know. It's our first time being alone together, and I want to enjoy it for a little while without having to share you with other people."

Jesus Christ, he couldn't take it when Percy was possessive of him. He reached down and nudged Percy's thigh down so he could readjust himself. He squeezed firmly, and couldn't believe he was squeezing his fucking cock with Percy right there.

"What do you expect me to do then?" He breathed.

He huffed a frustrated breath. "I don't know, okay, Junes? I just need you to stay. Need you to not go and get a boyfriend just yet cause then everything will be different."

"Nothing would be different," he rasped.

"It would. If you had a boyfriend, you wouldn't need me. You'd hang out with him every day, talk to him all the time, and play guitar for him. He'd become your best friend."

Winston's cock throbbed again. It seemed like it couldn't stop, and everything Percy said made it worse. "Don't want a boyfriend. Just hook-ups," was all he could get out.

"That somehow doesn't make me feel better," he said.

Winston groaned and dug the heel of his palm into his shaft. "I'll do whatever you want, Percy. Just tell me, and I'll do it. You know that."

He could feel frustration rolling off Percy in waves. "I don't want to share you at all," he snapped. "With anyone."

The palm of Winston's hand slowly but firmly rubbed against his shaft. He couldn't even help it. The shit Percy was saying was making his brain go hazy. It was hard to form a logical thought, and he was having trouble not shooting his load in his briefs.

"So you expect me to do what? Just jack off forever?"

"Not forever," he whispered, lips grazing against his neck because Percy couldn't be any closer than he already was.

His hand moved a bit faster. Only a bit. "How long?"

"I don't know. Is it really so bad?" He knew Percy was frowning, and Winston hated it.

He used his other hand to grab the nape of his neck, fingers tangling in Percy's long brown hair as he held him in place. Percy groaned and melted into the touch. Most guys didn't like being handled like that, but he did.

"It's not bad, Percy, but it can't last forever. Don't you want to have sex too?"

Percy's hand trailed along his side. He knew it was just an absentminded thing, but it still sent goosebumps across his skin.

"No... I mean, not really," he muttered.

"Not at all? What are you thinking of when you get hard then?" He asked even though he definitely didn't want to know the answer.

"I don't know. What I mean is that there's never been a girl that I wanted to do that with. Never got that feeling."

Winston blinked, trying to make sense of that. "It's just cause there weren't many options back home. That's all." It pained him to say that. The thought of Percy being with someone else made him violent with rage.

"Maybe you're right," he said.

He dug his fingertips deeper into Percy's neck.

"Is that what you want? You want me to find someone, so I'll leave you alone? I've been clinging to you for a decade now. It was bound to happen—"

"Stop," he interrupted. His next words came out strangled, but he really needed Percy to quit saying shit like that. Not only did it hurt, but it scared him. A deep, gut-wrenching fear. "Percy, I don't want you to go anywhere. I don't want you to even leave this fucking house. I don't want to share you with anyone, but I was trying to be reasonable. This isn't... it's not normal. Not healthy."

Percy shifted around, and then he felt it. Percy's dick was hard and digging into his thigh. He tightened his hand around his shaft harder than ever before, gritting his teeth. Why was he suddenly hard when he'd been soft just a moment ago?

"You don't want normal and healthy, do you?" Winston asked, already knowing the answer.

Percy's response was soft. "I don't care what it is. I just want to keep my Juney."

His cock pulsed in his hand at that, and his mind was clouded with it. He shoved his hand under his briefs and fucking finally wrapped his hand around his cock without a barrier. He slid his hand down lower and grabbed a handful of his sac, but his knuckles bumped into Percy's thigh.

He froze.

Shit, what was he doing? He couldn't rub one out right now.

He cleared his throat and tried to get up again, but he felt the soft press of Percy's hand on his crotch. His hips lifted from the bed, chasing the touch on instinct, but he forced himself to still. "Percy, what—"

"I can do it for you," he whispered.

Blood roared in his ears. "You what? Why? No," he stammered.

Percy's fingertips slid beneath his waistband. They brushed against his leaking cock head, and his body spasmed.

"You don't want me to?" He asked, actually sounding offended. "You said this wouldn't work because you need to have sex, but I could help."

"Help?" He panted. "Percy, you're straight."

"So?" He wrapped his hand around him and at that very moment, fire blazed out from the point of contact to each of his limbs. He felt it explode behind his eyelids. "If that's your only issue then I'm doing it."

Percy's hand moved, sliding up and down his shaft tentatively. "Am I doing okay?"

Sweat beaded on his forehead, and his breaths were uneven. He could've fucking laughed at that question if it weren't for the fact that he was so genuine. "You're doing good," he said hoarsely. "Better than good."

Percy's hips jerked forward, pushing his own erection against Winston's thigh. His mouth was open at his neck, hot breaths fanning over his skin. This was too fucking much for him. He shoved his boxers down just enough, wrapped his hand around Percy's smaller one, and guided his movements. Made him go faster and harder. He was fucking Percy's fist, thrusting his hips up into it.

"This isn't what friends do," he ground out between thrusts.

"But you like it, right?"

He groaned. "Doesn't make it okay."

"Do you still wanna find someone to hook up with?" He asked, daring him to say no.

Winston felt delirious. His mouth had fallen open, and his eyes rolled back into his head. "I don't," he said, but he knew this wouldn't happen again. Knew he'd end up needing someone soon. "Your hand feels so fucking good."

Percy whimpered. It was muffled by his neck, but close enough to his ear that he heard it clearly. It was the softest, sweetest fucking sound he'd ever heard. He needed to hear it a million times over. "Fuck," he groaned. "It's been so long."

"You can have it whenever. Whatever you want."

Percy had no clue what he was saying. Whatever he wanted? He huffed a laugh.

Percy whimpered again. That one noise made his orgasm surge through him. Endless ropes of cum shot from him while his body trembled through it. His hips were still jerking when he said, "Don't stop. You're gonna come too."

He grabbed Percy's hip with his wet hand. His grip tightened, and he forced him to keep moving.

Percy fumbled around before he found purchase on his shoulder, and used it to thrust against him. His strokes were long and hard, punching.

He guided his hip back and forth, resisting the urge to slide his hand around and grip his ass. A strangled groan left his throat.

"I'm close, Juney," he whined.

Winston was drenched in sweat, and the muscles beneath his skin were tense from all the restraint he'd been using. But he couldn't hold it back this time.

He yanked Percy's head back with the grip he still had on his neck, and brought his mouth to Percy's ear. "I fucking love it when you call me that," he growled roughly. It was almost animalistic.

Percy's hip stuttered beneath his palm, and a broken moan bubbled from his perfect lips.

They lay there, Winston with his briefs still halfway down and cum drying on his stomach, and Percy with a whole load in his briefs. There was no way that was comfortable. This didn't feel as awkward as it should—not for him, anyway.

"We should go get cleaned up," he said.

Percy was limp at his side, still holding him. He felt him shake his head no. "Just stay."

So he gritted his teeth and didn't move, but this whole situation was bothering him. He'd just gotten a handjob that he'd fantasized about having for a sad number of years. He should feel happy, for once in his fucking life, but he felt worse. Percy did that because of a weird sense of obligation. It was almost like a bribe.

He didn't want Percy to feel used.

This shouldn't have happened, but he was never able to say no to him. And with Percy's hand on his cock, he never stood a chance.

He wanted a drink. Wanted to forget this ever happened, so it would be easier to not let it happen again.

"Stop thinking so hard," Percy mumbled.

"Don't you regret it?" He blurted out. "You just did a lot of gay shit with me, your best friend. That doesn't bother you at all?"

"Not really, no. I meant everything I said. I don't want to share you," he said with so much conviction.

He pulled his lip ring between his teeth while he tried to form a coherent thought. "But I'm a guy."

"You're my Juney."

He never wanted to stop being his Juney. Couldn't even stomach the thought.

Percy spoke again. "I know how messed up it sounds, and I don't care. If it's unhealthy, then so be it. That's just how it has to be for now."

For now.

Not forever. This was only temporary for Percy until he found another person who he needed this badly.

Maybe Winston would have to make sure that never happened.

Two

PERCY

SIX MONTHS LATER

P ercy blinked his eyes against the afternoon sun blinding him through the windshield. He'd quickly learned that Florida and Georgia's weather weren't all that different. It was either hotter than hell or pouring rain with tropical storm-force winds. He reckoned the only difference was winter. They didn't really experience a true winter here. It was November and not a jacket in sight. Either way, he would always prefer sunshine.

His heartbeat was unsteady as he turned down their street. He used to look forward to coming home. Being away from Juney for any length of time was more than awful. But they'd been here for half a year now, and over the last few months, things had started to change. Percy had sort of expected that, but he'd held on to hope anyway.

He parked and got out quickly, slamming the door shut. The front door swung open and Torin and Gage stepped out, looking every bit like the troubled musicians they were.

"Hey, Percy," Gage said before wrapping him in a big hug. The smell of weed was permanently embedded in Gage's clothes. He wasn't sure how often he actually washed them but figured it wasn't a lot.

Torin gave him a quick hug too. He wore Birkenstocks like Percy, and his wardrobe was significantly less black than Gage and Juney's. "Winston is buzzing a little high today," he said.

Percy frowned. "Yeah, he's been ramping up all week." A sick feeling churned deep in his stomach.

They parted with shrugs and walked back to the apartment across the street from them. They were Danny's roommates and Winston's bandmates.

He heaved a sigh and went inside the house. It would be nice and bright in there, but Juney insisted on covering the windows with black sheets. He liked it better this way. He did leave the kitchen window and Percy's bedroom window untouched because Percy said so.

The air was heavy with smoke. He internally winced as the thought of his parents seeing the apartment like this crossed his mind. He thought about that a lot actually.

Juney put his guitar down when he walked in and looked at him with glazed-over eyes. He was wearing the faux leather jacket he'd bought when Percy decided to be vegan. Juney went vegan too, claiming it'd be easier for them that way. "How were English and Psych today?" He asked. Usually, he was genuinely interested in his day, but not lately. He looked distracted like a million thoughts were racing behind his eyes.

He walked over and collapsed on the other side of the

couch. "Not bad. Only a few more weeks left in the semester," he said, but his head wasn't really in it.

"Why are you all the way over there?"

Percy avoided his best friend's eyes and grabbed Eleanor from the coffee table. There was a bowl already packed. Juney did that for him on days he had off. He landed a job doing commercial landscaping, and he hadn't voiced any real complaints about it. He went to work super early and got off at one p.m., so he had a lot of the day to himself.

He put the lighter's flame to the green buds and filled Eleanor with smoke before inhaling it all.

"Percy," he repeated.

Finally, he met his pinched gaze. "I just wanted to sit alone for a minute if that's okay with you." He laughed lightly and let his heavy lids slide shut.

Percy was starting to feel insecure about his attachment to him. Juney *never* touched him first. Didn't hug him or hold him. Didn't ask him to sleep in his bed. Percy initiated all of it, and it took him a while to realize that. What made it hurt more is when he thought back to all the time they'd spent together growing up, it had always been like that.

Juney had always insisted that he was possessive of him, but Percy could tell it wasn't the same.

Percy *needed* to be held by him. He needed to be touched, loved, and given all of his attention. Juney didn't need any of that—probably didn't even want it. He was only possessive in the way that his life depended on Percy being safe. He hovered and wouldn't let him talk to certain people. He constantly needed to know how Percy was feeling and if he was okay.

He didn't mind any of that. It was the opposite. It made him feel loved and cared for which was always the feeling Junes invoked in him. He knew it was bound to end someday. That much was certain.

"You never want to 'sit alone for a minute.' What's wrong?"

There it was.

Junes only wanted to make sure he was okay. He didn't actually miss holding him. His heart panged. Sure, it was a ridiculous thing to be upset over, but he couldn't help it. He knew his constant need to be the center of his best friend's world wasn't normal.

"Everything's fine," he lied. "I'm assuming we'll be going to Danny's tonight?"

"You're lying to me," he said, surprise pitching his voice higher.

Percy's eyes flitted to Juney before his gaze landed on the collage of musicians they'd covered the wall with. Posters, magazine pages, records.

"Look at me." Juney's voice was hard.

He hesitated but slid his eyes over to him in the end.

Juney's brown eyes took in every little detail, then he scoffed and shook his head. "So it's happening?"

He tugged on his fingers. "What are you talking about?"

"You got a girlfriend, didn't you?" It was more a statement than a question.

He gasped. "What? No, Junes. When would I even have time to do that? You're with me every minute of the day unless I'm in class."

Juney sagged back against the couch and looked at the ceiling, the ounce of emotion he'd shown was completely wiped from his face. "Exactly. Class," he said stiffly.

He wanted to scream at him for being so stupid and for making him want to give up already. Couldn't even resist him for an hour, especially not when he was upset. Juney's reactions—good or bad—tended to consume him dangerously.

Percy knew how stupid it was, but he'd do anything, so he said, "You can look through my phone. I swear there's no girlfriend. There isn't even anyone in my life who you don't know."

"If that's the case, then what you're saying is you don't need me to comfort you anymore? That's what it is?"

He winced internally and tried to sound as confident as possible. "I don't. You're finally free from my clinging." His voice only shook a little.

Junes swung his head around to look at him, and what he saw written in every hard line there made him flinch. "This means I'm free to hook up then, yeah?"

A lead weight sunk in his stomach, but he had to follow through or this was all for nothing. He knew this was the right thing to do, and they'd be better in the long run if he got this over with now. "I don't care what you do. It's time for both of us to get more... independent. I should probably try dating too."

"Dating," Juney echoed. "Independent."

He looked like he was having trouble parsing through it all. Meanwhile, Percy was gutted and barely refraining from flinging himself into Juney's lap right this very moment.

His eyes burned.

Why had he thought this was a good idea?

He couldn't help it. Maybe if he held him one more time, it'd help ease him into this major adjustment.

He moved across the couch lightning fast, threw a leg over Juney, and sat in his lap. The relief was immediate until hands landed on his shoulders and pushed him back. It shocked him.

"What are you doing, Percy?" He asked coldly.

Being this close to him made his voice softer on instinct. It was something he couldn't help. "Just one last time."

His brows were still set in harsh line and his jaw ticked, but he slipped his hands under the back of Percy's shirt and pulled him to his chest. Percy buried his face in his neck and committed the feeling of his rough hands on his skin. The feeling of gripping his body between his thighs and squeezing him back. A sigh turned into a moan when his lips met just below his jawline.

This was the hardest Juney had ever squeezed him, yet he wished he could do it even harder. Needed to be closer.

Juney's hand trailed from his back, up to the nape of his neck where he gripped his hair tightly. He'd been doing that forever, but it never failed to send shivers down his spine.

The longer he straddled his best friend's lap, the worse he felt. His brain was clouded and fuzzy, and there weren't any logical thoughts to be found.

Juney's hands fell to his hips. He gripped them tightly and hissed. "Stop moving like that," he ground out.

He hadn't even noticed he'd been moving, but that did happen sometimes if he was too dazed. "Sorry, Junes."

The hard-on beneath him was unmistakable, and it made him feel bad. Junes got them a lot. Percy had gotten them more often as time went on, and it made him think that he might not be a hundred percent straight. He was probably bisexual, but he still hadn't ever felt that way about anyone else. So, he just didn't know.

He would never tell Juney that, unless he absolutely had to —which would only be if he fell in love with a guy, but he didn't see that happening now or ever.

Everything was all messed up now. If he told Juney, it would probably ruin their friendship, or at the very least, put a stain on it that would last forever. All this time he'd been using Juney for comfort and it had always been platonic, but if he found out, he'd think Percy had been lusting after him over all these years and taking advantage of him.

His skin crawled and he felt like he might be sick, so he drew in a deep breath and peeled himself out of his best friend's lap. He could've sworn Juney's hands tightened as he did.

"That's it. That's enough. I promise I'll control myself from now on."

"You're giving me whiplash," he said. Percy frowned. "Well, since we're really doing this, will you help me out for old times' sake? My cock is fucking throbbing."

His breath hitched at how raw and crass Juney was being. He swallowed roughly, looking down at the massive thing in his jeans. That was when his own dick twitched and he figured it was the least he could do.

Juney saw his decision and tugged his shirt off. Percy knew it wasn't for his benefit, but his body was something he could look at all day. It was just perfect. Juney ripped open the button on his jeans, shoving them down just enough that his cock sprung free. It lay heavily on his lower abdomen, and Juney fisted it right away. His hold was always so tight when he jacked off. He strangled his shaft, choked it. Nostrils flared and short pants burst from him.

"If you wanna help me, get on the floor right here."

Percy slid off the couch so fast it should've been embarrassing, but he didn't think anything could be embarrassing with Junes at this point.

He situated himself on his knees, between Juney's spread legs, where he was eye level with his abused cock. His eyes followed the veins on his hand, up his forearm, to his strained bicep. The ridges on his abdomen glistened with sweat. When he met Juney's gaze, he found it already locked on him. Mapping his face, his body. Everything. All while he beat his dick a few inches from Percy's nose.

His cock ached now too, but he ignored it.

His palms landed on Juney's thighs, and he wondered how exactly he wanted him to help.

Juney's hand started jerking erratically, and he bit out the words, "Wrap your lips around the tip. I'm about to come."

He gasped, and his heart pounded in his chest as he leaned forward and wrapped his lips around the leaking tip. He'd only ever given him handjobs, so this was... new.

His cheeks colored as he thought about the picture he made, blinking up at Juney with the tip of his cock in his mouth. His best friend's eyes were fixed on him. Beads of sweat dripped down his face, getting caught in his eye, but he didn't wipe them away. Didn't blink.

He made a noise Percy had never heard before. It was a low, guttural groan, and it washed over him somehow. Then, Juney's heavy cock pulsed on his tongue. His cum spurted over and over again in thick, hot ropes. It seemed like it would never stop. But Percy let every bit of it roll down his throat. That's what Juney had wanted from him.

When he finished, and his cock began to soften, Percy still had his mouth on him with his head resting on Juney's thigh. Juney cupped his face gently and looked at him with something heavy in his eyes. He couldn't place it. But he knew this was the last bit of closeness he'd ever get from his best friend, so he didn't break his gaze.

That thought tied his stomach in knots. He couldn't take it anymore, so he pulled back, letting Juney's hand fall as he stood. He didn't even bother fixing his jeans. His eyes were dead in a way Percy had rarely seen them. It was a sign of bad things to come. Things had already been escalating, and all he could do was be there for him. Make sure he didn't do anything too dangerous. And most importantly, make sure he stayed living.

"Maybe you should stay in tonight. You look really tired," he said. It was the logical thing to do considering he hadn't been sleeping much at all these past few days. Percy would wake up to the sound of Juney's rough voice, singing over his guitar. He'd been spending a lot of time writing music.

"We're playing tonight," he said blandly.

"You play almost every Friday. You can take a break if you want to."

The corner of Juney's lips pulled up into a small smirk that was stark against its dead backdrop. "Don't want to. I'm fine."

He didn't sound fine, and Percy struggled to reconcile with the fact that it was his fault. Danny's house is the last place he wanted to be tonight, but he had to go. Wouldn't let Juney go alone in this state. Hell, maybe it would help him deal with sleeping in his own bed from now on. If he was out late, he'd have to spend less time in there. Less time alone. "Okay. I'll go too."

"If you insist," Juney said. He could already see the mischief on his face—the twinkle in his eye.

His hands shook at his sides. "Gonna go take a nap since we'll be out all night."

"In your bed, right?"

Percy swallowed. "Yeah."

Juney scratched his jaw absentmindedly before looking at him. "Good," he said, cold as ice. Percy's heart twinged, but he didn't say anything. He knew Juney had been wanting the bed to himself for a long time. He stood up and grabbed his notebook from the table, his guitar, and left without a word. Sun streamed in when he opened the door and cut out when he closed it. The darkness in their apartment hadn't ever felt so stifling.

Percy's eyes lingered on the door for too long until he was finally able to pull himself away and go to his room. He opened the door and flinched. It was so bright in there. Probably the brightest room in the house.

It felt like a cage, but at least it wasn't dark. He felt less alone. He heaved a sigh and went to the living room to get Eleanor, and cradled her in his arms until he made it back.

He reckoned if he smoked enough weed, he'd be comatose in no time. All the anxiety and racing thoughts and heartbreak would go away.

It wasn't long until his head was hitting the pillow and his eyes were heavy enough to fall closed. He curled in on himself, hugging his knees close to his chest, and hoped for good dreams.

He sprung awake to the loud beating of drums and so many overlapping voices. The party was in full swing at Danny's judging by the noise, but his room was bathed in darkness. He wrestled his phone from his pocket and checked the time.

Fuck.

Fuck.

He scrambled out of bed and yanked his shirt off. It took a minute for him to process that none of his clothes were in there, but he didn't have time to think about that.

When he opened Juney's door, he was engulfed in his

smell. It was hard to describe but it was everything to him. The smell of home and comfort and awe. Nothing tangible.

It will be okay, he told himself. Just because he wasn't going to be glued to Juney anymore, didn't mean he would have to lose this too. He's not leaving.

He pulled Juney's drawer open and grabbed a thin, gauzy button-up. He left the shirt open. His confidence had been boosted significantly since their move. Then, he grabbed his pack of joints from the coffee table, knowing he wouldn't be able to handle tonight without them.

Percy lit one up right there and took a couple of hits to steady himself and ease the bad energy eating away at his stomach. Based on the way his hand trembled as he opened the front door, it hadn't worked all that well.

He schooled his features anyway. A cool breeze whipped through his long hair and skittered over his bare stomach. The goal was to walk straight into the house where he heard Juney's band playing, but he kept getting pulled aside by people.

It was a new thing he'd been adjusting to since moving here. People actually wanted to talk to him. They thought he was interesting. Laughed at his jokes. People wanted to be his friend.

No one back home gave him the time of day.

There was one guy in particular who he always seemed to run into, and there he was, right next to the front door. "Percy," he said.

"Jazz," he responded as he passed the joint to him. There wasn't anyone back in his hometown that looked anywhere near as cool as him except Juney, of course.

Jazz planted a hand on the pole right behind Percy. The black tank top he wore was basically painted on over rigid muscles and tattooed skin. Percy seldom found people attractive, but Jazz had a way about him.

"I don't think I've ever seen your hair down," Jazz said.

The way he looked at his hair and face and bare stomach made Percy forget how to speak. He could feel the blush heating his cheeks, and it kicked him back into gear. "Thank you," he mumbled before hurrying into the house without even getting his joint back.

He hadn't noticed the music had stopped, but he didn't see Juney come out the front door, so he was either in here somewhere or in the backyard.

Danny's apartment was so filthy that Percy used to wonder how he lived in this level of squalor until he went over during a weekday and found the place looking nothing like it did on the weekends. Turned out that he and Gage and Torin cleaned up after their parties. It was a lot of mess to clean up every week, so Percy found their dedication to partying admirable.

He navigated through people as politely as he could with a litany of *excuse me's, sorry's,* and *thank you's.*

Gage wasn't sitting at his drum set and the guitars were propped against the wall near their amps. A lot of rowdy stuff happened at these parties, but no one ever messed with their equipment, so it was safe there. He saw Danny in the kitchen waving his arms around dramatically, probably telling one of his crazy stories. If Percy wasn't anxious as all get out, he would've patiently waited for Danny to finish talking. "Danny! Have you seen Winston?" His first name felt all wrong on his tongue.

"He's in their room," he said, not bothered by the interruption at all. It's a good thing he asked because he hadn't even considered that.

He didn't mind the weed smoke clouding the house, but

he grimaced at the foul stench of liquor. He wasn't a drinker. Never had been.

The closer he got to their bedroom door, the worse he felt. The gnawing in his stomach was impossible to ignore. The best-case scenario was that they were chilling and smoking weed away from the party for a minute. Taking a break. And he didn't want to think too deeply about the worst-case scenario.

His palms were sweaty. He steeled himself as best as he could before turning the knob and pushing the door open.

Gage and Torin kept their beds butted together in the corner. There was a small couch on the other side, so altogether it formed a U with a table in the middle.

He expected them to be on their beds and Juney to be on the couch, but Juney was on his knees, leaning over the table with a short straw in his nose. Sweat-soaked strands of his shaggy hair concealed his eyes as he plugged one nostril and snorted an entire line of what appeared to be coke.

Percy didn't care who was in the room. He was pissed. "You told me you weren't going to do coke anymore. That was only three months ago."

Juney swiped the back of his hand across his face and didn't even meet his eyes. He just got up and moved to the couch where a guy was sitting.

He hadn't noticed him sitting there before.

But then Juney sat right next to him and draped an arm around his shoulders.

He was *touching* him.

The last time Percy saw him touching someone like this was when he dated that idiot, Logan.

And he recognized this guy now. He'd just seen him with Jazz's tongue shoved down his throat last weekend.

Juney grabbed the guy's chin with one hand and kissed him hard.

All the blood drained from Percy's face, and he froze. He'd never been confronted with something like this before. His mouth went dry, and a cold sweat broke out on his forehead.

Gage and Torin were looking at him like it was out of their hands. They'd probably tried to stop him already.

Percy didn't really know what to say, and he was trembling. He could turn around and leave right now. That was what he should do, but the idea made his hackles rise.

He forced himself to close the door and ambled around the table to sit next to Gage.

Juney still hadn't answered him, but he reckoned there was no point. The proof was right in front of them.

He pulled out his pack of joints and lit one. He inhaled that smoke like it would heal all of this. Cleanse him of this confusing mish-mash of feelings that he couldn't articulate.

It settled over his skin like a warm blanket, and that's about all it did. He passed it to Gage.

He took it and wrapped an arm around his shoulders, pulling him into his side. Percy's breath hitched. He'd never touched him more than a greeting hug. They locked eyes as he hit the joint. Gage's eyes were heavy with something like sadness or maybe exhaustion. It was the same look he knew was on his own face.

Torin leaned into his ear and whispered, "We tried, but he's strung too high." He sounded just as gutted as he knew they both felt. This was only the beginning.

"Fucking *wow*, Gage," Juney's voice cut across the room, splitting right through the loud music in the house. Gage's arm stiffened. "You've been gazing into his eyes long enough. Go ahead and fucking kiss him already."

Percy's stomach hit the floor at his goddamn feet.

"Fuck you, Winston," Gage said without any bite.

Percy still hadn't looked back at the couch where Juney and that guy sat. There wasn't even a small part of him that wanted to, and he thought it might take decades to wipe away the memory of Juney kissing him. He knew he shouldn't care, and he knew that Juney wouldn't usually be this callous toward him no matter what happened between them.

"Is this another revelation you've had tonight, Percy? You're on a roll," his voice dripped with sarcasm. "Gage does it for you? Hate to break it to you, but he's a guy."

His heart raced, but he thought it better to not give Juney more ammunition. He'd only get worse.

"If you don't shut the fuck up and leave him alone, then I will kiss him. How about that, Winston? Why do you care so much?"

The gnawing in his gut had worked its way to his chest, and he didn't know what to do with it all. But he was angry. So angry that Juney was doing all this. Hurting him so badly.

"Do it," Juney said. "I dare you."

Gage looked at him tentatively, asking permission with his eyes. Everything was happening so fast, but he was going to do this.

Gage's hand wrapped around the nape of his neck—the same spot Juney always touched—and he pulled him closer until their lips met.

Percy hadn't ever kissed someone. He didn't know what it was supposed to feel like, but this was good. Gage moved his lips just right. It was almost like a dance. He was getting lost in it. He brought his hand up to cup Gage's cheek. He wanted more, and Gage anticipated it. He opened his mouth a little wider and let Percy's tongue slip past his lips. The slow slide of their tongues gave him goosebumps. He didn't want to stop. Still wanted more and deeper.

A thought crossed his mind, and it was a crazy one, but Juney was being pretty crazy tonight, so why should Percy hold himself back?

He swung his leg over Gage's and sank to his lap. Gage's groan vibrated through his mouth. His hand stayed at Percy's neck and the other slid under his open shirt, settling on his back.

A loud crash had him jolting away from Gage. The room was empty and they both looked toward the open door.

It sounded like...

Gage hurried out of the room and he followed, feeling like he might be sick.

Juney had destroyed Gage's drum set. Both the bass and snare drums were sliced open and Juney was smashing them with a hammer. Wood splintered everywhere, and he looked up at Gage through sweaty tendrils of hair with a twisted smile on his face.

Blood thundered in Percy's ears, and his mouth hung open. He didn't know what to do, didn't know what Gage would do. He couldn't let him hurt Juney, but he could tell Gage was a millisecond away from pulverizing his face.

Gage took a step forward, and Percy stumbled in front of him with his hands on his chest. He looked up at him with pleading eyes. "Please don't," he begged. "You know he's all messed up in the head right now."

Gage's dark eyes met his, and there was murder in them. "Get the fuck out, Winston," he said.

"Oh really?" Juney laughed. "Come on. Hit me. Let's fight about it."

Gage took another step forward, and Percy pushed him

back. "Just leave it."

He saw some of the red-hot anger clear from Gage's eyes. He was still furious, but it was enough to make him turn around and slam his bedroom door shut behind him.

Juney looked smug, and Percy couldn't take it anymore. Everyone stared at him with wide eyes as he made his way through the room—less politely this time around. He crossed the street with wide steps, thankful for the breeze cooling his scorching skin.

Percy was kind of desensitized to Juney's rage and unpredictability. There was a lot more to it. This is just how he was sometimes. Sometimes it was triggered by something, other times it wasn't.

Juney's footsteps followed behind him. "You're not getting let off from this either, Percy," he said.

He hadn't thought he would.

He opened the front door and headed straight for his bedroom. In a perfect world, Eleanor would help, and then he'd go back to sleep and escape this hellish day. He knew that wasn't how this was about to go down though.

The door slammed shut behind him and Juney was hot on his heels.

"Percy," he said. His voice was barely a whisper. If it weren't for the light on in the kitchen, they'd be in pitch-black darkness. "What was that, Percy? Huh?"

Juney was unraveling right in front of him, but he wouldn't give in so easily this time. Percy leaned against the wall and crossed his arms over his chest. Juney looked like he was employing every tactic he had to stay calm, and Percy knew he wasn't helping the situation by ignoring his question.

"What. The fuck. Was that?" He spoke through gritted teeth.

Percy's expression was blank as he watched him, and that was too much for Juney. He took a few quick steps, closing the space between them. His forearms landed on the wall on either side of his head, and once again, Percy was surrounded by his scent. His sweat. Everything. He bit the inside of his cheek.

"Do you want to tell me why you just made out with my friend, who's a *guy*, right in front of me?" Through the anger rolling off him, there was genuine confusion.

"You told him to kiss me," he said, and Juney pulled his arm back and smashed his fist against the wall behind Percy. Up close he could see every bulging vein in his face and neck. "Why does it even matter? You relapsed on cocaine!" That was the real thing they should be worried about right now, but even he knew it was futile. All he could think about was his best friend kissing some random guy at Danny's house.

"Who gives a fuck about the cocaine!" June tried catching his breath. "You... you... have you ever even kissed anyone before tonight? You haven't. I know you haven't. You would've told me."

Percy gaped at him. He couldn't believe this was even a topic of conversation right now. They both knew Percy was completely inexperienced, other than the very few things he'd done with him, and that Juney was the exact opposite. He didn't like thinking about it.

Juney didn't wait for an answer that he already knew. "What the fuck was that?" He asked for the millionth time. "Please, explain. I'm— this can't be right." He raked his fingers through his hair, tugging at it as he looked up at the ceiling.

Percy spoke clearly. "You snorted a lot of coke—definitely more than what I saw firsthand. You were kissing a guy whose name I don't even know. You told Gage to kiss me, and he did. Then, you destroyed his drum set. That's what happened."

"He wanted to kiss you. I could tell by the way he was looking at you," he said with so much conviction.

"No, he didn't, Juney. He was just comforting me because he could tell I was upset." As soon as the words left his mouth, he knew he'd made a mistake.

"He fucking WHAT?" Spit flew from June's mouth with the force of his yell and his fist slammed into the wall. Drywall crumbled to pieces, falling on his shoulder. "He *comforted* you?" His voice was strangled. "And you let him? You wanted Gage to comfort you, but not me?" His fist cracked against the wall again before he stumbled back a few steps.

"It's not like that, Junes," he said, a pleading edge to his voice. His heart was starting to crack right down the middle. "You know it's not—"

"I don't know anything," he said, resigned. "Do I even know you?"

Percy gasped and unshed tears stung his eyes. "Of course, you know me. Just stop this already. We can talk about everything tomorrow."

Juney grabbed Percy's chin and leaned down to look directly into his eyes. His nostrils flared with every huff of breath. "Do you want to fuck Gage?" Percy opened his mouth to answer, but Juney cut him off. "Don't you fucking lie to me. I saw the way you ground your ass down on his dick."

Percy balled his fists at his sides. "I don't want to fuck him, and if I did, why would it matter so much? He's your friend, someone you care about. You know he's a good guy."

Juney lips twisted up into a cruel smile as he slid his hand from Percy's chin down to his neck. He wrapped long, calloused fingers around his throat and tenderly brushed his thumb against his racing pulse. Juney looked down at him. "What makes you think I care about him? The only person I care about is you—Percy fucking Lovell. I don't even *see* anyone else. They don't fucking exist."

Percy's breath hitched at the vehemence behind his words. He knew Juney cared about him. He did. "Then why did you do things you knew would hurt me tonight?"

He shook his head slowly. "I didn't do anything to hurt you. I did it to help me." His hand tightened around Percy's throat, just enough to remind him it was there. "I've been hurting for a long, long time, and it doesn't let up. It gets worse every day, but *this* day will be one for the fucking books, Percy."

He unclasped his hand from Percy's neck and gently stroked his knuckles down his cheek, leaving a sticky trail of blood. There was so much pain behind his seemingly dead eyes that it choked the air from Percy's lungs.

Juney stepped back, and a chill swept over Percy's bare chest. Juney took all his warmth with him and tried to walk away, but Percy grabbed his arm—clung to it for dear life. His stomach twisted up in knots. He felt like something very, very bad was happening. "Please," he pleaded. "Can we just forget this happened?"

Juney wouldn't look at him. "You will. I won't."

He floundered, losing the little composure he had left. "But what did I do? Why are you acting like—why are you doing this to me?"

He finally turned his head and looked at him. His eyes were devoid of any feeling. Empty. Percy knew it was his mask, and he knew it was hiding something awful, but he didn't know what exactly. Couldn't pinpoint it.

It didn't matter at this point.

Juney had iced him out.

"This is what *you* wanted, Percy."

Three

WINSTON

Torin had been banging against the front door for a long time, but Winston wasn't going to get up any time soon. Percy could handle it.

His eyes burned. He'd been staring at the ceiling for the past couple of hours, watching the white popcorn texture morph and blur. There was a deep-rooted ache in each one of his limbs and a faint sting coming from the torn flesh at his knuckles.

Bang, bang, bang. "Open the fucking door, dumbass."

He barely heard it over the incessant ringing in his ears. If Gage was with him, and he wanted to finish what he started last night, he was in for a rude awakening. Winston was past the point of caring. The numbness in his mind was a much-needed balm that settled him low, low, low. He wanted to sink into his mattress, wanted it to engulf him in its warmth. His mattress was so good to him.

Torin barged into the bedroom, and Winston didn't even flinch. He could tell Gage was right behind him by the clinking sounds that the chains on his jeans made.

"Winston, you need to get up," Torin said. What a stupid fucking thing to say. "We need to show you something. This is serious."

He peeled his tongue from the roof of his mouth. "Talk to Percy. I'm trying to sleep."

Gage spoke this time. "You stubborn asshole. After the shit you pulled last night, I wouldn't be here if it wasn't important. Just go ahead and tell him, Tor."

Winston wished Gage would punch him in the face. Knock some teeth out. Make him bleed. If he were anyone else, he'd be comatose right now. That's what he deserved. It's not like any of them have a ton of money to throw around for a new drum set.

"We went viral," Torin said.

"What?" Winston had no recollection of anything before Percy showed up.

Torin thrust his phone in his face, holding it there for him. On the screen, he saw their band performing one of their original songs in Danny's living room.

"That's from last night," Torin said. "Someone recorded us and posted it. Look—a million views and counting. Thousands of comments. Hundreds of thousands of likes and who fucking knows how many shares."

Winston felt a headache blooming in his forehead. "Wow, that's great. Now leave me the fuck alone."

"There's more, Juney. We've received inquiries from multiple record labels. They want to sign you guys."

The sound of Percy's voice soothed him in a way that wasn't natural. A person shouldn't be capable of something like that. But he hadn't forgotten about yesterday. Things were different now—even if he wished Percy would come hold him.

He hadn't been lying when he said this was great, but he couldn't handle any of it right now. He'd been running on little to no sleep for too long, and he was crashing. He'd been spinning circles around everyone, and now he would fade away. That's how it always went.

He heaved a sigh. "Please, just give me a few days, and we can talk about it, okay? I just can't right now."

He was met with silence.

Percy cleared his throat. "That's fine. They won't make any decisions without you."

All he needed was Percy's reassurance.

His eyes drifted shut, and his head filled with thick fog. Finally, he could sleep.

He'd barely regained consciousness. It was just enough to know that he wasn't asleep anymore, but not enough for his eyes to open or for his body to move. He stayed there for a while, noticing the thin layer of sweat sticking to his body, and that his bladder was going to explode. If it weren't for that, he'd go back to sleep or lie there for a while, but he wasn't too keen on pissing himself.

Winston knew he was a pathetic sack of shit who couldn't handle a single day of life. He was lucky anyone tolerated him at all, but he wished they didn't because it left him feeling indebted to them. He felt like he needed to try harder, be more likable—give, give, give. That's why he defaulted to not giving a fuck, and even that stirred up guilt that lived in the back of his mind.

Right now, he had a lot to make up for. More than usual, and he wasn't sure he could.

Gage might brush it off for the sake of the band, but their friendship will be in tatters.

Torin would probably understand, but still be on Gage's side at the end of the day.

Percy... that hurt the worst. Everything that happened cemented what he already knew. He thought he could look past it, but this torture had gone on long enough. The wounds Winston had inflicted on himself would never heal. They couldn't. Being in love with someone who doesn't love you back, and having it dangled in front of your face every day for years would fuck even the strongest person up.

Percy treated him like they were already together. If anyone knew how close they really were, they'd think they were fucking crazy. Handjobs? Cuddling together every night? Best buds didn't do that.

Winston had been taking advantage of Percy. He wouldn't deny it. What was worse is that Percy had to have known, but he was that good of a fucking person. He swallowed Winston's cum for fuck's sake. He loved that hard.

When he kissed Gage... when he sat on his lap and looked like he would've let Gage fuck him right then and there, Winston didn't have a rational thought in his brain. His heart wrenched in half. It was a jagged split, one that had zero chance of healing right.

He didn't handle pain well. He'd wanted to kill Gage. Hurt Percy. Anyone. Anyone who got in his way would've gotten fucked up. Winston would be sitting in a jail cell right now without a single regret.

That was how he knew there was no way in fucking hell that he could watch Percy love someone else the same way Winston loved him.

There was a lump in his throat. His eyes burned, but he wouldn't cry. He hadn't cried since his mother died. Nothing could be as painful as that. Not even this. He needed to hold onto that fact. It was the only thing that would keep him together.

He'd attempted to commit suicide when he was fifteen. He lived, but the thought—the temptation—never truly went away.

Existing made him sick to his fucking stomach. It was pointless and exhausting. Painful and unfair.

The only thing that kept him here was Percy. He'd never forgotten how his attempt had affected him. It was tattooed behind his eyelids.

Percy was all he had, and even that was killing him.

Fiery acid clawed its way up his throat. He gagged on it and begged it to go back down. Pleaded with it to stop. His joints creaked as he hurried to lean over the edge of the bed. It was just in time for his sickness to spill onto the spotless tile floor. He coughed and gasped for breath, and a harrowed groan fought its way out of his raw throat.

His heart raced as he tried to steady his ragged breaths.

The bedroom door flew open, and Winston wanted nothing more than to be six feet under. Percy was the only one who'd ever seen him in this condition, and it was humiliating. Pathetic. Disgusting. It was no wonder Percy didn't love him back.

The bed dipped, and Percy gently rubbed his back. He gagged again, but there was nothing left. He dry heaved and wished he was strong enough to tell Percy to not touch him. To get the fuck out. He had to try.

"I'm okay. I can handle it," he croaked.

"No, Juney. Please let me help you. You need a shower and some food." Percy's voice was feather-soft. So, so perfect. It was already making him feel better which made everything worse.

"Just go."

"But, please—"

He moved a bit, knocking Percy's hand from his back. "I'm not dying, unfortunately, and I'm not a child, so I will handle it."

Winston was terrified.

He could barely see Percy's face through the pitch-black, but his small gasp was enough to inflict more injury on Winston's heart. He got out of bed, ignoring the aches in his body and making sure to not step in the mess he made. The room was so quiet all he could hear was the low hum of the air conditioner. It was unsettling as all hell, and he needed to get out of there. He crossed the hall and shut himself in the bathroom.

He'd sooner die than look at himself in the mirror, so he walked past it and turned the knob to get the shower going. There was a twinge in his lower abdomen. He remembered he needed to piss, so he kicked his briefs off and did that. Then, he put the seat down with more force than was really necessary. It didn't matter that only guys lived here, Percy wanted the seat down.

Winston always did whatever Percy said—even something as minor as this. Listening to Percy came naturally to him. Hell, he trusted Percy more than himself. He was Winston's walking conscience.

As soon as his foot hit the shower floor of the tub, he knew he was in for a long bout of thinking, and he hated thinking. Preferred when his head was empty. He spent a lot of time brushing his teeth and letting the toothpaste foam down his chin. The water was scorching his skin, and he leaned his forearms against the wall and let it pour over him until it ran cold.

He dried off and came to some brutal realizations. He would never cut Percy out of his life, but he would need to create boundaries between them. He wrapped the towel around his waist and registered that he still felt like death incarnate. But, hey. At least he was clean.

His room smelled like bleach. Of course, Percy had cleaned up his vomit. He was as thankful as he was irritated, but he put on some gym shorts and headed into the living room. Percy was sitting on the couch, and he flinched when he saw Winston. His eyes were bloodshot, and he was stoned out of his fucking gourd.

Percy was so cute when he was stoned. Usually so affectionate and happy. His happiness wasn't bright or stifling. It was calm and assured, but he didn't look so happy at the moment. He was frowning at Winston with round, sad fucking eyes.

Winston scrubbed a hand down his face and sat on the other couch. Percy shook his head. It was like he'd gotten his hopes up and was let down, but he took a hit from Eleanor and looked at him with more resolve.

"How are you feeling," Percy asked.

Winston wanted to skip this bit. "I'm fine."

Percy blinked at him. "If you're worried that I'm upset over last night, don't be. It's okay—I promise. We both made some mistakes, but we can move past it."

He settled into the couch with his legs spread wide. Percy's eyes dropped down, and Winston cleared his throat before speaking. "We can move on from it or whatever, but some things have to change. For good."

"Like what?" He sounded so small.

Winston clenched his fists to ground himself. "We need to be normal. Regular friends like Gage and Torin. Just like what you said yesterday after class. That's what we need to do."

"But we're closer than Gage and Torin," he said.

Winston swallowed. "We still can be, but there comes a point when we need to have some space. We need to live our lives."

A wrinkle formed between Percy's dark brows. Neither of them could process it. That's how unimaginable it was. Winston couldn't help but get lost admiring him—even at a time like this. Winston could never ignore him.

His hair had grown past his shoulders, and his face was softer than Winston's. Percy's nose was perfectly straight, and his was crooked with a bump on the bridge. He was just beautiful in every way. He'd never met anyone who even came close to looking as flawless as his Percy did.

"I don't like this," Percy said solemnly.

They met each other's eyes and gazed long and hard as if it would change anything. Winston wouldn't let it. "Me neither," he responded. For once in his life, Winston was trying to do the right thing.

Percy nudged Eleanor toward him and fixed his gaze on their Led Zeppelin poster. "Looks like a lot of things are about to change."

Winston took a ridiculously big hit, wanting to get as high as possible. So, he took another. Weed made him feel soft around the edges just like Percy did.

It took him a minute to catch on to what Percy had said. "What are you talking about?"

Percy's eyes widened incredulously. "Your band is a viral internet sensation. Millions of people want your music just as much as they want to fuck you. Life's about to change for you, Junes."

Winston could tell that he was trying to be positive and happy for him or some shit, but there was a bitter edge to his words. "It's going to change for all of us," he corrected, looking at the side of his face pointedly. "If we sign with any record label, you're part of the deal. You can be our manager."

"I'm sure the label will give you one of those."

He scoffed. "Fuck their manager. As I said, if we're as hot of a commodity as you say we are, we'll stand our ground." He set Eleanor back on the table. "What do the guys have to say about this?"

"They're ready when you are."

All Winston ever wanted to do was make music. Percy had always told him that he was going to make it big someday, and Winston always told him that was a pipedream. Most musicians never got a taste of stardom, and considering the cards he'd been dealt, he didn't have high expectations for himself.

He shouldn't be surprised that Percy was right. He somehow always was. That's why he needed to be their manager.

He wouldn't get his hopes up about any of this seeing as how it was all too good to be true, but he didn't have anything else to do with his life. He reckoned this was exactly the distraction he needed. "Invite them over."

"The record label in Miami seems to be our best bet. Think they're called Heatwave Records," Percy said.

The room was tense. Winston still hadn't talked to Gage about what went down, and the wound was still fresh. So, Gage was brooding. He was really good at that.

Torin held the other end of the conversation. "Yeah, they're only an hour away, and they're a pretty big deal in the industry. Especially for rock 'n roll."

"Okay, for fuck's sake," Winston blurted out. Torin and Percy's eyes snapped to him, but Gage had already been glaring in his direction. "I'm sorry about the fucking drum set."

Gage's arms were crossed in front of his chest, and he looked entirely unconvinced. "You're a goddamn lunatic," Gage said succinctly.

Winston shot to his feet. "No shit! If you hadn't noticed yet, let me clarify: I haven't been doing well. There's something wrong with me." He was getting increasingly louder. "The fact that I didn't sleep for three days and wrote ten songs should've tipped you off. But it should've definitely been obvious when I relapsed and snorted an eight ball of cocaine in your bedroom with Casey-motherfucking-Claremont of all people."

"Juney—"

"I'm not finished, Percy." He was red in the face, and blood thrummed in his ears. "So, why, on God's green fucking Earth did you think it was a good idea to listen to a single word I said?" Each word was like a punch.

A muscle was jumping repeatedly in Gage's jaw, and his nostrils were flared. He was ready to fight. Winston knew it.

"Juney," Percy hissed. "That was the furthest thing from an apology I've ever heard."

He snatched his cigarettes from the table and walked

outside, slamming the door shut behind him. If they were going to fight, they might as well do it outside.

He smoked angrily, with jerky movements and venom in his eyes. How many times would he need to relive his mistakes? No one ever wanted to move on. No one ever wanted to brush it under the rug.

And he knew he fucking deserved it. His lips curled. It didn't matter that there was something wrong with him or that he wasn't always in full control. Actions had consequences, especially when they hurt other people. But what everyone failed to notice, was that it hurt Winston even more.

The front door opened and out stepped Gage, looking no more pleasant than he had when Winston left.

Winston ran a hand through his hair and planted his feet on the concrete. "Go ahead. Punch me one time. Maybe twice if you don't knock me out the first time."

"Shut up," he grumbled.

Winston beckoned him with his fingers. "No, come on. You really should. How often do you get a free pass to rock my shit? I know you've always wanted to."

Gage sighed and lit a cigarette of his own. He looked out past the palm trees, face set in stone. "You were right. We knew you hadn't been well. It's not an excuse, but it can't be ignored. Have you at least tried to get help?"

There was no such thing as help. Nothing could fix him. It was just like his dad said.

June had problems even Jesus couldn't fix, try as he might.

"Save it for someone else, Gage. I'm not the one."

Gage growled in the back of his throat and crossed his big arms in front of his chest. "Stubborn. Asshole."

Winston chose to give him that one. "We'll get you a new drum set. Heatwave Records will, I'm sure."

"Better be top of the line," he grumbled. Winston had no doubt it would be. "Looks like we're gonna be fucking famous, Winston. Telltale Dream will be known worldwide."

"Telltale Dream," he repeated to himself. Guess some of them did come true.

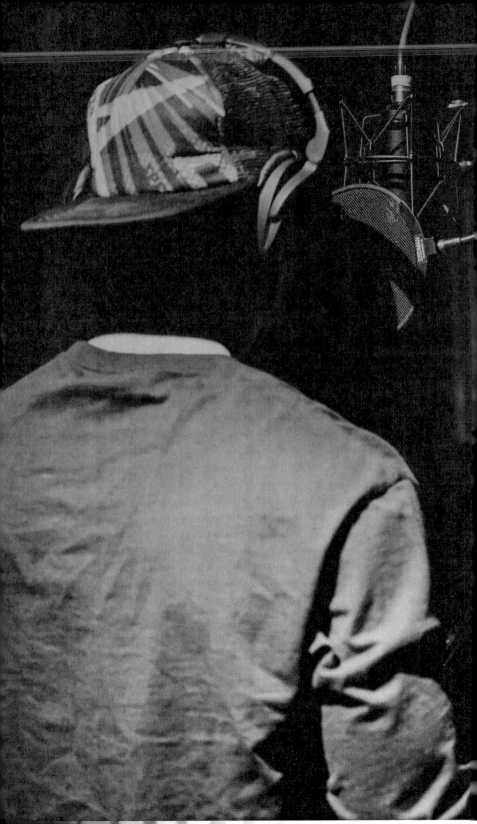

PART TWO
Telltale Dream

Four

PERCY

THREE YEARS LATER

"After a kick-ass North American tour, Telltale Dream is back in the studio working on their second album. As it would turn out, they're more than just a viral internet sensation. They've established themselves in the industry as a progressive metal band with no distinct genre. With a lead singer whose voice can make anyone cry, a soulful bassist, and a lightning-fast drummer, this band has been topping the charts with every single they release. So, it's no surprise that Telltale Dream will be doing their first international tour later this year. Dates to be announced soon."
—Electric Metal Magazine

Percy shut his laptop.

"Sounds great," Torin said.

"Lovely's bubbly bullshit hasn't steered us wrong yet," said Gage.

Percy looked at Juney for confirmation he knew he wouldn't receive. Juney was laying on the faux leather couch in their in-home studio with a throw pillow over his head. Percy nodded his head once and cleared his throat. "Right. I'll give her the okay to publish the article."

Lovely Toussaint was a *lovely* Haitian woman who was a writer for the most popular metal mag around. They trusted her to keep their reputation as clean as possible, and she sure had her work cut out for her. They all had their own set of issues, but Junes caused the most problems for them.

Gage threw another pillow at him.

"Quit." Juney's words were muffled.

"Get the fuck up. We still have three songs to write before the album's complete."

The album was supposed to be finished two months ago, and Heatwave had been hounding Percy for updates.

Juney tossed his pillow to the floor. "So fuckin' write 'em then. You and Torin can handle it." His words slurred together with his southern drawl that was stronger when he was tired. It was a slow, lazy way of speaking that Percy didn't get to hear from him much anymore. Hadn't for years since Juney drew a line in the sand and never once wavered from it.

Torin spoke up, way calmer than Gage, who was fuming. "We all like getting fucked up, Winston, but we still have to work. And really, it can hardly be considered work because we love doing it."

Juney stood up and stretched. The hem of his shirt rode up and showed a sliver of his toned abdomen. Percy's heart thudded once, and then he looked away. He felt bad whenever he missed *his* Juney. Despite everything they'd been through together and the past few years of distance, he still yearned for him. His touch. His attention. All of it.

It might not have been a raging fire anymore, but it was an ember that refused to go out. Percy knew it would burn forever.

Percy had been forced to realize how needy he truly was without having Juney there to fix it.

So he'd moved on.

Juney opened the door, letting in a bright stream of light. "I'll be ready to put pen to paper tomorrow. I promise. But it's Saturday night, and I'm going out. Feel free to join me."

The problem was that Juney didn't only go out on the weekend. He could be found drunk or high on any given day of the week. Percy rarely participated. After so many failed attempts at getting him help, he couldn't stand by and watch as his best friend got worse and worse.

"Fuck it. I'll go," said Gage, not putting up much of a fight at all.

Torin nodded. "Count me in." He went wherever Gage did.

They all looked at him, and his mouth went dry. He hated bringing up his boyfriend. "Emilio planned a dinner for us tonight."

He didn't want to see the look on Juney's face. Tried to avoid it, but he couldn't.

Juney was smiling—a perfectly normal, if not a little tired, smile. "Have fun."

Even Torin and Gage looked confused. In the six months they'd been dating, Juney hadn't ever acknowledged their relationship. It was as if it didn't exist. "Thanks," he said, but it sounded like a question.

"Actually, invite him over for drinks afterward. Gage and Torin have met him. I reckon it's about time I do, too."

Percy was having a mixture of feelings he didn't understand. "Oh. I don't know about doing that today—"

"Ten o'clock. We'll be here," Juney said. Then walked out of the room without another word.

Torin looked like he was going to say something but closed his mouth and shook his head. Gage spoke for him. "You know Winston's been somewhere between depressed and numb for many, many months."

"Yeah," he said, already anticipating his next words.

"I wouldn't be surprised if he shoots back up again. Remember what happened last time... with Gage?" Torin asked.

"That was different," Percy said even though he didn't know how it was different.

None of them were experts on Juney's mental health. All they could do was observe him and help in whatever way they could. And Juney wasn't the only one who struggled mentally either. Gage and Torin did as well.

"Hey, at least we'd get the songs done," Gage said, trying to lighten the mood.

Torin facepalmed.

"This will be fine," Percy said. "There's no reason why it wouldn't. Emilio is very likable."

Juney had no reason to cause any problems tonight. They might've been under each other's skin in the past, but it'd been three years. It was rare that they were even alone in the same room, and Juney had fucked his way through the U.S. and Canada.

So what if Percy dated?

Percy tied his hair up in a bun. It'd been flying around in his face from the breeze coming off the water. They were out on the deck of an oceanside restaurant. It was ridiculously expensive to eat there, and if it weren't for Emilio, he never would. It didn't matter how much money Percy made, he didn't think it should be spent on a meal that he could make at home for a fraction of the price. Maybe he'd go out every once in a while, but this was how Emilio exclusively dined.

But just like Percy, Emilio hadn't always been wealthy. He clawed his way up from the bottom without the help of going viral on social media. It was admirable, but they had different outlooks on some things.

"How was work today?" Emilio asked. "Are they making progress on the album?"

For some reason, Percy never wanted to paint Junes in a bad light. He didn't think anyone needed to know how he struggled unless Juney himself wanted them to, but Emilio asked about this often. It was Percy's job after all. Percy just kept dragging it out. "The guys were hungover from last night. Weekend warriors. We'll be back on it come Monday," he said.

Emilio nodded and took a bite of his steak, and Percy took a bite of his salad. It was loaded with all kinds of nuts and fruits and drenched in a raspberry vinaigrette. This restaurant didn't have many meat alternatives or a diverse menu at all, but Emilio loved it. Sometimes they went to places he liked too, so it was a fair trade-off.

"You're good at what you do. I could never keep those guys on track. They just don't have a determined mindset. No discipline," he said offhandedly. He didn't dislike them and had been nothing but nice. This was just Emilio's view on things because of the way he grew up. Those were things he valued.

"They're also very good at what they do. That makes it easier for me." He took a sip of his water.

It was nice being able to look out over the water from the deck their table was on. He could never get enough of the beach. When he moved his gaze back to Emilio, he was smiling at him. "You're so stunning, love." There were hearts in Emilio's deep brown eyes.

Percy's cheeks reddened, and he reached across the table to grab his boyfriend's hand. Emilio's fingers were soft against his as his thumb stroked circles atop Percy's hand.

Emilio looked up at the sky, so Percy followed his gaze. It was free of clouds and painted orange and pink and yellow as the sun set in the distance. Percy was getting lost in its beauty, feeling far, far away from life.

Then, his view was interrupted by a plane flying across the sky. It was one of those planes that carried banners, and Percy squinted to read it.

WILL YOU MARRY ME, PERCY?

Percy's heart catapulted into his throat. He knew there was little to no chance of that being for a different Percy, and when he turned to look at Emilio, his chair was empty. He hadn't even noticed that he'd let go of his hand to kneel on the deck. Right there. In front of everyone.

His mouth went dry, and he felt a bit faint.

"You're the best thing that's ever happened to me. I thank God every day for bringing you to me and keeping you here. I can't think of a better way to spend the rest of my days than with you."

Tears sprung to Percy's eyes. He didn't know why. He wasn't feeling as happy as people always looked when they were proposed to, but Emilio's words meant something to him. They were so sincere. Percy avoided looking at anyone else on the deck. He hated having this kind of attention directed at him, and he wanted it to stop. "Yes," he blurted out. "I will."

A single tear tracked down his face, and Emilio swiped it away with his thumb before proffering the ring. It was a sweet gesture. He was always so endearing. Percy let him slide the silver band on his finger and clasped his cheeks, pulling him down for a kiss.

People were clapping and congratulating them, and all Percy could do was try not to feel mortified.

He stood up with Emilio and let himself be engulfed in his arms. He gave good hugs that made Percy feel warm inside. Emilio slid his hand up to the nape of his neck, and his skin immediately crawled at the contact. He recoiled, pasting a smile on his face. He felt guilty, but Emilio didn't seem to notice. It wasn't his fault that Juney had always held him there. That his body rejected that touch from anyone else.

They sat back down, finished their dinner, and had some dessert. All the while, Percy felt a strange sort of detachment. It wasn't right. He should've been soaring with happiness.

Percy reckoned he was just scared of the unknown.

"Well, are you ready to go back to my place?" he asked.

Emilio nodded easily. "I'll be meeting the other band member right? What's his name? Winston, I think? Your best friend."

There was a lump in Percy's throat. He held out hope that Juney would give Emilio a fair chance.

They stood on the front porch of Percy and the band's Mediterranean mini-mansion. Emilio was holding his right hand, and Percy privately thought that they shouldn't do that, but he didn't want to be disrespectful to his new fiancé.

That's when he remembered the silver band on his finger. He shoved his hand into his pocket. He had a bad feeling about this despite doing nothing wrong. Juney didn't see logic sometimes. Percy had always been there to help him with that, but now he was on the other end of it.

Emilio reached forward and opened the tall, arched door. They stepped inside. "Shoes off," Percy said. He didn't know why he was whispering.

"I don't allow shoes in my house either. That'll make things much easier for us when you move in."

Percy nearly choked. He hadn't thought of that yet. Hadn't even processed the engagement, but he kept walking, leading Emilio through the foyer into the massive living area. More faux leather couches. Sleek furniture and instruments scattered about. Everything was black or varying shades of green—even the walls and vaulted ceiling.

"Well, you can definitely tell that rockstars live here. Oh, a full bar," Emilio said, getting distracted. Percy wished he could drink his way through this get-together, but he'd just have to smoke weed instead. Yeah, he was going to do that now.

"Help yourself to a drink, Emilio," Percy said. He would've made Emilio's drink for him if he knew anything about alcohol.

He crossed the room to grab Eleanor off the shelf. Eleanor was so finely crafted that she looked like expensive decor. He didn't think to feel nervous about smoking in front of Emilio because he'd been fully transparent about it with him until he saw the expression on Emilio's face. His brows climbed into his hairline, nostrils flared slightly. Emilio looked at him with contempt.

"I told you that I smoke weed," he said as he sat on the couch to pack a bowl.

Emilio cleared his throat but sat down next to him with a crystal glass. It was half-full with amber liquid that Percy assumed was whiskey. "I guess it's just strange being confronted with it, love."

Percy considered him for a minute. "Did you want me to go to a different room? I'll go if the smell or smoke or whatever makes you uncomfortable."

The distinct sound of the front door opening made Percy's heart trip over itself. He forgot what they'd been talking about immediately.

Torin glided into the room. Percy always thought Torin moved so fluidly. Emilio stood up to greet him. He shook Torin's tattooed hand which struck Percy as odd, but whatever. Emilio was a bit formal like that. Gage followed behind him. He was shirtless and his skin shone with sweat, pierced nipples on full display. He shook Emilio's hand roughly and dismissively before turning the other way and grabbing a beer. They had partnered with Bud Light, so they had a reach-in refrigerator that was always stocked.

Emilio was still frowning after Gage when Juney walked in, but he recovered and extended his hand. "You must be Winston." He was casual and relaxed.

Juney probably looked relaxed to Emilio, but Percy could tell he wasn't. Not at all. He didn't shake Emilio's hand. Instead, he openly scrutinized him. His eyes tracked over every inch of Emilio before settling on Percy. The corner of his mouth was curved into a smirk that spread into a full-blown smile. Percy's brows knitted together. Juney thought something was very funny.

He maintained that unsettling smile as he swung his gaze back to Emilio and finally shook his hand. Black nail polish and fingers covered in chunky rings met Emilio's neat and polished hands. "It's so nice to meet you. Emilio, right?"

Emilio had the same assuredness as he did with the other bandmates. "Yes. Emilio Alvarez."

Juney shook his head. "Winston Jennings, but Percy calls me Juney. Sometimes Junes."

Emilio nodded slowly, and Juney patted his shoulder a few times before snaking past him to make himself a drink which was just a full glass of vodka. His go-to.

"Will you roll me a joint, Percy?"

Percy was ashamed at the way he nearly clambered to do anything for Juney, but he kept a straight face and said, "Of course."

Emilio was still standing there sipping his drink when Percy sat down. Gage was laying on the other couch with one leg planted on the cushion and the other sprawled widely on the floor, messing around with his drumsticks. Torin had one leg crossed beneath the other with a hand atop Gage's sock-covered foot. Gage always looked ready to fight, and Torin was the exact opposite.

Percy was distracted with opening his jumbo-sized jar of weed and pulling out just enough for the joint when Juney sat so close to him that their thighs touched.

His breath hitched, and his cheeks flushed. It was a full-body sensation. Juney draped his arm across the couch behind Percy's shoulders and spread his legs wide. Percy's flooded with heat from Juney's proximity alone, but the touching? He couldn't remember the last time they touched at all. Percy was having trouble pulling in air.

His eyes searched for Emilio and found him on the other side of the room, looking at all of their guitars. So, he steeled himself and risked a glance at Juney who looked imperturbed while watching Emilio's every move.

Percy's heart ached painfully. He hadn't felt something like this in a long time, and it was tearing him apart. He wanted to sit on Juney's lap, bury his nose in his neck, and whisper softly to him about his day.

But, even though his body resisted it, he leaned forward and away from Juney's arm to grind the weed. Finding a coherent thought was impossible, so he zeroed in on the process. Emilio was oddly keeping his distance, not even looking at them.

"He doesn't like that you smoke," Juney said from behind him. Percy bit down on his lower lip as he nodded. "He doesn't like that you call me Juney either."

Percy made sure to keep his left hand hidden from him as he rolled the joint, shielding it from Juney's eyes with his body. "I don't think that's true. He seemed perfectly fine with it."

He could hear the smile in Juney's voice. "He wasn't."

"Whatever. I don't care if he doesn't like it." He folds the paper over the weed, tucking it in before licking the other side and sealing it closed in one swift movement.

"You're so good at that. You roll the best joints." The tips of Percy's ears reddened. Why did Juney have to say it like that? So low and rough. He didn't want to acknowledge how much he missed Juney's praise. It mattered so fucking much to him.

Percy put the joint between his lips and lit it with his right hand. He took a couple of puffs to get it burning evenly before passing it to Junes. Then, he grabbed Eleanor and took a long, slow hit, clearing all the smoke. Tingling warmth skittered across his skin. He wanted to relax back against the couch, but Juney's arm was there.

Emilio finally turned around. His eyes darted between all four of them but landed on Juney. He didn't seem put off by Juney's proximity.

"Do you listen to our music?" Juney asked easily, but there was an almost imperceptible edge to his words.

Emilio shook his head. There was a single lock of black hair grazing his forehead that Percy had always liked. Perfectly neat hair except for that one bit. Percy had difficulty being around perfectly conventional people. "I'm not into that kind of stuff. I like music that's a little less loud."

Juney tilts his head to the side. "Do you like Led Zeppelin?"

Emilio shrugs with a lofty air about him. "Never put much thought into it. 'Stairway to Heaven' was good, I guess."

Junes laughed.

Percy's favorite band was Led Zeppelin, and that song was his least favorite. Their music taste didn't have to align. That sort of thing didn't matter.

Juney wasn't done yet. "As someone who has known Percy his entire life, I'd just like to know why you want to be with him. You two don't seem to have very much in common unless there's something I'm missing."

Juney's calloused fingertips grazed over the nape of his neck, and he had to fight to hold back a whimper. He tried to stay composed—begged himself to lean away from his touch, but he was desperate for even the most meager amount of Juney's affection.

Emilio saw where Juney's hand was, but he still seemed unconcerned.

With the torrent of loud thoughts Percy was having, his fiancé should've been concerned.

"Oh, that's easy," Emilio said. "Percy is the most genuinely kind person I've ever met. You're correct in saying that we don't have much in common, but that hasn't caused us any issues thus far. Right, love?"

The casual endearment he'd said right in front of Juney felt so, so wrong. He didn't know why he felt like he was being unfaithful to Juney. Despite their intensely deep friendship, they'd never been in a relationship with each other. If anything, he should've been feeling unfaithful to his fiancé.

Juney looked at Percy with his eyebrows lifted. His lips were curved in disgust, but his fingers tightened in his hair.

Percy nodded. "Yup. We get along just fine."

Gage and Torin seemed to be doing their best to ignore the conversation, but even they looked a little tense.

Emilio smiles at him. "Are you ready to go? It's been a long day."

Percy gaped for a second. He hadn't realized Emilio wanted him to stay over but of course. They'd just gotten engaged. It made perfect sense. "Yes. Yeah. I'll go get some things together."

He stood up and walked toward the hallway. It was on the opposite side of the house from Juney's, per Juney's request.

"Oh! Did Percy tell you the good news?" Emilio asked, and Percy stopped dead in his tracks. All the blood drained from his face, and a chill worked its way around his body. He forced himself to turn around, and what he saw shocked him.

Emilio was looking at Juney with smug satisfaction all over his face. Maybe he hadn't been so unconcerned after all.

He cleared his throat. Every pair of eyes in the room turned on him, and he did his best to keep his on Emilio. Percy tried to speak, but the words kept getting stuck in his throat. His hands trembled in his pockets.

He had to say it.

Percy cleared his throat. "We're engaged." He did his best to look excited, but he felt like he was going to be sick. His stomach wrenched tightly, and a lump swelled in his throat.

The room was so silent that he felt like he was outside of his body. None of it felt real. How could it be real?

Juney's voice brings him back down a little. "You're engaged to a man you've been dating for—six months come next Tuesday?"

Percy was taken aback. He hadn't realized... Juney never even acknowledged their relationship, yet he knew the exact day they began dating. "Yeah," he said, even though everything inside of him screamed *NO*.

"The heart wants what the heart wants," Emilio said.

Juney stood up and poured more vodka into his glass. He swallowed most of it without flinching before filling it again. He leaned against the wall with one foot crossed over the other and looked at Emilio intently. Percy didn't want to think about the painfully attractive picture he made.

"What's Percy's favorite color?" he asked.

Emilio's brows pinched. "I don't see what that has to do with anything," he said.

Juney nodded slowly with pursed lips. "Okay, sure. It's sage green, by the way. What's his favorite song?"

Emilio looked down his nose at Juney despite their distance from each other. "I'm guessing you'll tell me."

"'I Need You' by Lynyrd Skynyrd." He pointed his glass toward the Lynyrd Skynyrd record that hung on the wall among many others.

Juney was questioning him so quickly and smoothly that

Percy was having trouble processing any of it. All he knew was that his heart was racing.

"This should be an easy one, Emilio. When's Percy's birthday?" Juney still looked casual as all hell, but a muscle in his jaw was jumping repeatedly.

Emilio scoffed. "This has nothing to do with you."

Juney toyed with his lip ring with his tongue, looking far too calm for Percy's liking. It was unsettling. "You really want to marry this guy?"

"He said yes—"

Juney cut him off. "I wasn't asking you."

Juney finally looked at Percy, and Percy almost wished he hadn't. What he saw there was agony. His entire body was tensed, veins bulged in his forehead, and his eyes... His eyes barely concealed it.

Percy felt like he'd been stabbed in the chest, right through his heart. He opened his mouth to speak, but Juney was faster. "You don't," he stated.

"I—"

"Percy, you don't." He wasn't jumping for joy at the prospect of being married to Emilio, but he did care about him. It felt secure. Stable.

Juney's face was set in stone. "Let me make this clear, Emilio. You'll marry Percy over my cold, dead body. Give up while you're ahead. You understand?"

Percy was too stunned to speak. Juney hadn't been this possessive of him in forever. It stroked that ember inside of him, and heat radiated from his core. He wanted to drop everything and do whatever he said.

No. *No.* Juney had no right to do this to him.

Right?

Percy never had a say over who Juney fucked, but Juney

hadn't ever dated anyone—let alone gotten engaged. The vaguest thought of that happening made Percy want to die. He wouldn't be able to handle it. That'd be the end of them.

But Juney only wanted to protect Percy. It was different.

"You've really got some nerve, thinking you can tell us what we can and can't do. Threatening me? It'll take more than that, Winston." Emilio glanced at Percy with concern. "Way to go, jackass. That's how you treat Percy? Look at how upset he is."

When Juney looked at Percy, he smirked. Percy swallowed. Emilio thought he was upset, but Juney knew he was melting on the inside. Knew what Percy wanted and needed.

Percy realized that he was getting angry. After three whole years, Juney chose now to do this. He should've done it a long time ago. This engagement would've never happened.

"Juney, let's go talk. It'll only be a minute, Emilio. Then we can go," he said with resolve that he didn't truly feel.

Juney didn't spare either of them a glance as he strode past him, disappearing in the hallway. Percy gave Emilio a conciliatory smile before following him.

Juney let himself into Percy's room and picked up the picture frame that was on his nightstand. He shook his head and brandished it at Percy. It was a picture of them at their high school graduation. They had their arms around each other, smiling like no one was watching. Juney only ever smiled at him like that anyway.

He tossed the picture frame on his bed and crossed the room. Pulled out the drawer in his nightstand and tossed his photo album right next to it. How did Junes even know that was there?

He went into the walk-in closet and ran his fingers across the shirts that were hung up. He grabbed one and tossed it on the floor. Percy swallowed when he saw it. It was one of Juney's old shirts. Another one landed on the floor. Then another. Then, there was a hoodie. He ransacked the folded laundry and found two pairs of sweatpants and pajama pants.

All the clothes in the pile on the floor belonged to Juney at one point in time, and Percy still wore them regularly.

"Do you think Emilio's gonna be okay with all this stuff? You have an entire photo album filled with pictures of us. You still wear my clothes," Juney seethed. "Do you wear his clothes now? Not in front of me, you haven't."

He couldn't get a word in, and even if he could, he had nothing to say for himself.

Juney moved until he was directly in front of him. He grabbed Percy's shoulders and spun him around to face his full-length mirror. He still hadn't adjusted to Juney suddenly touching him. He wanted to touch him back. Touch him all over and smell him. Skin to skin.

He stood behind him, looking at Percy through the mirror. There was still space between them—the only point of contact was his hand on Percy's shoulders, but he swore he could feel heat radiating from his body. He wanted to sink into it— wished Juney would wrap his muscular arms around him. He'd forgotten how it felt.

"Are you in love with him?" Percy froze, unable to speak. "It's a yes or no question."

"I... I care about him," he replied.

Juney huffed a laugh. "That's not what I asked. That man out there—that fucking suit—has nothing in common with you. He knows nothing about you. After six months, he can't tell me a single detail about you."

"You know what, Juney? It's none of your concern who I choose to be with. I don't owe you an explanation." Percy was fuming because he wanted to tell Juney everything. He missed leaving everything in his hands, no matter how unhealthy he knew that was. "You've been doing whatever you wanted to these past few years without a word to me about it, so why should I listen to what you have to say now?"

Juney took a step closer. His broad torso crowded Percy from behind. Percy shuddered, eyes falling shut. There was a sob stuck in his throat.

So long.

It'd been so damn long.

Juney whispered hotly in his ear, "You're not gonna marry him." His nose was grazing Percy's cheek, and he wanted to fall to his knees. "I won't let you."

"You won't let me?" Goosebumps raised the hair on his skin. "Why do you think you can tell me what to do?"

Juney pressed his forehead against Percy's temple and wrapped him in his arms. Percy couldn't breathe. "I'd do anything you told me to do without a second thought," Juney responded. "That's why."

Percy knew that wasn't true. There were things he wanted from Juney that he'd never give him, and it was better that way. "You wouldn't. I promise you wouldn't."

Percy watched Juney's side profile in the mirror. His sharp, stubbled jaw. Lips parted. Eye's shut against Percy's skin. "You're the one who wanted this. You wanted us to stop being codependent. Wanted us to be normal. I did what you asked," he bit out. One of his hands glided up over his chest to his neck and grasped it lightly, just like that night.

"Don't act like it was only because of me."

"Every-fucking-thing is because of you, Percy." The vehemence behind each word felt like shrapnel pelting his heart. "Whether we're distant or not, I've had enough of this charade you have going with Emilio. He won't make you happy. He'll never be able to give you what you need."

No one can, Percy wanted to say.

Juney pulled back so suddenly that Percy stumbled a bit before regaining his footing. Juney was out the door before he could blink. He rushed after him, cursing himself inwardly. That wasn't how he intended the conversation to go, but whenever Juney was like that with him his brain stopped working. It went cloudy and soft around the edges.

Juney waltzed into the open living area and pulled out a cigarette as he said, "Leave."

That was it. Just the one word.

Emilio set his glass down and slid his phone into his pocket. "Excuse me?"

Juney spoke with the cigarette hanging from his lips. "Get the fuck out of my house." He didn't yell, and he wasn't even looking at Emilio. He was focused on lighting his cigarette.

Percy was walking toward Emilio—still unsure of what to do or say. There was so much conflict inside of him. Emilio placed a hand on his shoulder, right where Juney's had been. "Did you get your things ready? I'm not going to argue with this psycho. He's fucking crazy, Percy. I don't like you being around him."

"He's not—"

Juney grabbed his glass of vodka from the table and moved closer to them, taking a long sip. "Looks like you aren't as fucking clueless as you seem." Percy hated when people called him that. Despite what Juney believed, he wasn't crazy. "What was the last part you said, though? I'm not sure I heard it quite right."

The edge that wove between his words was undeniable.

Emilio stepped in front of Percy, and Percy knew that was

the worst decision Emilio could've made. "You heard me loud and clear. I'm not playing these childish games with someone like you."

In one swift movement, Juney's cigarette was crushed between his lips, he shoved Percy out of the way and smashed his glass against Emilio's head. It didn't shatter until it crashed on the terracotta-tiled floor. Vodka drenched Emilio's face. He stumbled back a few steps, grunting and roughly wiping his eyes to get rid of what Percy could only imagine felt like fire.

Percy gasped and stepped forward to get between the two of them, but Juney held him back with a forearm braced against his chest.

Percy trembled. He knew Emilio would fight back. He might've been a suit, but he was rough around the edges and spent most of his spare time in the gym. Juney was drunk and high and somewhere else entirely.

Emilio steadied himself and threw a punch that connected with Juney's nose. An unimaginable amount of blood poured from his nostrils, sluicing down his chin to his bare torso. All Juney did was groan and smile with crimson teeth. "Thanks for sobering me up a bit."

Fuck, fuck, fuck. Percy didn't know what to do. Juney got into fights regularly, but this was worse than any of them. This one was personal.

Juney powered toward Emilio and wrapped his hands around his throat. Emilio shoved at his shoulders, but Juney brought his knee up and into Emilio's stomach.

He coughed and dropped to his knees, cheeks puffed like he might throw up.

Where the fuck were Gage and Torin? Percy shouted for them. He knew he didn't stand a chance at breaking up this fight.

Juney wouldn't stop. He didn't give Emilio any time to catch his breath. He kicked Emilio square in his chest, and Emilio's back met the floor. "You fucking lunatic," he spat as he scrabbled to get up. Juney stood over him and grabbed Emilio by his hair, wrenching his head back.

Veins bulged in Juney's forehead, and the tendons in his neck pulled tight against his skin. He spoke through his teeth. "You're preaching to the fucking choir, Emilio. I don't give a fuck, and neither does Percy. The engagement is off."

"Fuck you," Emilio seethed before spitting in Juney's face. "You don't tell him what to do."

"Juney, please. Just stop already. You made your point," Percy begged him. He tried to grab Juney's shoulder but Juney didn't budge.

"You won't look at him again. Touch him. Breathe the same fucking air as him. Your first mistake was thinking you had more sway than me. Your second was implying that I'd ever hurt him." Juney was dark red. He looked more furious than Percy had ever seen him. "No one—and I do fucking mean no one—comes before me. Do you need me to repeat it?"

He wrapped his hands around Emilio's throat again, straddling him. Emilio's eyes bulged from his face. Percy jumped into action and tried his hardest to pull Juney off of him. He gave it his all, but it didn't work.

"I should've stopped this bullshit a long time ago. I could fucking kill you for this." Spit flew from his mouth. Emilio's blunt fingers scratched against Juney's forearms. "Why, Emilio? Why is this my fucking life? Why do I have to experience this kind of pain? I'm fucking sick of it. This is the last of it, right here." He slammed Emilio into the floor over and over again. "What's wrong with me? Why am I like this? I'm done. Can't do this anymore."

For the first time ever, Percy saw tears fall from Juney's eyes as he released him. Emilio gasped, hands flying to his neck as he curled onto his side. Percy fell to his knees, scrambling over to him to make sure he was okay. "I'm sorry. I'm so sorry. You didn't deserve this." Emilio wasn't saying anything back, still wheezing.

Juney grabbed his bottle of vodka and upended it. Chugged and chugged, and Percy stood up to yank it from his hands, but he didn't get there fast enough. Juney smashed the glass bottle against the wall. It shattered into large shards in the puddle of acrid liquor.

Gage finally rushed into the room. Torin was right on his heels.

Percy's eyes swung back toward Juney's, and there was a shard of glass in his hand. Time slowed, and no one was fast enough. No one could've stopped it when he dug the sharp point of it into his forearm and sliced.

A sob ripped from Percy's throat. His chest was collapsing. The pain was so insurmountable that Percy didn't feel the glass cutting his knees as he collapsed. He dragged them through shards and grabbed Juney's unwounded arm. Juney dropped the glass and looked at Percy through bleary eyes. "I'm so sorry," he said.

Percy couldn't hear it, but he knew he was screaming. He hyperventilated around choked sobs. "Help him. Call an ambulance. Please. Please. Please. He needs help. My Juney. Don't do this to me. Don't. I can't take it. I'll come with you." Strong arms were pulling him back, and he fought against them. Clawed and scratched and screamed. "He's going to die! Please!" Snot flew around his face as he gagged on each ragged inhale of breath. Juney's limb's that were propping him up lost their strength, and he fell back to the floor. His head cracked against the tile, and Percy ripped through Gage's arms.

Percy's arms were around Juney in no time, holding him close and tight. Squeezing him as hard as he could. How could Juney do this to him? How could he?

His heart couldn't take this kind of pain. It was going to rip from his chest. He wailed into Juney's neck, begged him, and cursed him. His head pounded with the force of his pleas. Maybe if he put all of his energy into it, he could save him. He could do it. He knew he could.

There were arms around him again. They weren't Gage's. They wrenched him back. "You have to stay calm. We're taking him. We'll do everything we can." The man was telling him things that he couldn't fully process as he watched paramedics lift Juney's lifeless body.

Percy screamed but nothing came out. All he could hear was Juney's agonized questions. *What's wrong with me? Why am I like this?*

He wanted to tell him that nothing was wrong with him. That he had the most beautiful soul. It was just locked away. He wasn't a monster. No matter what he or anyone thought, Juney was not a fucking monster. He wasn't bad. He was someone who needed help, and that was okay. Juney didn't have to let that define him.

He needed Juney to see himself the way he did.

His head spun with it all, and darkness closed in, narrowing the scope of his vision. His skull cracked against the tile just like Juney's had, and he lost consciousness.

Five

WINSTON

Winston's arm burned like hellfire, but unfortunately, he hadn't made it to hell yet. This was probably the closest thing to it though. Black Diamond Recovery Center. He wasn't on the resort side of the island. No. Of course not.

No matter how much money, success, and fame he'd found over the last three years, he never felt good.

Yeah, there were times when he was on top of the fucking world. So high up, no one could touch him. But those instances were fleeting. When he thought back to them, they were like a dream. Like they never happened.

Most of the time, Winston felt like there were heavy weights on his shoulders and a boulder strapped to his back. For him, existing was more exhausting than it was worth, and it was about to get a whole lot worse. He didn't need to be told how majorly he fucked up this time. His regret was bone-deep and sharp as that damned shard of glass.

He squeezed his eyes shut.

Percy.

He'd done it in front of Percy.

Winston could still see a blurry vision of Percy grabbing at him, trying to pull him away from death. He could hear Percy's shrill screams as an endless river of blood poured from his arm, drenching both of them.

What he'd done to Percy was inexcusable. Even if Percy tried to forgive him, Winston wouldn't let him. He doubted Percy would try anyway.

Winston had traumatized him—no question about it. He knew he'd scarred Percy worse than he scarred his own forearm.

Percy had a heart as vast as the ocean, but even that wouldn't be enough to wash him clean of this.

There was a knock on the heavy door directly in front of his bed. Nurse Miles' head popped in before he pushed the door all the way open. He stood at the foot of the bed, dressed in grey scrubs with a clipboard in hand. "How are we feeling, Mr. Jennings? Pain level?" he asked. He always sounded both kind and uninterested.

"Ten," Winston replied. He just wanted more pain meds, really. Being in his mind right now was more than he could bear. The thought alone had a cold sweat breaking out on his forehead.

The nurse paid him no attention as he flipped through his chart, taking notes. Winston couldn't blame him. He didn't want to look at himself either.

"You've been in this room for a week, and you've had the same pain level every day," he said drolly. "With your history of substance abuse, we're going to be stricter about your treatment plan."

Winston glared at the tiny, square window on the door. "When can I get out of this fucking room?"

Nurse Miles flicked his eyes at him over the clipboard. "You've certainly detoxed enough. Are you willing to see Dr. Weaver yet?"

Winston grumbled to himself. It'd been one week without weed, vodka, cocaine, and worst of all—not a single goddamn cigarette. It was ridiculous. He didn't like using his fame to pull strings, but he'd resorted to that and they still left him for dead. No wonder he'd been combative. He couldn't remember the last time he went without any of those things. It must've been his last juvie stint before he and Percy left Georgia.

He clenched his teeth. If he could go one fucking minute without thinking of Percy, maybe his pain wouldn't be a level ten. Maybe he wouldn't be begging to die.

"Guess so," he said. It was about time he started playing along, or else he'd be stuck in this room forever. He swung his legs over the bed and stood up with creaky bones. "When do I get to wear regular clothes again?"

He had to admit that the hospital gown they had him in was higher quality than they usually were, but he was over it.

The nurse led him through the door. "When you become stable enough to not be a risk to yourself."

Winston hadn't bothered putting on the slides they'd given him, so he padded beside Nurse Miles in his standard-issue grippy socks. This was the first time he found himself in a mental health center, and he was surprised to be there. They should've thrown him in jail.

The halls were just as cold and white as any hospital, and

his arm throbbed painfully since blood was rushing to the wound. He needed to sit down already.

They pulled to a stop in front of a wooden door with a plaque that read, 'Fonda Weaver M.D.'

Miles rapped his knuckles on the door, and then there was a "Come in."

He followed the nurse into the room. "This is Mr. Winston Jennings." He set a file down on the doctor's desk.

Dr. Weaver didn't look at the manila folder. Instead, she smiled warmly at Winston. His stomach twisted into a tight knot. No one should look at him like that—not after what he'd done. She probably wasn't fully aware yet.

"Have a seat, Mr. Jennings. That'll be all, Miles."

He sat down stiffly and heard the door shut. Then there was silence. Her office was bright, not from the fluorescent bulbs, but from the large window that overlooked a crystal clear ocean. Winston had a tiny window in his room, so the view was nowhere near as good as this.

Percy would love this place, he thought.

He balled his fist which made his arm hurt worse.

"I'm Dr. Weaver. It's nice to meet you." Winston swung his eyes toward her. Her dark hair was pulled back into a slick bun and wire-framed glasses rested on the bridge of her nose. She looked young enough that he reckoned she hadn't been doing this very long.

He stared at her blankly before remembering that he needed to bullshit his way through this. "Nice to meet you, too," he replied. Try as he might, he couldn't fake enthusiasm.

She hadn't stopped smiling at him.

His knee bounced up and down as he resisted the urge to bolt.

"I'm not going to make you rehash what landed you here.

You'll be talking to your therapist about that, but I do want to look closer into your mental health, so we can figure out how best to treat you."

After a beat, he said, "You want to put me on crazy meds."

She frowned. "Mr. Jennings, there's no such thing as crazy meds. Medications are life-saving for many people." When he didn't respond, she spoke again. "Have you ever been on any psychiatric medication?"

His lips thinned. The psychiatrist at the juvenile detention center tried, but he'd refused every time. "No," he said.

She nodded. "Have you ever received a psychiatric diagnosis?"

His heart began to race, and he felt faint. He'd been diagnosed, but he'd refused to acknowledge it. He wanted to lie, but he knew it wouldn't get him anywhere. "Yes," he said. Dr. Weaver waited patiently for him to continue. Her eyes dropped down to his trembling hands, and he really wished he had some pockets. *This fucking hospital gown.*

His gaze locked onto his forearm which was tightly bandaged from wrist to elbow. It didn't make him feel better, but he didn't want to ever forget what he'd done. He didn't deserve that kind of peace.

Winston felt like he was going to be sick. "Bipolar disorder type one and borderline personality disorder." He wished he could take the words back immediately. He'd never told a soul —not even Percy. He still held on to hope that they weren't true, but speaking them aloud felt like an ice-cold realization.

The longer he stared at his bandage, the more his eyes burned, so he cleared his throat and met Dr. Weaver's eyes. She didn't look like she was pitying him, but he still felt like a sorry piece of shit.

"Do you agree with that?" she asked.

His brows knitted together. "Well, something's fucking wrong with me. Maybe you can figure it out."

She didn't flinch. "How often would you say you're depressed?"

He shrugged. "Almost always. Ninety percent of my life, at least. It's hard to tell. I'm either depressed or numb."

"What's the other 10%?"

Winston instinctively tried toying with his lip ring but remembered they'd taken it from him when he was admitted. He didn't know how to explain this. It wouldn't make sense. "The other 10% is perfect."

She tilted her head. "Would you say it feels euphoric?"

He nodded. It was as if all the good chemicals in his brain that he missed out on for months and months slammed into him all at once.

"Do you sleep well?"

He scoffed. "All I ever think about is sleeping. If I'm not in my bed, that's where I want to be."

"That's when you're depressed, but what about when you're feeling happy?"

He felt like he was digging his hole deeper with every answer he gave. "No," he said. "I barely sleep then." That was when he wrote most of his songs. They didn't always turn out, but when they did, they were hits. Those songs were the ones that topped the charts. The ones he wanted to sing.

"Does it generally last a couple of days or longer than a week?"

He thought back over the years, trying to distinguish what was what. It was almost impossible. There were minor instances, and there were a couple that stood out. A couple that lasted a while and hadn't ended well. "Both," he said.

She looked at him softly. "Do you find that you regret anything afterward?"

He couldn't help the sardonic laugh that ripped from his throat. "You do know what I did right?"

Dr. Weaver's brows formed a hard line. "Mr. Jennings, what you did is not because of your mental disorders." His face must have conveyed how stupid he thought that was, but she continued anyway. "You have gone your entire life without treatment. You have no tools, no awareness, and no knowledge of the way your brain works. Anyone would have a hard time with that, but you are also an addict. That makes it even more difficult for you. Neither of these disorders is a death sentence or a prison sentence. Mental disorders do not make you a bad person. There were many factors at play that night."

He narrows his eyes at her. "If my mental disorders aren't to blame, then why am I a bad person? Why would I beat someone nearly to death, and then slit my wrist in front of the only people who seem to give a fuck about me?" Winston had no actual recollection of what he did to Emilio. Most of the night was blacked out from his memory, but that was what he'd been told.

She took a deep breath. "Because you are untreated and unequipped, and you were on a multitude of substances that impaired your brain function."

He raked his fingers through his shaggy hair. "So, what? I'm just supposed to be on meds for the rest of my life?"

Dr. Weaver's tone was softer. "Not necessarily."

Winston wanted to go back to sleep.

"I hope that you open yourself up to embracing treatment here. It could make all the difference for you."

All Winston could think about was going home. It didn't

matter that he'd have to be in the place where he made his biggest mistake yet. It would be a reminder, same as the scar on his arm will be. He couldn't forget even if he wanted to.

He needed out of this place. "Just give me the meds."

They spent an even longer amount of time discussing the different options he had. There were mood stabilizers and antipsychotics and antidepressants. Most of them sounded like they had awful side effects, but Winston's life was an awful fucking side effect.

"It might take a few tries to find the medication that's right for you, but you have to give each one a fair chance to properly assess its efficiency," she said.

That sounded fucking exhausting.

What was new?

By the time that they decided on a combination of two medications, Winston didn't want to think about it anymore. The more he processed it, the worse he felt. The shame. The regret. The humiliation.

Sleep. He just needed to sleep.

He stood up, and so did she. She reached her hand out for him to shake, and he had a flashback from that night. Emilio wanted to shake his hand, and when Winston felt his soft skin against his, he wanted to squeeze until he heard the *crunch* of his bones breaking. All he'd been able to think about was the fact that those hands had been all over his Percy.

Winston clasped her hand in his and followed a nurse that led him back to his room.

It was one thing to know Percy had a boyfriend, it was another thing entirely to see him in the flesh. Before that night, he'd been able to ignore his existence. A nameless, faceless person.

There hadn't been a single part of him that was delusional

enough to think he'd be okay when he met the man Percy had been fucking for six months, but when Winston locked eyes with Emilio, he didn't feel hurt.

The thoughts that had consumed him in that fraction of a second were alarming to even himself. He was no stranger to violence, but he'd never contemplated homicide as seriously as he had at that moment.

He wasn't sure what condition Emilio was in currently, and he was okay with that. There was a big part of him that didn't regret what he'd done. Matter of fact, he wasn't sure if he regretted it at all.

Winston didn't think there was a man on this planet that Percy could date who he wouldn't want to put into a coma. Whenever anyone touched Percy, Winston wanted to break their fucking fingers, and that wasn't even the half of it.

He knew none of those feelings were okay, but he also knew they couldn't be helped.

A knock on the door startled him awake. "Breakfast," said a nurse on the other side.

Winston blinked his eyes open and was met with a whole lot of nothing. White walls and frigid air. He was shivering beneath the world's thinnest sheet. Luckily, it wasn't scratchy —it just did fucking nothing in the way of providing warmth.

Fuck, he'd rather stick nails in his eyes than get out of this rubbery bed. After talking with Dr. Weaver yesterday, he skipped lunch and dinner. He'd been exhausted before entering that room, but after? He was wrung dry.

Everything about this place was uncomfortable—he

wondered if it was meant to make patients cooperate faster if only to get released.

His stomach twisted with hunger, so he forced himself up with his good arm and threw his legs over the bed. The linoleum flooring was ice cold beneath his hospital socks.

It seemed like the walls were the only unsafe thing in the room. He wanted to ram his head into one of them. Maybe he'd end it all if he did it hard enough.

Winston sighed. He knew that wasn't the case. How many more failed attempts would he have in his lifetime?

Knock, knock. "Let's go."

Running on someone else's time was not going to mesh well with him. Percy was the only person he'd ever let push him around like that.

Percy.

Percy.

Percy.

Everything was fucking Percy.

Reinvigorated with anger, he stomped over to the door, shoved his feet into the slides they gave him, and walked out of the room. Pain shot through his retinas. The lights in the common area were blinding. He missed his bedroom. Missed the soft, ambient lighting in their house. The only room with an overhead light was the kitchen, and that was bearable. But this? This was too much. He could already feel his brain buzzing.

He sat in his usual seat at one of the circular tables that had chairs affixed to them. There were only three tables and plenty of room to have your own space since there weren't very many patients. Winston didn't know if it was always like that or not, but seeing as how this recovery center was meant for rich people, it wasn't a surprise. He reckoned most of them ended up in rehab—not the mental health ward.

Winston did abuse drugs and alcohol, but the more pressing issue was his fucked up brain.

There were two other people at his table, and they both appeared to be in their twenties as well. They ate in perfect silence together. It was the table to their left that annoyed him to no end. Four patients sat there and all of them boasted about their issues loudly. Money, fame, scandals, and all as if it were something to be proud of.

A plastic tray was set in front of him, and he removed the lid and tucked in. He needed to distract himself so he didn't slam those loud motherfucker's heads into their table.

The stuff they served was gourmet, and they accommodated his vegan diet. It wasn't regular bland, microwaved hospital food. If there was any plus side to this place, it was that. He downed the meal in record time and chugged a glass of orange juice that he wished had vodka in it.

"Jennings." He didn't bother turning around, just tilted his head a bit. It was an older woman in scrubs. She proffered a tiny plastic cup with two pills in it. "Morning meds."

Winston looked at the pills. One was a brown circle and the other was a white rectangle. There was a spike of fear that prickled at his neck, but he clenched his teeth. The meds weren't going to do anything anyway, he thought. He'd take them if it meant getting out of there any sooner, so he swallowed them quickly before he could change his mind.

"Open," she said. He opened his mouth and stuck out his tongue. She nodded and went on to the next victim.

He took the last couple of bites of his food, then mosied over to throw the plastic silverware away and put the tray on the rolling cart. He'd resolved to shut himself away in his room again, but he stopped at the nurse's desk first. "Any chance I could have my clothes yet?"

Nurse Miles scrutinized him closely before opening a door to what appeared to be a long, narrow closet. He came out with a clear trash bag that was half full of clothes. "Your manager followed the proper guidelines for clothing and packed these for you."

Winston's heart palpitated in his chest, and his lips thinned. He grabbed the bag without a word, turned on his heels, and went to his room.

He poured out the clothes on the bed.

After the incident, he woke up in the hospital with his arm stitched up. Gage and Torin were there, but Percy wasn't. Percy wanted nothing to do with him anymore. It'd been the last nail in Winston's coffin. He knew it was the right thing. That was what was supposed to happen. But that didn't make it any easier. Didn't alleviate the pain in his heart that was worlds worse than the slash in his arm.

So he didn't understand why Percy had gone through the trouble of packing this for him. Maybe it wasn't him who did it. Maybe Heatwave Records already appointed Telltale Dream a new manager. That had to have been it.

He grabbed a pair of sweatpants that the drawstring had been removed from and his Black Sabbath long-sleeve shirt and swallowed around the lump in his throat.

Percy definitely packed this.

It was one of the shirts Percy had stolen from him.

Winston clutched the faded black fabric, trying to refrain from burying his nose in it. He bit down on his lip hard enough to draw blood. He knew it'd smell like Percy.

He sat down on the edge of the bed, and really thought about it. What did it matter if he dragged himself through more agony? He'd been doing it his entire life. Yeah, he had ended up here, but that was inevitable. Percy or not, he'd have ended up institutionalized at some point. It was just the card he was dealt.

Winston covered his face with the shirt and fucking whimpered. He needed it so badly.

It was the one thing he'd allowed himself all these years. Sometimes, when Percy wasn't home, Winston would let himself into his room just to lay on his bed. The pillow was laden with his scent and knowing Percy laid in the very spot he was in was like a giant band-aid for Winston. It helped him to not feel like he'd lost Percy entirely.

Sharing a bed with Percy had always been that way. No matter what happened throughout their day, he could fall into bed with Percy and just *feel* him. Breathe him in. Hold him close.

It twisted the knife in his chest to the point that it was beyond repair, and yet he wouldn't undo it.

This place was beating him down, but at least he had this now. All of these clothes were from Percy's closet. It wasn't a gift either. Giving Winston his stuff back was Percy's way of letting him know that they were through. It had to be.

He relished in the heady scent of the fabric for a little while longer before stripping his gown and entering the bathroom. The shower was rudimentary with a couple of bars to hold on to and a tiny nub of a showerhead. The water pressure was weak, and the water didn't get hot enough. If anything, it was an incentive to get in and get the fuck out as quickly as possible. And he had to keep his left arm dry.

He hated it.

At home, Winston boiled himself in a whirlpool bathtub. It wasn't very often since showering was usually the last thing he wanted to do. He'd never understood why it was that one thing that seemed like the most impossible mountain to scale when he was depressed, yet he always felt a little better afterward.

He dried off with an overly small towel and threw on the clothes. It was almost like Percy was right there with him, and he didn't want to think about how hopelessly desperate he was.

The bed was calling for him, but there was another fucking knock at the door. They never left him alone. "Therapy," a nurse said.

Winston had refused therapy every day this week. Everything in him wanted to skip out and curl up in bed instead, but he needed to bite the bullet and do it.

He shuffled out of the room and was led through the same hallway as the psychiatrist's office. They passed it and came to a door at the end of the hall. It was wide open, so the nurse announced herself and led him in.

"Thanks, Jan," he said nicely, and the door clicked shut behind him.

Winston, once again, fixed his gaze on the view outside of the window. "I'm Ian Kang."

"Winston Jennings," he mumbled before meeting the man's eyes. He had distinct East Asian facial features and a colorfully patterned button-up shirt—the kind that Percy tended to wear.

He realized he was glaring at the shrink's torso. There was a comfortable-looking wicker couch along the wall facing the window, so he cleared his throat and sat down. The man rounded his desk and gracefully lowered himself into the wicker chair directly in front of Winston.

They sat there in silence for long enough that Winston's knee started to bounce. He itched to make it stop. "So what are we doing here, Kang? How does this work?"

"Call me Ian, please," he said firmly.

"Sure."

Winston watched one of Ian's delicately slender hands tap the woven arm of the chair.

"If you're willing, I'd like to start from the beginning. Your childhood."

Ian's voice was smooth and calm and not judgemental at all. Not even a little abrasive. He found he preferred that over the therapists they tried to stick him with in juvie who were fed up and impatient.

But Winston didn't want to do this at all. The mere idea of reliving anything here threatened to make him sick. He'd rather lean toward anger, but Ian was so gentle that he found it difficult to retaliate.

He could feel the wrinkle forming between his brows as he gave the man a short nod.

"Thank you for leading with an open mind, Mr. Jennings—"

"Winston," he interjected.

A small smile curved Ian's lips. "Of course. Winston, would you tell me about your parents?"

His voice was so fucking soft. Winston strangled his thigh, just above his knee. "My mother was named Farah June Jennings and my father's name is Hunter Boone Jennings. They were born and raised in bumfuck Georgia, and so was I. Mom died when I was eight. Dad's still living but barely," he said bluntly.

Ian waited for a beat before asking the inevitable question. "How did she pass?"

It was straightforward, and Winston didn't sense any pity. It made it easier for him to answer. "She was a lot like me, or I'm a lot like her. There was something wrong with her... mentally. She was mentally ill. Killed herself."

Ian pursed his lips, and Winston's eyes dropped to them. "How did your father handle that?"

That was... different. People tended to ask how he'd handled it—not his father. "After she died, he never mentioned her again. *Poof.* She never existed. The one time I asked him about her was a waste of time."

"The only adult in your life wasn't there for you. He was grieving but so were you."

Winston knew that. "He still hasn't come around. He works and drinks himself to sleep. He was like a drunk room-mate." He laughed. "I got out of there as quick as I could."

Ian crossed one leg over the other and rested his chin in his hand. "I don't blame you. That's a natural reaction. When did you start noticing signs of your own mental illness? Depression or unhealthy behaviors?"

Winston absentmindedly stroked his thumb along his bandaged forearm. "I was always a bit of a problem, but when she died, I stopped caring. Got in trouble more. That kind of thing."

"You were not a problem. You were a child who was alone," he said firmly. Winston gulped. There was something about this therapist that got under his skin. He was saying things that were obvious that no one had ever vocalized to him. It set him on edge while also making him feel seen. He'd never talked this candidly with anyone other than Percy, and even that was rare.

"Feel free to pass on this question, but I do think it would be beneficial that you answer honestly."

Winston stared at him blankly.

"Was this the first time you attempted suicide?"

"No." That was easy enough until Ian watched him patiently but expectantly, and God, Winston could really use a fucking cigarette right now. He was having trouble figuring out what to say about that night, but he tried anyway. "I swallowed a bunch of my dad's pills when I was fifteen."

Ian rubbed his hand in small circles on his thigh. It seemed to ground him. Winston knew what that was like. "Did you want to talk about the events that led up to it?"

"No." The denial was out before he could even consider it.

"Okay," Ian said, and Winston was shocked that he didn't press him about it. "What you did to Mr. Alvarez—was that your first act of physical violence?"

Winston couldn't help his sardonic smile. A lot of his altercations have circulated through the tabloids over the past few years. They were out there for anyone to see, but maybe Ian didn't pay attention to that kind of thing. "I have a long history of being physically violent," he said.

"When did it begin?"

Winston thought about that. "I got into my first fight in kindergarten."

Ian smiled, and it threw Winston off so hard that he didn't hear his next question.

"Winston," Ian said. He snapped out of it and met his waiting gaze. "Would you tell me about one of the incidents that stand out to you the most?"

Immediately, Winston saw Percy sitting on Gage's lap. Gage's hands all over him and Percy's hips rotating shamelessly.

His jaw ticked multiple times. It didn't matter how much time had passed. He still wasn't over that night.

What hurt the most about it was that that's when Percy realized he was attracted to men. He hadn't realized any of the times he was nuzzling Winston's neck or humping his thigh to get off. Nope.

It was Gage.

Not him.

"No," he responded with a harder edge than he'd taken on with Ian thus far.

Ian uncrossed his legs and looked at him softly. "I respect your decision, but if you won't tell me, then you should tell yourself." Winston's brows knitted together. "I get the impression that you've never spoken about it before. It might help if you tell yourself, out loud, what happened."

Winston gaped at him.

"At the very least, attempt it. Our next appointment is Wednesday, so that gives you some time." Ian stood up and clasped his hands in front of him. "You did an amazing job, Winston. I look forward to speaking more with you."

"Uh. Okay," he said.

Ian smiled again. "You may go back to your room. It's nearly lunchtime. My favorite."

Winston nodded dazedly and let himself out of his office. He ran his fingers through his hair and began the trek back to his wing. It was the first time he'd gone anywhere without being escorted, and he wondered if it was a mistake. Didn't fuckin' matter either way. He had no intention of being anywhere other than his bed for the hour until lunch.

When he collapsed onto his bed, he felt like all the life had been sucked out of him. There was an ache in his temples and a loud ringing in his ears. He considered skipping lunch today but knew that would count against him. Miles told him from the beginning that if he cooperated, followed their routine, and made notable progress, he could go down to a level green. That'd mean he can get out of this fucking white box and into an oceanside bungalow. He'd rather go home, but that wasn't possible. He had sixty mandatory days at Black Diamond.

Winston couldn't see the end of this hell, so he planned to watch the back of his eyelids instead.

WINSTON

Winston was sitting on one of the various chairs in the common room surrounded by most of the other patients in his ward. Most of them were wrapped in blankets, including himself, and they were watching *The Goonies*. He'd been informed that they watched the same three movies here. The other two were *Elf* and *Back to the Future*. If he had to rank them, *Elf* would be last, and *Back to the Future* would be first.

He wanted the movie to be over with already so he could go the fuck to sleep. He wasn't sure why daily, after-dinner movie time with his fellow crazies was even a necessary part of psychiatric treatment.

The nurse was calling them back one by one to have their phone time. Winston was actively trying to ignore the stabbing feeling in his chest and the compulsion to pull the TV off its cart and smash it on the floor. In the eleven days he'd been here, no one had called him, and Winston didn't have anyone's number memorized except Percy's.

He didn't have many people in his life, so it bothered him that he clung to a scrap of hope that someone would want to talk to him or see if he was okay. Of course, they didn't. They were the ones who weren't okay, and he was at fault for it.

The movie's credits finally rolled down the screen, and Winston promptly sprung from his seat and shuffled to his room, but the nurse called for him. He heaved a sigh. He wanted this day to be over with already—another day to take off of his sixty.

He turned around and headed to the desk. Listening to what people told him took a concerted effort and never failed to worsen his already sour mood.

"Someone by the name of Torin called for you earlier today. Would you like to call them back?"

Winston bit down on his cheek. He hadn't been expecting that. He silently nodded, and she led him into a mostly empty room with a corded telephone on a table. She handed him a sticky note with Torin's cell phone number written on it. "Fifteen minutes," she said before walking out and closing the door.

Winston sat in the rolling office chair and picked up the phone. He had no idea what awaited him on the other end but figured it best not to fuck around.

The phone rang twice before Torin picked up, and Winston's stomach dropped. He halfway hadn't expected him to answer, and somewhat looked forward to that outcome.

"Winston?" Torin asked.

"Mhm."

There was a healthy pause before Torin spoke again. "How are you doing in there?"

When confronted with it, Winston found that he didn't

want to talk about himself at all. "Fine. How are you and Gage doing?"

Torin sighed, and it crackled in his ear loudly. "We're okay. It's Percy that's—"

Winston hung up the phone and promptly showed himself back to his room.

He found himself in bed, holding one of Percy's shirts to his chest like a sad sack of shit. Sleep was evading him no matter how hard he squeezed his eyes shut.

This place was poison.

They put him through the wringer and then confined him in this empty, white cage every spare minute of every day. Just left him to simmer in his thoughts if he couldn't sleep them away.

He ducked his head down, burying his nose in the shirt. He didn't know how to handle any of this. Didn't know what to do. It went against all of his instincts.

It was visceral—the way he could imagine Percy in his arms, and just how much better and worse that made him feel. But it was all he had. All he'd ever had. No matter how wrong he knew it was, he clung to any vestige of Percy he had. That's why he didn't want to hear whatever Torin had to say about Percy. He knew he couldn't handle it. Didn't want to tarnish the little that was left.

There was a persistent swelling of emotion every day that passed. It grew and grew and Winston was afraid of what would happen when it exploded. He didn't know how to feel that much, but he knew this was the consequence of what he'd done.

He had to live with himself.

Another day, another fucking dollar. Many dollars, actually. Heatwave was paying the big bucks for his stay here, and he still hadn't seen where the fucking luxury was other than the soft linens and decent food.

Supposedly, he'd get a taste of it when he finished his stay here in the facility, but Winston wasn't buying it.

It was Wednesday, so he had a quick breakfast and shower before heading to his appointment with Ian. He wasn't looking forward to therapy, but he was looking forward to Ian's company. So far, he was the only person in this place who was bearable to be around—maybe even a little more than bearable.

"Winston! So nice to see you again," Ian greeted with a smile. He seemed to genuinely mean it which didn't sit right with Winston. No one should ever be that happy to see him.

He gave Ian a grunt of acknowledgment and collapsed onto the couch. He wanted to melt into it and live in it for the duration of his Black Diamond incarceration.

Despite his grumpiness, Ian's smile didn't falter.

Winston's eye twitched.

"How are we feeling today?" Ian asked.

Winston shrugged.

His therapist crossed his legs like he did, looking very interested in whatever Winston had to say. "Try to identify the loudest emotion you've felt in the three hours you've been awake today."

He could already tell that his brain would be on fire by the time he walked out of that door today. He attempted to do what Ian had asked but only came up with one thing. "Exhausted."

"Lack of sleep exhaustion or general exhaustion?"

Winston could never anticipate what Ian would say next. It almost always caught him off guard. "A mixture of both. I couldn't sleep last night, and I'm sick of this place. It's an empty cage."

Ian hummed. "Perhaps we could talk outside. Would that help at all?"

Winston's breath hitched almost imperceptibly. He stood up quicker than he would've liked to. "Show me the way, man."

His therapist passed him and opened the door, grinning. They took a right at the end of the hall and arrived at a heavy door with a neon 'EXIT' sign. He waved a badge in front of a sensor and bright, blinding sunlight shone on his skin. Its warmth and energy radiated through him so abruptly that it stole the breath from his lungs. It was overwhelming in a way he hadn't expected, but he kept his expression neutral as they stepped out. They were on the east side of a courtyard brimming with lush, tropical plants and flowers as colorful as the ones on Ian's shirt.

Ian noticed his awe as he led him to a picnic table. "The landscapers do an amazing job with bringing the outside in. This is a small taste of the beauty of this island." They sat across from each other and Winston relished in it, tipping his head up a bit toward the sky while maintaining eye contact with him. "They don't usually take the patients in your ward outside since your stay is so short, but once you enter level green, we can have our sessions outside if the weather permits."

Winston liked his home to be dim and his room to be dark. Bright lights made his head hurt, but he'd always appreciated sunlight. They had plenty of it in both Florida and Georgia, and he'd never want to live in a place that didn't.

"So, why were you having trouble sleeping last night?"

"Why don't you ever take notes?" Winston asked.

"I don't need to. I summarize afterward."

Winston nodded. "Last night..." He didn't want to talk about this. Ian wouldn't understand, and it was humiliating. He wanted to change the subject, but no matter what, they'd have to start talking about things he wasn't ready for. He never wanted to or planned to talk to anyone about his friendship with Percy. That shit was strictly his own brain rot, and it was no one else's business. "This is... I don't like talking about this," he said gruffly.

Ian nodded. "There are many things we'd like to keep to ourselves, but there's only so much you can bottle up before it explodes from you. I'd like to be a safe space for you and remember, everything we discuss in our sessions is completely confidential unless your safety is compromised."

He knew that was supposed to be the case, but he didn't trust him or anyone for that matter. Especially with his newfound fame, everyone wanted some behind-the-scenes information about him and his bandmates, and they'd gone to great lengths to get it. "I had a phone call last night with my bandmate, Torin. I hadn't expected anyone to call me, and Heatwave put me here to rehabilitate me so we can get this album finished in time for our sold-out world tour, but I don't know. I think it's best that I quit the band."

Ian's perfect eyebrows furrowed. "Why?"

He scoffed. "Isn't it obvious? I'm a loose fucking cannon. A danger to myself and others or whatever the hell they say. I traumatized them with what I did that night. It was beyond selfish of me, and I'll probably do it again."

"But Torin did call to check on you, yes?"

"Yes."

Ian tapped a manicured fingernail against the wooden table. "What you did can't be considered selfish because you weren't of sound mind."

He shook his head. "I don't think you understand. I wanted to crush Emilio's skull in. I wanted to kill him." He probably shouldn't have said that, but Ian didn't flinch.

"Wanting to do something and actually doing it is not the same thing. You didn't kill him. That was your choice to stop and had you been in your right mind, it wouldn't have gone as far as it did."

Sure, he did choose to stop. He thought about it more closely. "Sober or not, I've always wanted to fuck up anyone who even looked at Percy."

"But you hadn't until then. What was different this time?" he asked softly.

Winston squeezed the edge of the bench he was sitting on. Rough wood dug into his palms. "They got engaged," he said, low and rough. He didn't want to speak those fucking words into existence. They weren't real. Couldn't be real. "I should've killed him."

"You're angry," he said. Winston didn't respond. "You're hurt." Winston blinked away the burn and focused his gaze to the right of Ian's slender shoulder. "What is Percy to you?"

And wasn't that the question of the fucking century. What was Percy to Winston? The answer to that was as vast as the universe with the depth of the Mariana Trench. "He's oxygen. He's blood. He's water." Winston replied. "Without him, there is no me."

When he met Ian's sharp eyes, he saw something flash in them. They widened briefly. "Have you always felt that way?"

Winston's teeth cut into his bottom lip as he recalled the memory.

"Every day, Farah. I work outside in the hot sun to keep the bills paid, and I come home to you in bed. Dishes spilling out of the sink. I can't even find clean clothes to wear to work," his father said. He didn't sound angry. He sounded tired, like this had been going on forever, and Winston supposed it had. "I know you aren't well. I know, but when will you get better? I miss you."

Despite Winston's young age, he knew what his dad meant by that. It wasn't that his mom had gone anywhere. She was right there and always had been, but she used to be different. She used to take Winston outside to play. She used to pick out his outfits for school and brush his hair in the morning.

Now, she barely left her bed, and that was okay with him. When he got home from school, he'd lie there with her. When she asked him to get her some water or a snack, he'd do that too.

Sometimes she would try to get up and do a few things before his dad got home from work. She'd cook something for dinner and sometimes clean up the kitchen. He didn't understand why it wasn't enough for his dad, but he knew that his stomach hurt when his dad made her cry.

"Hunter, you know I'm trying. I'm sorry, okay? I'm sorry." Her voice cracked, and a single tear slid down her face.

Winston wished he hadn't seen it. He felt just as upset as she looked, so he swung open the screen door and crunched through the dry blades of grass with bare feet. He never knew what to do when he went outside since he didn't have anyone to play with. Sometimes he'd just sit there and pluck the grass from the soil just to see its tangle of roots. Each one was different enough that he wouldn't get bored of it for a while.

When Winston's mom used to come outside with him, she would ask him to stay where she could see him, so he never ventured off. So, although she didn't come out with him anymore, he still stayed right in the front yard. Her bedroom window over-

looked it. She would pull up the blinds and check on him from time to time.

Today he didn't want to do that. Today he wanted to escape.

He approached the woods on the far side of the yard, eyeing them carefully and wishing he'd worn shoes. He swatted spider webs away, but they clung to his skin. He gritted his teeth, wanting to turn around. There were probably spiders crawling on the back of his neck. He held his breath, rushing through until he emerged on the other side.

He was surprised to see that it was his neighbor's yard. Winston froze. He wasn't supposed to be here. What if his parents were looking for him right now?

No. They weren't, he thought. He would've heard them calling for him.

There was a big yellow house, and the grass was thick and green. Winston wanted to feel it, so he took a few hesitant steps forward.

"Hey, you!"

Winston jumped, and he looked around to see where the voice had come from while walking back the same way he came.

"No! Please don't go. I'm over here." Winston squinted his eyes, scanning the yard until they landed on a boy who appeared to be around his age. A silent thrill went through him. A friend. He could have a friend. If the boy liked him, that is.

He trekked through the yard toward him slowly. The grass cushioned the soles of his feet, and it was better than he'd imagined it'd be. The boy was lying on the grass beneath a tree, propped up on his elbows to see him. He wasn't wearing shoes either.

"Do you live over there?" the boy asked.

Now that Winston was closer, he thought the boy looked familiar. Maybe they went to the same school, but he had to be a *grade below him. He was smaller, and there was something about his face. He had dark hair that resembled the same bowl cut Winston sported.*

He nodded, still standing there, towering above him.

"Wow! I've seen you at school. Didn't know you were my neighbor. That's so cool," he said with a wide smile. Winston couldn't stop looking at it. "My name is Percy. I'm seven years old."

Maybe they were in the same grade then. "I'm Winston," he replied quietly.

Percy frowned. "Are you sad?"

Winston's mouth fell open to respond, but he slammed it shut. How could Percy tell? "No."

Percy collapsed back into the grass. "Come lay with me. It's super awesome." He pointed up at the tree.

Winston wasn't sure about that, but he laid down anyway. They were shoulder to shoulder, and Winston didn't think he'd ever been this close to a person who wasn't his mom. But it was... it was nice. Warm.

"My dad told me this is a live oak tree," Percy said. "Isn't it so nice?"

Winston was looking up at the tree's canopy. Its spindly branches were dense with leaves, and the sun shone through them in dappled rays. He turned his head to look at Percy, and Percy turned to look at him. A beam of sunlight hit Percy's eye, and Winston's breath hitched. He'd never seen anything like it. He didn't know how to describe the shade of blue that Percy's eyes were, and he was positive that no one could.

The view from beneath the oak tree wasn't nearly as nice as Percy's eyes.

Percy's lips twisted up into a self-satisfied smile. "Not sad anymore, are you?"

No. He wasn't sad, but he didn't know what this feeling was. He only knew that he didn't want Percy to stop looking at him, and he didn't want to leave.

Ian was tearing up, and Winston bristled. He'd never talked about that day before.

It was becoming clearer to Winston that he hadn't ever talked about much at all. "Percy has meant everything to me since that day. No matter what has happened, that has never changed."

There was a silence only broken by wind gusting through palms. "How do you think Percy feels about you?"

"For a long time, he needed me. It was unhealthy. But now? I reckon he wants nothing to do with me, and I don't blame him. If he didn't make that choice for himself, I'd have to make it for him."

Ian tilted his head, parsing through what he'd said. "Were you afraid that if he got married, he wouldn't need you anymore?"

His jaw hardened. "He hasn't needed me for a while."

"Are you certain?"

Winston carded his fingers through his hair, recalling Percy's collection of his belongings. The pictures. Everything. He still remembered what happened after the incident with Gage. Percy hadn't wanted to put distance between them, but Winston knew it was the right thing to do. The only thing.

He shook his head. "It's not the same," he mumbled. Ian did that thing where he waited so long that the silence made Winston feel the need to keep talking. It ticked him off. "Percy needs me in a different way than I need him, and I can't be the one who gives him that because I'm in love with him."

Ian didn't look like Winston had just revealed his deepest

secret—the one he planned to carry until death. "You haven't told him," he stated.

Winston's face contorted. "Of course I haven't fucking told him. Are you kidding me? We might've been distant these days, but at least he was still there. I'm not great at handling things to begin with, but if I had to endure that, I wouldn't make it."

The therapist's face softened. "You said he needed you. In what way?"

Winston roughly dragged his palm down his face. "It ain't right," he sighed, and Ian looked at him expectantly. "Percy has clung to me our entire lives."

"Physically?"

Winston nodded. "And every other way possible. It's... he always used me for comfort. Just—never mind. You wouldn't understand." He pinched the bridge of his nose. He knew how crazy it sounded without having to say it out loud.

"You can't make decisions for other people, Winston," he said pointedly. "If you'll tell me, I'd like to know."

Winston slowly exhaled, looking forward to his pillow and one of Percy's shirts. "Percy has always been physically affectionate with me. No one else but me. He always wanted to put his head on my shoulder, wanted to sit as close to me as possible—even on my lap. He never liked sleeping alone, so I let him sleep with me. He didn't want any space between us in bed either. Percy wanted to live in my skin much the same way I wanted to live in his. But he wasn't in love with me. It wasn't the same."

Winston's heart ached deeply. He hadn't been able to forget the way they used to be, and it hurt. But it hurt less this way.

"Do you know much about his childhood?" Ian asked. Winston didn't see how that was relevant.

"The Lovell's were great. A totally normal family who loved Percy and gave him everything he wanted and needed. They treated me like a second son."

"Sounds like he had a stable childhood with healthy attachments with his parents, and yet he leaned on you for love and affection."

Winston didn't know how to explain it. "Percy had always been that way. I think he just needed more than a lot of people. He needed that safety and comfort. Percy felt things so deeply, and I think it drained him. He needed someone to be his pillar."

"And he chose you," Ian stated. "When did he stop choosing you?"

Winston cleared his throat. "He, uh. He didn't. We were toxic as toxic can be. Codependent. He latched onto me right where I wanted him, but I also wanted him to be mine, and he was always out of reach. I couldn't bear it anymore."

"Having said all of that, do you still think that he wants nothing to do with you now?"

The answer came easily. "Yes."

Ian sighed. "I have an assignment for you. I know you didn't do the last one, and that's okay, but I want you to try this one."

Winston was already dreading whatever torture the man had cooked up for him.

"I'm going to send you with a notebook and a pen. I want you to confess all the things you'd like to say to Percy in a letter. Tell him everything."

Winston's heart constricted in his chest. "I don't know about that, man."

"It's my understanding that you enjoy writing music. Everything that you've bottled up about Percy is taking up an enormous amount of space inside of you. Getting even some of it out onto paper might help you in ways you hadn't expected."

He still didn't want to do it. "What if I stab myself with the pen or something?" he tried.

Ian looked unimpressed.

Winston's nostrils flared, and he clenched his teeth. "Sure. I'll attempt it. No promises."

Ian rose from the table and smiled warmly. "Your progress in only two sessions is tremendous. I can see how hard this is for you, and I appreciate your effort. I can't magically heal you, but I want to help you identify your feelings and cope with them. We have a lot of ground to cover, and with your open mind, it's definitely achievable."

Winston didn't know why that made him feel a little choked up. He hadn't ever considered that he could be helped at all, and he still wasn't sure he could. But Ian was emphatic about his devotion to trying. There was a tiny seed of hope tucked away in his ribcage, and he already wanted to crush it because hope was dangerous. Life was easier when you had no expectations.

That night, Winston wrote the letter.

He balled up many failed attempts. He quit numerous times. He considered snapping the pen in half.

But he wrote the letter.

Seven

PERCY

Percy took a long, slow rip from Eleanor. It bubbled and filled with smoke that he shot directly into his lungs.

"Are you getting high?" Amir said exasperatedly through the phone that was on speaker. "I need you to take this seriously. This could make or break everything."

Amir was his higher-up. He was the person who constantly hounded Percy, but he'd never heard as much from Amir as he had over the past few weeks. And it just so happened that if there were three weeks out of his entire life that he didn't want to be bothered, it was these. "Please get to the point," he said after exhaling a thick cloud of smoke.

"You need to go to Black Diamond to keep an eye on him. Make sure everything's okay."

Percy passed Eleanor to Torin. "No," he said.

"No isn't an option. If you think I'm on your ass, you should see how the directors are coming down on me."

Percy blinked hard. His eyes burned from the lack of sleep over the past few weeks. "There's no reason for me to physically be there, Amir. I get weekly updates from them. During the first week, Winston didn't cooperate at all. In the second week, he attended both of his therapy sessions and participated in all group activities and meals. He would've been out of the facility after two weeks, but he spent a week of it holed up in his room. They wanted fourteen good days."

"So he's out now then? It's his twenty-first day."

"Yes. They moved him to his private bungalow today. So, you see, I don't need to be there. They have it under control," Percy reiterated.

He heard Amir's pen hit his desk. He must've thrown it down like he tended to do when he was at his wit's end. "Have any of you been able to get ahold of him?"

Torin, Gage, and Percy looked at each other.

"Torin did, but Winston hung up."

Amir scoffed. "That's the fucking problem. Right there! Who knows what he's thinking—he's probably gearing up to walk away from the band as we speak."

Percy pinched the bridge of his nose. He was beginning to realize that he had no choice in this matter.

"I'll have the jet ready for you to take off tonight. You're the only one who can get to him, and you know it," he mollified.

Amir hung up before Percy even had a chance to speak. "Is he joking? Tonight?" he yelled. "I can't do this shit. One of you has to go."

Gage smacked the table with the palm of his hand, nearly sending Eleanor over the edge, and Percy looked at him witheringly. "We were there just the same as you, but you know him better than us. Of course, you should go. Winston probably already mentally quit. I mean who fucking knows where his head is at right now? No one."

Torin interjected calmly but firmly, "Amir's right this time. None of us can even begin to heal until we get this figured out. That night affected us all." Torin sniffled a bit and wiped his nose with the back of his hand.

"If this is about Emilio, then you need to cut the shit, Percy. I swear to fucking God. Winston comes first. Above anyone else," Gage bit out.

Percy's chin wobbled and he looked away, focusing his gaze on his favorite record. Emilio was fully recovered now. Juney had given him a mild concussion and strangled him hard enough that there were blown blood vessels and dark bruises. He had a large knot on the back of his head from being slammed into the floor so many times. Luckily, there wasn't any brain damage and nothing life-altering.

It was a hard pill for Percy to swallow. He cared about Emilio a lot—enough to get engaged to him, and Winston had nearly strangled him to death.

Winson almost murdered a man for wanting to marry Percy.

That was already painful, but everything after that moment nearly killed Percy himself. He might as well have been on the other side of Juney's hands.

There wasn't a soul on this planet who Percy cared about more than Juney—not Emilio, not Gage or Torin, probably not even his parents. So as he watched the life drain from Juney's eyes, he felt his life fading away, too. He hadn't gotten it all back yet, and he didn't know if he ever would.

This was Juney's second attempt, and Percy wondered if

each time, he regained less life back, too. Juney must be only half-full now.

Percy wanted to help him—needed to help him hold on for dear fucking life, but he wasn't sure he had enough life in him to do it now. For the first time, Percy didn't have enough to give Juney.

He'd gotten so used to being the sun behind his storm cloud.

"Will Emilio keep you from going to him?" Torin asked gently.

Percy's vision blurred. "No one can keep me from Juney."

Torin grabbed his shoulder, attempting to comfort him, but it didn't work. No one did it like Juney. "Then why don't you want to go?"

He didn't know how to convey all of the immense feelings he'd been having since that night. "I'm just not ready to see him yet, but I guess it doesn't matter." Fat tears rolled down his flushed cheeks. "I nccd to be there for him in whatever capacity I can."

Torin dropped his forehead to Percy's shoulder. "I understand."

Percy looked up at the ceiling, breathing through the sobs threatening to wrack through him.

Gage grabbed his beer and guzzled the rest of it down. "Percy, look at me."

Percy's eyes found his.

"If you get there, and it's too much—if you need to leave, then do it. Heatwave, Amir, the band—none of it matters more than your own health. Your life. Winston might be out there healing, but you haven't had a chance to even lick your wounds between being there for Emilio and managing every-thing with Heatwave and Black Diamond. If you need to tell everyone to fuck off and take time for yourself, please do it, okay?"

Percy swallowed roughly. It was a rare show of sincerity from Gage and one he hadn't known he needed to hear. In all of this, he hadn't taken a moment to consider himself until now. Three weeks had passed, and he still felt as if it were yesterday that Juney grabbed that shard of glass and sliced both of them wide open.

Maybe it was only right that they did heal together.

No matter what, Percy knew he would always be there for Juney.

"I love you guys so much. We'll figure all this out together."

"Yeah. Love you," Gage grumbled under his breath.

"Everything will be okay. We love you," Torin said. He had a way of putting people at ease, and Percy needed that more than anything right now.

Percy stood up and tied his hair into a quick bun. It was time to go pack and catch his plane.

"These bungalows are for guests. The patient's bungalows are down that way." Lawrence pointed toward a cluster of bungalows further down. His finger landed on a specific one. "That's where Mr. Jennings is staying."

Percy swallowed roughly. Juney's lights were on, and he was right there behind those walls. "Got it. Thank you," he said. "Have a great night."

The man looked like he'd rather be anywhere but here as he spun around and boarded his golf cart. Percy watched him drive back the way they came, disappearing into the jungle.

He stood there long enough that he realized he was stuck. He felt like he couldn't go inside without checking on Juney first. It was like there was a magnetic force between them.

He was also uncomfortable with the idea of sleeping somewhere new, in the middle of the jungle, on an island. At least he could find comfort in the salty air and the distant sound of waves crashing. Wind gusting through palm trees. Those were things he knew, so Percy heaved a sigh and straightened his back. He was an adult, and he'd get over it.

He reached out to open the door but froze. Someone was strumming a bluesy melody on the guitar. He'd recognize it anywhere. Juney was playing Percy's favorite song.

He roughly swiped a hand down his face. His heartbeat was getting harder to ignore.

He let go of his suitcase and took to the path. Every step was both too fast and too slow. Percy was at war with himself. He didn't think this would go well.

He hadn't seen Juney since the moment they carried him away. Everything was still raw and fresh. His nerves were still frayed, and he was still plagued with visions of him bleeding out whenever he closed his eyes.

Maybe he needed to see Juney in one piece to start feeling better.

He came to a stop in front of the door and tilted his head up toward the night sky. This was his best friend, he reminded himself. He knew him inside and out. There was no reason to be nervous.

He steeled himself and knocked. Juney didn't stop playing the guitar. "Go the fuck away," he yelled.

Percy very nearly rolled his eyes, but when he opened his mouth to speak, nothing came out. So, he knocked again.

He heard the hollow clatter of Juney slapping his guitar

and putting it down. "It's ten o' fucking clock," he grumbled as he swung the door open. The air whooshed past Percy. Loose tendrils of his hair fluttered around his face, and his breath caught in his throat.

Juney looked like he saw a ghost. "What—No. God, no. Please. Why are you here?" He dug the heels of his palms into his temples. Percy couldn't help but notice the long angry looking scar that ran the length of his forearm. Tears sprung to Percy's eyes, face flushing with heat. "Amir must've put you up to this."

"He did, yes," was all Percy could manage.

"Well, tell him I'm fine."

Percy's lower lip trembled. "You don't want to see me, Junes?" Juney stood there with his mouth hanging open. That was all the answer Percy needed. "I'll make myself scarce. Don't worry. You don't have to see me while I'm here."

His chest was shaking as he turned to leave. He was beginning to panic.

A rough hand wrapped around his arm, stopping him in his tracks. "I didn't mean it like that," Juney said. He sounded pained. It hurt him to get those words out. "Just—come in."

How had they ended up like this?

They'd meant everything to each other.

Percy tried to force calm breaths through his nose and looked at his shoes as he crossed the threshold into Juney's room. Juney stood a few feet in front of him, but Percy refused to look up. He couldn't do it.

This was never going to work.

"Percy," Juney said firmly. "You don't have to do this. I know you don't want anything to do with me now, and you shouldn't. What I did was not okay. Don't let it be okay."

Percy shook his head, hiding the lower half of his face with a hand. He knew Juney would paint himself in a worse light than even the slimiest tabloid could.

"I don't care about any of that right now. All I care about is the fact that you're standing in front of me. You're breathing. Nothing else matters."

Juney sat on his bed, and a tense silence stretched for far too long. "If that were true, you'd be able to at least look at me."

He had it all wrong. Percy didn't want to look at him because he was afraid of what he might do. He had so many urges. They were the same ones he always had, but now they were more amplified than ever. "I'm trying to be respectful," he mumbled.

For the first time in years, Percy had experienced Juney's touch, and he hadn't been able to forget it. He was back to point A again, desperate for whatever Juney would give him. Percy didn't think he'd ever needed to be held quite as badly as he did right then. He shook with it.

"You're so stupid. How can you possibly think for even a second that I'd ever want nothing to do with you? Is it that easy for you to wash your hands of me? Of course, it is." His voice cracked. "You did it three years ago."

Juney growled through his teeth and grabbed Percy's forearms, pulling him to stand between his legs. "This isn't something that warrants forgiveness, Percy," he stressed each word.

He finally met Juney's gaze with determination. "The three of us only care that you're alive. Everything else can be worked through—like you're doing right now."

Junes still hadn't let go of his arms. Percy watched his face fall and shoulders slacken as he dropped his forehead to Percy's stomach. He gasped at the rush of warmth that engulfed his body. It was enough to knock the air from his lungs. "I'm so messed up."

Percy hadn't ever heard Juney sound this broken.

Percy couldn't take it anymore. He was going to explode. He threaded his fingers through Juney's messy hair and held on tight. He fell to his knees, bringing their foreheads together. "Juney, please. You don't deserve to be thrown away. I know you're beating yourself up way worse on the inside than you'd ever let on. It's too much. All of the people who cared about you still do."

Juney's breaths harshly plumed over Percy's lips. They were so close to each other that Percy felt like he was melting into him, just like he used to.

"Keep caring about me, and you'll only be hurt and disappointed."

Percy's nose grazed against Juney's stubble as he brushed it down the side of his face. He kept going, sinking into Juney's neck and gulping down the scent of comfort and home. He wasn't sure, but he thought they both shivered. It pained him to move away from the skin there as he felt like that was where he belonged forever, but he kept moving down, dragging his cheek down the plane of Juney's torso, feeling the firm muscle beneath his skin. It wasn't enough. There was too much separating them. Percy slipped his fingers beneath Juney's shirt, urging it off. "Please," he murmured.

Juney's expression was unreadable, but his eyes looked sad and his jaw looked angry. It was how he always appeared.

But he pulled his shirt off and tossed it to the floor before grabbing both sides of Percy's head and crushing his face into his stomach. Percy's sigh of relief came out like a moan, and his power drained away as he felt Juney's hot, smooth skin against his. He nosed around his navel, feeling the trail of sparse hair.

Juney kept his hold on him with his fingers threaded through his hair.

Juney's abdomen tensed against Percy's cheek with every short huff of breath he took. "I just missed you so bad, Juney." He spoke into his skin. He moved down to his thigh, and Juney's fingers tightened in his hair. But he didn't stop him when Percy laid his cheek on his upper thigh, just a hairsbreadth from his groin. That was where he wanted to be. Right there with Juney's legs on either side of him, Juney's hand in his hair, and Percy's arms wrapped tightly around Juney's back. He was surrounded, caged, consumed.

He breathed him in. "I'm sorry. I couldn't take it anymore. I thought I lost you for good," he said softly but heavy with anguish. "Need you right now. Forever. Always." He didn't want to stop. He wanted Juney to understand that what he felt for him was unconditional. He'd have Juney in whatever capacity.

But now he needed to move. They hadn't done this in years, and he knew Juney was only tolerating it for Percy's sake. It wasn't enough, but that was okay. It had to be. He dropped his arms and attempted to pull away, but Juney's legs tightened around him, and he used his grip on his hair to press Percy's face even harder into his thigh.

Percy whined.

"Don't move," Winston bit out.

Percy nuzzled his groin. He was so soft and warm.

"Percy..."

"Don't you fucking say it, Junes. I know this isn't normal, and I don't care. I haven't had you in three years."

Juney's fingers tightened, tugging his scalp enough to sting. "You seemed to do just fine."

Percy forcefully pushed back against his hold and glared at

him. "And what about you? It was like nothing changed for you, but my entire life got rearranged."

"Mine did too," he shot back. "But I had to make music and tour the country. I never had time to ruminate. We'd been one way our entire lives, then it changed overnight. Of course, it fucked me up. I'm still fucked up. You saw what happened."

Juney grabbed his chin, hard and unyielding. "I can't accept the fact that I'll lose you to him. To fucking anyone. Nothing has changed since back then, I still don't want you to have anyone but me. I'm selfish, but you don't deserve to be dragged down with me." His eyes were turned down at the corners. "I'm sorry for everything, Percy. I'm trying to work on it so I won't be like this anymore. Just because I'm fucked up and possessive over you, doesn't mean you should let it hold you back. I'm the one with the problem. I don't even trust myself and neither should you."

Percy's face hardened. "I wouldn't be going anywhere if I had you," he seethed. "You took yourself from me."

"I did the right thing," Juney stated with finality.

"You don't get to make that choice for me. I know that I've always left a lot in your hands, but that wasn't—"

"You came to me first. You wanted to cut things off. All I did was follow through because you were right. Here. I'll show you."

Percy's eyes widened before Juney pushed him down, shoving Percy's face into his crotch. Once Percy felt the warmth right there between Juney's legs, he melted into it. Inhaling and rooting around. He held Juney so tight. He just wanted to be the center of his world. Percy felt the almost imperceptible thrust of Juney's hips as he groaned through his teeth. "Do you see? What do you think Emilio would say if he were here right now? Do you think he'd still want to marry you?"

At that moment, Percy didn't care what his fiancé thought of him. He didn't care what anyone thought of his friendship with Juney. For him, it was never something that would be up for debate, and if that left him alone? Good. If Percy had Juney, he would be okay. He shook his head against the cotton of Juney's sweatpants.

Juney laughed, a short hysterical laugh. He was in disbelief. "You're shameless."

"Always have been. Did you forget?" he asked, muffled.

Juney let go of his hair and leaned over him, trailing his large hands down Percy's back—touching him everywhere. "You make it so hard," he said. Percy was able to hide from the truth and the severity of what he was doing to Juney. He didn't have to look at him. "But there's a reason why this decision was made three years ago, and it hasn't changed. If anything, this situation proves that we can't keep doing this."

Percy felt his heart split in half. He'd gotten a fix, and now, Juney was taking it away again. He said there was a reason, but Percy failed to see what could possibly be important enough to keep them apart like this.

He cleared his throat and moved from Juney's hold. His cheeks were warm, but a chill froze the rest of his body without Juney there to hold him. "It's time for me to get going," he said hoarsely. He met Juney's hard eyes. "I'll be here for you. Whatever you need, Junes. I'm here."

Percy rushed through the door and stole away down the trail back to his bungalow.

He wouldn't be getting any sleep tonight.

Eight

WINSTON

It was Winston's second day outside of the main facility. His second day as a level green.

Birds were chirping incessantly, and someone had knocked on his door with food. It sat on the table untouched.

It was also a Saturday so he wasn't expected to do anything. No Ian, no group activities, no stupid fucking movies. If he wanted to, he could lie in bed for the rest of the day.

They'd given him his medications, and he was responsible for taking them—which he actually planned to do. After two weeks on them, he was noticing something of a difference in himself, and he'd yet to have an awful side effect. The worst he'd experienced was dry mouth. That was a small price to pay for how he felt.

The change wasn't drastic, but it was in the little things. He wanted to stay in bed right now, but a larger part of him didn't. He thought it was because overall, he felt more present lately. It made him realize just how much of his life he'd spent disassociated.

So at first, he didn't understand what this feeling was or how to describe it. He just knew that he used to feel like a wraith, but now he was opaque. It wasn't so easy for him to fade away. He wasn't sure what he thought about that yet.

All he knew was that he could get up today. He didn't have to rot. The choice was up to him.

His eyes gravitated to his guitar propped against the wall, but they also flitted to the door. He knew Percy was a stone's throw away. Yet another thing Winston was conflicted about. The safest thing he had going for him was Ian, but he only got to see him on Mondays and Wednesdays.

He groaned. He needed to do fucking something, so he forced himself out of bed and got half-assed ready. Cut-off sleeve t-shirt and cut-off jeans. He brushed his teeth without looking in the mirror, grabbed the guitar and notebook that Ian had given him, and left.

He wasn't sure where he was going, but he followed the beaten trail further into the brush. The breeze that rolled off the water provided a constant balm against the heat. It shook through the palms, bending their flexible trunks. The sun flitted through them in flashes and Winston hadn't felt this good in a long time. Ever since their music took off, he had less time to do the few things he enjoyed.

It became work. His favorite thing to do became a contractual obligation.

The fame. Knowing millions of people perceived him however they wanted. It was a cage. It wasn't a surprise that money didn't change how fucked up he was on the inside, and how that colored everything he did. He would always fail.

There was a fork in the path. One led to a cliff that overlooked the ocean, and the other looked like it trailed around and down the incline to get to the beach. Winston didn't feel like walking that far. This outing was supposed to be relaxing, so he decided to venture further another day.

He headed toward the grassy knoll that was close to the cliff's edge. He scoffed. "Can't believe they put a bunch of crazies this close to a cliff," he said to himself, and wasn't that just great? After twenty-two days here, he was talking to himself. Considering the only soul he spoke to during his stay in the facility regularly was Ian, and most of his time was spent alone in his room, it wasn't surprising.

Winston was no stranger to being alone, but he'd always been able to be high or drunk. Stone-cold sober isolation was a different beast that he was starting to take solace in.

There was a palm tree that grew out horizontally over the edge of the cliff like a hand reaching for the sun on the horizon. He sat with his back to the trunk. Its hard ridges dug into his spine, but it wasn't so bad with the heat on his skin.

Percy had been right about living at the beach. It suited both of them well, and Winston never had to open his front door and see miles of farmland.

Now, he had a house with a private beach as his backyard. A small part of him was proud that he was able to do that for Percy. Make that dream come true. If anything good had come from Telltale Dream's money and fame, it was that.

His eyes fell closed, and he tilted his head to the sky.

On the outside, he felt like a flimsy version of serene. On the inside, swords were clashing and cannons firing. Chaos. He might've had a chance at being calm if it weren't for Percy showing up at his door last night.

Winston considered his feelings for a moment. He'd been trying to do that more lately.

He wanted to chain Percy to his bed and swallow him whole, wanted Percy embedded in his skin. He wanted him to be happy, and it didn't matter if Winston could give him that or not. Percy should be his regardless. That was how selfish he was.

Winston clutched the neck of his guitar. Those feelings couldn't be healthy, but that didn't make them any less valid. He was supposed to work through those kinds of thoughts, but Winston didn't believe they could be worked through.

They could work on his mommy and daddy issues all they wanted, but Percy was a fucking brand on his heart. If he weren't, Winston would've moved on by now.

And at the end of the day, he didn't want to move on from Percy. He wanted to hold onto him forever.

Winston's eyelids were getting heavier, so he forced them open and readjusted himself. Sleep was not his friend last night.

It'd been so long since he was able to write anything worthwhile, but he'd been feeling something brewing inside of him. Some energy was circling in his gut that he knew could be put on paper if he was able to get it out. Of course, his first attempt would be a waste because he couldn't stop thinking about Percy.

Of course.

The wheels turned in his brain until they started to jam. It was on fire from straining so hard. He stared at the blank sheet of lined paper until his vision blurred, and his limbs grew heavy. He tried to fight it by readjusting but felt himself giving up, and it wasn't long before his eyes drifted shut.

"Juney. Fuck, fuck, fuck. I thought you..." Percy trailed off, and even through Winston's dense fog of sleep, he thought it was strange that Percy was swearing so much. It was rare that he did.

He forced his eyes to open just enough to tell that the sun was setting. There was a subtle chill. He hugged his arms around himself.

"Mr. Jennings," said another voice. "Please, get up. It's past dinner time."

The stranger got his attention. Winston propped himself up on his elbows. "Damn. What's with the fucking search party?"

Percy glared at him with flinty eyes, and the man next to him who was in a Black Diamond uniform—tan shorts and a collared shirt—looked bored. "You were missing when the dinner cart came through, so he reported it to the unit. You have to be in during breakfast and dinner. It's a very important rule for psychiatric patients."

Winston nodded, staring off into the choppy surf. The waves were rough, there was a chill and a breeze. It was going to storm soon. It bothered him that even though he was a code green, he still had to follow their schedule all because he was a suicide risk. He knew that was what the guy was implying, and they found him right here on the cliff where he could've very easily jumped. He shook himself out of it and stood up.

After grabbing his guitar and notebook, he breezed past them, following the trail back to his bungalow. He didn't want to talk about it or think about it any longer. There was something about the fact that people were watching his every move because they thought he might try to take his own life that made his stomach turn. It was pathetic that he needed to be monitored like a baby. So fucking pathetic.

And he didn't even want to talk to Percy. It would only bring him more shame than he already felt.

He opened his door and locked it behind himself before throwing the guitar on the ground. It clattered loudly, and his notebook slapped against the table. His heart dropped into his gut, and he truly felt sick. Felt like retching. This is what his life had become.

This.

He had everything anyone could ever want. He had his dream career and more money than he knew what to do with. But, still, he couldn't guarantee to anyone that he wouldn't attempt suicide again. He knew himself. Knew the way that his mood could plummet at any time. It was something he had no control over. He'd be locked to his bed with the same thoughts on a loop.

What's the point of living? It's too hard. I'll die someday anyway, so why not now? Being here... hurts too bad. It's hard for me to even take care of myself. I'm wasting space. Wasting every-one's time.

I wish something would take me in my sleep, so I'd never wake up.

When he was that low, even the thought of Percy wasn't guaranteed to keep him from doing it.

He flirted with death often. He'd do unnecessary amounts of cocaine in the hopes that his heart would stop. Sometimes he'd take more pills than he needed. Alcohol? Until he blacked out.

Winston didn't consider himself an addict. He knew he wouldn't be doing any of that if he didn't constantly want to die. He figured if he was still alive, he might as well say fuck it. What did he have to lose?

He knew he was weak and a coward and a selfish piece of

shit. That much had always been obvious, and all of his guilt made it even harder to keep two feet on the ground.

He lived like that. Every day. His dwelling was a bleak, lonely forest where he hoped the fungi would take him as he rotted.

Winston grabbed the pills that were supposed to be good and swallowed them quickly. It always had to be quick, so he wouldn't have a chance to think too much about it.

He stood there in silence, but the buzzing in his ears was loud, almost deafening. He was alone, and there was nothing left to do. Maybe he'd be able to fall asleep, so he could lock all his feelings back up again. He'd let them out but didn't have a way to fix them. Pointless.

He stripped down to his boxers and turned off the light before slipping into bed, hugging the blanket to his chest and Percy's shirt to his nose. The shirt had a permanent home under his pillow. It got a lot of use.

Since he slept for so long outside, he wasn't entirely sure he'd be able to fall asleep now, but there wasn't another option.

He stared into pitch-black darkness for long enough that his vision swirled, and the ringing in his ears had gotten so loud that he almost didn't hear the soft knock on the door. He knew it was Percy, and he wanted to scream. So, he didn't get up. Maybe Percy would leave.

Nope. He knocked louder and louder until he resorted to shouting, "Open up the door you fucking asshole! I know you're in there. Stop ignoring me!"

It really was concerning how much Percy was swearing these days. He considered whether he should continue to ignore him or not, but there was something about the way he sounded that compelled him to open the door and see if he was okay.

Percy's brows were pinched. It wasn't a good time because he knew Percy was about to scold him, but the wrinkle between his brows was cute. He wished he could smooth it away with his lips.

Percy took in his current state of undress and cleared his throat. His eyes were glassy, and his arms were crossed over his chest. Percy was ready to ream him the fuck out, but Winston didn't understand what the big deal was. Either way, he stepped back and beckoned him. "I'm not turning the light back on," he grumbled before sitting on his bed. Percy heaved a frustrated sigh and stood in front of him. He could just barely make out his form in the dark and figured Percy could see about the same. "Go ahead, Percy. Let it out."

Winston's hands fisted on top of his thighs. He was sick and fucking tired of not touching Percy.

"How could you be so careless? You scared me to death." Each word was emboldened with anger.

"It was an accident. I didn't get any sleep last night, so I was tired and drifted off. There's really nothing to it," he answered, even though he knew Percy didn't want it.

"There's nothing to it?" he repeated. "What the hell were you doing there anyway?"

Winston frowned in the dark. He didn't see how that mattered. "I was trying to write. You saw the guitar and note-book," he bit out. That much should've been obvious.

Percy didn't respond. They fell into complete silence, and Winston dropped his head into his hands. This was making everything worse. He'd disappointed Percy enough in their lives —he didn't need him there to add more damage.

After a while, Percy's breaths started to get increasingly louder until he was panting. There was a choked sob, and Winston hopped up quickly. "What's going on? Are you okay?" The words poured out of him thoughtlessly as he grabbed Percy's upper arms.

"I-I... can't..." He struggled to speak.

Winston realized Percy was hyperventilating, and hugged Percy to his chest. He wound his fingers in the hair at the nape of his neck hard enough to sting a little. He wanted to give him a feeling to focus on—something he could latch on to.

A choked sob shook from his chest as he cried on Winston's shoulder. There was snot and spit, and Winston couldn't care less. He just needed his Percy to be okay. He shushed him softly as he slipped his other hand under his shirt to rub circles on his back, squeezing him tight. Percy liked to be squeezed tight, and Winston didn't like how badly Percy was trembling in his arms. He kneeled, bringing Percy with him, so Percy didn't have to worry about standing up on weak legs.

Percy immediately sat in his lap, still crying on his shoulder. Winston's heart was in his throat. Now he was finding it hard to breathe. Percy wasn't the type to cry. It was rare that Winston ever saw him do it. He could name each time, and the last time was when Winston was dying. He hardly remembered any of it, but the sound of Percy's sobs and pleas still echoed through his head. It was gut-wrenching.

He didn't want to keep making Percy cry. "I'm sorry," he said. "I'm sorry. I'm sorry. I won't do it again. I promise, okay? It's okay, darlin'." He searched for the right thing to say to make Percy feel better, and it must've worked.

Percy's voice was hoarse and shaky. He hiccuped and sniffled. "D-darlin'?"

Something swirled in Winston's chest. He hadn't ever called Percy that, and he hadn't even realized what he was saying. Darlin' made sense to him though. It did. "What of it?" he said.

Percy huffed a short laugh and squeezed him harder. "I can't believe you," he said. His voice hadn't leveled out yet.

"I'm sorry," he said.

"I'm still... it's hard after what happened. You don't seem okay, and I'm worried."

It was like a knife in the chest. These were things he knew, but he didn't ever want to hear them from Percy's mouth. They took on a more solid form now, and he supposed he deserved this pain. He knew Percy and everyone would be traumatized. After seeing what they saw, who wouldn't be? "I have no intention of doing it again," he said, but it was only a half-truth. He had no intention right now, but he knew that someday he would again.

More guilt.

"I know that you're participating and being receptive in therapy. I'm sorry for not having more faith in you. I know you're trying."

Winston thought that was incredibly stupid. Percy should apologize for nothing ever, especially not this. Winston should be on his knees begging Percy for forgiveness day in and day out. "Would you quit that shit? You don't need to be supportive of me or consider my feelings or any of it. I hurt you. You have every right to feel angry and sad or whatever else. Don't shove it away on account of me."

Thunder cracked through the sky, shaking the floor beneath Winston. Percy jumped and Winston cursed. The loud sound of a torrential downpour pelting against his straw-covered roof began. Percy buried his face in his neck harder. This wasn't the time for a storm. They'd always made Percy nervous, and Percy did not need that right now.

"Juney," he said. "You're an idiot. A blind idiot."

Winston hummed. "Yes, thank you. I know."

"You don't need to tell me what I should and shouldn't feel. I'm healing at my own pace, and that doesn't make what I'm feeling any less real. I don't understand why you can't grasp the concept. I will never leave you. You can't convince me to do that. It'd be like severing a limb, like ripping my heart right from my chest," he said.

He was sure they hadn't exchanged this many words in years, and it seemed like every word Percy said disarmed him more and more.

He felt his resolve crumbling too often. "What do you want me to do?" Winston asked.

After a beat, Percy said, "Whenever you leave this bungalow, I want to be with you. I need the reassurance that you're okay. I can't live in fear twenty-four-seven—"

"You—" Winston tried to cut in.

"No. I don't want to hear it. We've been over it already. We're trying to solve things now, not keep harping on the same problems. Just give me this. I'll give you your privacy or whatever when you need it, but I need to be aware at all times."

Winston sighed against Percy's shoulder, still reeling over the fact that Percy was in his arms again.

He didn't think Percy was asking too much of him. Not at all. If things were the other way around, he wouldn't even give Percy the courtesy of a choice. He wouldn't tip-toe around his privacy either. Fuck that. "Sure," he responded. "But you're staying here tonight."

Percy stilled against him. Winston hadn't really thought that through before he'd said it, but it was a matter of not feeling comfortable letting him out of his sight if he's been having panic attacks like this. It wasn't something he would budge on.

"What?" Percy coughed.

"It's non-negotiable."

Percy pulled back. "Yesterday you told me we needed to keep our distance."

"That was before I knew you're an anxious wreck and having panic attacks. I'm under supervision, and you should be too."

Percy scoffed and mumbled, "I'm not an anxious wreck."

"Sure you aren't, darlin'. Actually, you might as well stay here every night. We'll get your things tomorrow."

"That's probably not even allowed, Juney. Come on."

Percy was just scrambling for a reason. They both knew that didn't matter. "Have Amir throw more money at them. It shouldn't be a concern anyway."

Percy was silent, and Winston knew he was thinking in circles. Thunder cracked again. It was even louder this time, and Percy jolted. "Fine. Whatever. I'll stay tonight."

"Every night. You'll stay every night," Winston corrected.

Percy shook his head and stood up. "I'm going to sleep. It's been a fucked up day. Do you have some sweats I can wear?"

"You've got some foul language lately," he said as he moved to turn the light on. His bones were achey, and he was having some kind of adrenaline crash that he imagined Percy was feeling too.

Percy had puffy eyes and a red nose as he gave Winston an unimpressed look. "Says you."

Winston almost grinned. "Sweats are in that bag over there." He hadn't unpacked anything yet, and he wasn't sure he was going to anyway. Percy noticed as much and poured them out of the bag. "That's not really necessary," he said as he sat on the mattress.

Percy didn't say a word. There weren't many clothes there, so Percy folded them and stacked them in the dresser drawer quickly. It took probably five minutes in total. It wouldn't have been difficult to do himself, but that wasn't why he hadn't done it. He'd been reluctant to settle into this place, and he thought Percy figured as much since he didn't say anything about it.

Then, like it didn't matter at all, Percy kicked off his shoes, pulled off his shirt, and dropped his pants. Winston gritted his teeth but couldn't peel his gaze from the span of Percy's back. His muscles were plain to see, they just weren't as obnoxious as Winston's. He loved them. Loved his long legs and narrow shoulders.

Percy stepped into the sweatpants and pulled the tie out of his hair. It was long like it always had been—a thick, dark curtain of hair that Winston knew was unrealistically soft. It was fucking beautiful and magical and all the rest of that bullshit. There wasn't another person on this planet that Winston would ever describe that way.

He wanted to tell Percy how perfect he was but couldn't. It didn't matter anyway. Percy was still engaged and still just his best friend. Nothing had changed.

Percy turned around and locked those dream-blue eyes with his. Winston knew there wasn't a shade of blue called dream, but he hadn't ever found a better way to describe them.

Percy noticed he was staring, but Winston didn't stop. Maybe he didn't actually give a fuck about Percy's engagement. It was feeling like he didn't. Percy's tongue swiped across his lips.

Emilio was nobody. He didn't matter. Winston would do what he wanted. He had a new lease on life.

He stood up directly in front of Percy and crossed his arms. "Were you able to sleep last night? It's a new place. I know how hard that is for you."

Percy rubbed his eyes with the heels of his palms. "Not a wink," he replied.

Winston turned toward the light switch. "Guess you better lay down then."

He saw Percy chewing his lower lip just before he turned the light off. Percy laid down, and Winston was right behind him. He didn't hesitate at all before putting an arm around Percy and sticking himself to Percy's back. His nose was right in his hair. It was that fucking smell that he loved. He missed it so badly. It centered him, and he didn't have to use the shirt tonight. He had the real thing.

Percy gasped quietly. "What are you—I thought..."

Winston squeezed him tighter. There wasn't an inch of space between them. He spread his palm and dragged it across Percy's skin, up to his chest. Percy latched onto it, holding it there just like he used to.

Winston's half-hard cock was resting against Percy's ass. He knew he could feel it, but he didn't seem to care. Hadn't moved. Percy's heart raced beneath his palm. "Is this okay?" he asked.

Winston slid his palm up further to wrap it around Percy's neck. His grip was soft, but just enough that Percy could feel it. He'd always liked being wrapped up in Winston in every way possible.

He felt him swallow before answering. "Yes." The single word was a barely audible whisper over the rain pounding the bungalow.

Percy relaxed against him, leaning back. "I think you're wearing too many clothes. I know you'd rather be held naked."

He hadn't always wanted to be naked. It took a while for him, but eventually, he'd said he wanted to be closer. It wasn't close enough with clothes on. It was the worst form of torture he'd experienced at the time, but he did it anyway. How could he not?

Winston started pushing Percy's pants down, and Percy didn't stop him. In fact, he helped kick them off. Now they were both in their boxers.

Nine

PERCY

Percy was on fire.

He burned hotter than he ever had.

Juney was holding him, getting him naked, whispering in his ear, and Percy's heart was going to burst. Juney brushed his calloused fingers near his waistband, grazing it back and forth. He pushed them beneath the waistband, and Percy's breath caught in his throat. He knew Juney was waiting to see if he'd stop him, but he was paralyzed. He couldn't stop him even if he wanted to.

There was nothing that could stop him now. He was done for.

For three years, he'd wanted this. Three long years.

Juney's fingertip grazed the head of his dick as he pulled the boxers down, and he couldn't breathe. Juney roughly ran his hand up the length of his inner thigh.

"Should I take mine off?" he whispered hotly. Percy's

mouth was so dry he wasn't sure he could speak. "What do you think your fiancé would say if he saw you right now? Do you think he'd still want to marry you?"

There was a sharp edge to his words that made Percy's chest hurt. They both knew the answer to that question. Guilt lodged deep in his gut, twisting it into knots. He was conflicted. He knew that this wasn't the right thing to do, knew it'd hurt Emilio. It made him sick to his stomach.

But there was a much louder feeling consuming him. It was something he didn't feel like he could fight. He was desperate for Juney's attention. He wanted to talk to him and be his person again. He wanted to be touched by him. He'd take the tiniest scrap of it.

He needed these things, and he'd been deprived for so long. Percy didn't know how he was supposed to resist.

Juney rocked his hips, pressing his hard shaft against him. Without a word, Juney slid his boxers down, and Percy didn't stop him. Not even when Juney's hard shaft seared into the crease of his ass. A small whimper escaped him, and he wasn't proud of the way he pushed back against Juney's cock. The groan that rumbled from Junes made his hairs stand on end.

Percy remembered when he realized what this feeling was. For the longest time, he didn't think anything of it. He thought he was straight, and he was okay with getting a boner. He figured it was a natural reaction. He knew Juney was gay, and he still didn't mind at all. Percy was always the one to initiate things. Junes never ever touched him first.

That was okay until it wasn't. A point in time came when he understood more about himself and his sexuality. He knew that there was no way he was straight with the feelings he'd been having about Junes, but he hadn't felt that way about another guy before, hadn't felt that way for anyone at all.

He was wanting more and more from Juney. Nothing was ever enough, and it was crescendoing. It was too dangerous. That was why he'd wanted to stop it. Juney didn't want him that way, and Percy didn't want to ruin everything.

But Percy wasn't strong enough to stick to it.

Juney was.

It had cemented everything he'd already thought which hurt more than anything.

"Juney, what's going on?" he asked. He didn't understand why he suddenly wanted to touch him. Juney initiated this. Juney wanted it.

Then it dawned on him, and his heart sank. Juney was doing this out of some sense of obligation or penance. He was doing it for forgiveness; he felt like he had to. "You don't have to do this," he said. The words burst from him, leaving anxiety in their wake.

Juney wrapped his muscular arm around his middle and grabbed his chin, forcing Percy to look at him. He could barely discern his facial features in the dark, but it didn't matter because he had every little detail about him memorized. Juney was so close that his breaths puffed against his lips. "I want to do this," he said.

Percy clenched his teeth. "I'm telling you it's okay, Junes. We can just lay separately."

He gripped his chin harder, and it sent a thrill down Percy's spine. "You don't need me anymore? Your fiancé has it all covered, doesn't he," Juney words were sharp as nails. Percy slammed his mouth shut to restrain his moan, but he knew Juney heard it. He cocked his head to the side. "You don't want me to stop, do you? You're just trying to do the right thing."

Percy kept his lips sealed tight even though Juney was

slowly thrusting against his backside. He couldn't say anything. It'd be a lie.

"You don't have to do the right thing with me, darlin'." There was a dark lilt to his southern drawl that made Percy's cock ache.

Juney's fingers dug into his chin as he moved his hips. His shaft slid through Percy's crack dryly. They were eye to eye, and this was sexual. This was different. It was more than they'd ever done.

Juney was... Percy's brain was on fire. All he knew was that he'd never felt better in his fucking life.

He'd never been this turned on.

Never been this desperate and needy.

He'd let Juney do anything to him right now as long as he didn't stop, and he knew it wasn't right. "In your nightstand," Percy croaked. "There's lotion."

"That's an answer if I ever heard one," he responded as he let go of him to grab it. Percy didn't like it. Immediately, he felt the edge of panic settle in, so he lifted his leg and brought it back to hook around Juney's thigh. Rationally, he knew Juney wasn't going anywhere, but he didn't like feeling like he was. It scared him.

He heard the slick sound of Juney stroking his dick with lotion, and his cheeks flushed hotter than they already were. Juney situated his cock in the crest of Percy's ass, right at his taint. Then, he put Percy's legs together again, with his dick between Percy's thighs.

Percy's heart raced. He'd done this before. He didn't want to think about it, but this was something he and Emilio did since Percy hadn't let him fuck him. Percy had never been fucked by anyone.

Juney was pressed against his back again. His big arm

wound around his front, so he could hold Percy's throat. He'd always loved how it made him feel owned—like he belonged to Juney and could trust him with everything. That fact had always been true, but it was another thing to feel it physically.

His nose was buried in Percy's hair again. He knew Juney was inhaling him the same way Percy liked to do to him.

He slowly thrust, dragging his cock along the sensitive skin there, along his balls, fucking himself between Percy's thighs. It was euphoric knowing that Juney was getting himself off, that Percy was doing it for him.

"So, you've been with men now, huh?" Juney bit out, squeezing his neck tighter.

"So have you," he said.

A low growl emanated from Juney's throat. "How many?"

His cock twitched. He reached down and wrapped his hand around it. "Not many."

"Give me a number, Percy. I'm just curious."

Percy had only been with Emilio, but he didn't want to admit it. "It doesn't matter, Junes. You couldn't give me a number if you tried."

Juney fucked his thighs harder. "You're engaged to be married," he said harshly. He let go of Percy's throat and roughly grabbed his shaft. Percy moaned loudly. "He must not be all that great."

"S-stop," he panted. He was trembling, and Juney's grip on his shaft was hard as he stroked him. It was taking him apart. He'd never had Juney like this. Percy was the one who gave him handjobs.

Juney's calloused hand felt way better than Emilio's soft one. Guilt lanced through his gut again.

"Does he make you tremble like this? Don't think you'd be here if he did," he said. His voice was low and gravelly. Juney was driving him crazy from three different angles. His hand around Percy's cock pumped at the same rhythm with which he slid his dick between his thighs. He couldn't take it.

"Who makes me feel what doesn't matter. I'd always be here for you."

Juney's movements stuttered, and he let out something akin to a whimper. More blood rushed to his cock as his pleasure mounted. "You'd come to me no matter who you were with?" Juney asked.

Their breaths were ragged, hot, and gusting over each other's lips. Their faces were dangerously closed. If he moved an inch they'd kiss. "I need you always. I told you it'd never stop, no matter who I was with," Percy replied.

Juney's moan was a strangled, painfully beautiful thing. He didn't think anyone could sound like that. Juney's hand tightened, and he punched into him one more time before Percy felt the hot burn of Juney's cum on his sensitive skin. Juney was still moaning, long and low, when he dropped his forehead to his. His dick was still moving between his thighs, squelching through his cum obscenely, and Percy's eyes rolled back into his head. He gasped as his release exploded from him. Thick ropes of cum coated Juney's hand. Some landed somewhere in his bed.

There was still a cyclone behind his eyelids when he noticed their lips were brushing together. They were breathing in each other's panting breaths, and Percy wanted to kiss so badly. He wanted to feel Juney's tongue against his own.

But Juney turned his head and scrubbed his cheek against Percy's, nuzzling into his hair again.

Juney's flaccid cock was pressed firmly against the crest of his sticky thighs, and he was still holding Percy hard enough that he couldn't move very much. It was exactly how he liked it.

"You're so fucking good, Percy. So fucking perfect for me," Juney murmured.

Percy swallowed as the cyclone moved to his chest, wreaking havoc on his heart. "For you," he repeated. A lump was swelling in his throat, and he was worried he might choke on a sob. He didn't want that to happen, didn't want Juney to feel like he'd done something wrong because he hadn't. He was perfect.

"My Percy," he said aggressively, like a kid hoarding their favorite toy. "Always."

As their breathing returned to normal, the silence stretched, but Percy could tell Juney wasn't asleep yet. He never went to sleep before Percy did. He was naked in bed with his best friend, covered in his cum, with an engagement ring around his finger.

Percy had never felt more disgusted with himself. It swirled in his stomach inky black and thick. Would he be able to look Emilio in the eye again?

What about Juney? This would change them forever. What they'd done years ago didn't even come close to this. Maybe he'd fucked everything up with both of them.

But that would be up to Juney himself because Percy would never turn his back on him.

"Juney—"

"Stop thinking. If you're going to tell me you regret it, don't," he grumbled.

Percy set his jaw and hugged Juney's arm harder.

How would he live the rest of his life with a weakness as great as this one?

In the morning, he woke up alone. Percy blinked the sleep from his eyes and took stock of the room. The lights were off, but he could make out Juney's guitar where he'd left it last night. His notebook wasn't on the table though.

As soon as he stood up, he was reminded of what he'd done last night. Juney's dried cum between his legs made him feel filthy—inside and out. *Shit. Shit. Shit.* He rushed into the bathroom and turned the knob until it was as hot as it could go. He avoided the mirror and stepped into the large walk-in shower. It was the extra fancy type they had in their house back in Miami.

He grabbed a washcloth and roughly scrubbed himself clean, but he didn't feel any less disgusted with himself.

He cheated on his fiancé. There had been so many opportunities to stop, but he hadn't had the willpower. If Emilio had been knocking on the door, he still didn't think he could've stopped.

God, no.

He was mindless in Juney's arms, barely even conscious.

That wasn't a good enough excuse, but he didn't think anyone could understand how he'd felt last night. If they did, maybe they wouldn't condemn him for it.

Was this how every cheater felt? Like they didn't even have a choice in the matter? Maybe it was just him and his marrow-deep need to be the center of his best friend's attention, to be possessed by him.

The more he thought about it the sicker he felt. As Juney had always said, it just wasn't right. Percy hadn't realized just how much he needed Juney and what that meant until it'd been too late. Juney had cut him off completely. Now he understood why.

This was his cross to bear now.

He shut off the water and quickly toweled himself dry. He stepped out of the bathroom with the towel around his waist and located the sweatpants he'd worn for all of five minutes last night and put them on. He stole one of Juney's t-shirts too. It was one he'd already claimed as his anyway—they all were.

Anxiety was starting to swirl with the guilt that was already in his stomach. He didn't think Juney would go and do something... he didn't think he would...

He couldn't even think about it. He threw the front door open and smelled cigarette smoke. Juney was sitting at the table on the porch with a pack of Marlboro reds on his thigh.

It was sad how relieved he felt. He wondered if he'd ever stop feeling like he was on the precipice of grief.

There were two untouched food trays on the table, and Percy quietly moved to sit down. The air was thick with humidity. It was already clinging to his skin, but Percy didn't mind it. The smell of wet soil and salt and all the tropical plant life relaxed him. He loved going down to the beach at dawn and dusk after a storm had blown through. It was something like relief and awe. He tried to never take the wonders of the world for granted, no matter how nervous they made him. They reminded him that he was so small, and there was a big picture if he looked for it. That was the only thing that helped him maintain peace of mind since he'd first met Juney.

When Juney had walked into his yard for the first time, Percy realized how lonely he'd been. When Juney laid in the grass with him, their shoulders were touching, and Percy hadn't been used to that feeling. He loved his family to death, but they weren't a physically affectionate bunch. So, he hadn't even realized that he missed it until it was right there next to him.

Juney had always looked sad, even before Mrs. Jennings passed away. Percy hadn't ever seen a kid who looked so dismal, and he'd figured that was why everyone avoided him at school. That only dug Juney deeper. Percy had watched his progression from elementary school on, and Juney had only gotten more troubled as time went on.

Percy had known how Juney and Mr. Jennings struggled. They were always against each other even though they were together in their shared pain.

Juney had attempted suicide at fifteen years old, and that was when Percy found out that he could be cut down. His life had always been perfect. He'd been happy and bright and his family loved him endlessly. But all of that could fade to black in the blink of an eye. Someone had the power to crush him to death, and it stunned him. Shot him right into the real world like he'd never been before.

From that day on, Percy's world tilted on its axis, and he hadn't felt true peace since then. He still struggled to find it. Percy was always worried about him, obsessing over him, and trying to do any and everything he could to ease Juney's life. Percy knew he didn't owe Juney that. He knew it wasn't his responsibility. But Juney was his heart and soul, and he suffered. He'd always suffered. Percy might not have always known how to define what Juney went through, but he knew that Juney needed help, and he would never ask for it or accept it from anyone but him.

Juney's pain was his own.

That was why he needed to find peace in the small things. The constants.

"Are you going to eat your breakfast? I made sure they

knew that you're a vegan too," Juney said, bringing him right back down to this heavy moment he wanted so badly to avoid. Percy didn't respond. Even if he wanted to, it felt like there was something lodged in his throat.

Palm fronds brushed against one another.

Waves crashed.

A light breeze swept through.

Percy lifted the lid from his plate, and his stomach roiled. Neither of them ate dinner last night. He could feel Juney's eyes on him as he started eating an acai bowl. It was topped with fresh fruit, nuts, granola, and honey. It was almost delicious enough to take his mind off of the giant, life-changing mistake he'd made last night and what it said about him as a person.

He risked looking up only to take the cigarette from Juney's fingertips and put it out in his makeshift ashtray. "Eat," he said sternly.

Juney scoffed but wordlessly removed the lid from his plate.

"How did you get cigarettes?" Percy grumbled. His curiosity got the best of him.

He paused his shoveling and said, "They confiscated them when I arrived at the mental health facility. Took my lip ring too, but they gave both back. I'll be out soon. Need to figure out how to get more."

"I'm sure there's a way," Percy said.

Juney nodded. "I bet one of the staff can get me some." He continued eating. Then he randomly stopped. "Did you bring Eleanor?"

"Of course I brought Eleanor. No way I'd go weeks without her."

"That's contraband. Criminal."

"Take me to jail," he said noncommittally around his final bite of food. Percy wasn't able to find humor in anything right now—not when there was a giant elephant in the room. He tapped his foot absentmindedly, faster and faster until he couldn't hold it in any longer. "We fucked last night," he blurted. Heat rushed to his cheeks. Somehow, talking about it in the light of day made him feel even worse.

Juney pushed his tray away and lit a cigarette. He inhaled it like it was better than oxygen, and Percy could understand that.

"No, we didn't," he said plainly.

Percy's brows pulled together. He didn't have the patience for this. "Whose cum did I just wash off of my thighs then?"

The corners of Juney's lips ticked upward, but his eyes bored into Percy's. He shook his head. "You certainly don't look like you've been fucked by me. I don't see any marks, and you sat down just fine." Juney trailed his eyes from Percy's face to his lips and down to his neck. Percy's heart raced. "'Cause here's the thing, darlin', you would know if I fucked you."

Percy's breath caught. He could easily imagine being covered in marks from Juney, and he could've whined at the fact that he wasn't. Cold realization trickled down his spine. Juney had fucked people. A lot of people. He did it all the time like it meant nothing to him.

"Like that makes a difference," he said weakly.

Juney stood up. "You feel guilty."

Percy covered his mouth with a hand. He didn't know what would show on his face. "A little bit, yeah." He saw no reason to lie about it. "I'm not a cheater. I don't want to hurt him."

Juney's eyes drilled into his, scrutinizing. Percy swallowed roughly, already feeling unsure.

After what seemed like forever, Juney said, "I'm going for a walk."

Percy shot up from his seat. "O-okay. Do you still want me to move into your place?"

"Yes."

Juney was being short with him. He could tell. It was the same way he'd been treating him the last few years. Percy had gotten as used to it as he could over time, but it was devastating in the beginning. Maybe he'd already started getting his hopes up that their relationship would go back to how it was, but it was clear now that it wouldn't. He cleared his throat. "I'll go get my duffel and come with you on your walk." Juney's jaw ticked. Percy could tell he didn't want him to come. "I'm going," he repeated—this time with a sterner edge of finality.

Juney didn't say another word. He walked into his bungalow and shut the door behind him. Percy didn't care if Junes was angry at him. His safety would always come first. Percy tried to shake it off as he followed the path back to his bungalow. None of his things were unpacked since he'd only stayed one excruciating night here.

A loud buzz startled him. He knew that sound. With a heavy sigh, he crossed the room and grabbed his phone from the nightstand. He begrudgingly answered the call. "Amir," he said.

"How is he? You've been there for two days, and no one's heard a word from you." Amir started the interrogation right away.

"There hasn't been anything to report back. He's doing well. Still cooperating," he stated dryly.

There was a scoff on the other end of the line. "Look, I know I've been up your ass and it's annoying. It's annoying for me too, but I need answers. My *boss* needs answers. Does he want to quit the band? Are you going to find a new singer or break up Telltale Dream altogether?"

Juney wouldn't quit. He might want to right now, but Percy would never let him do that. Telltale Dream was the only thing tying him and Juney together. It was something he didn't like thinking about. He didn't want to face the fragility of their relationship. "He's not quitting," he replied with all the confidence he could muster.

There was a long pause and then the *whoosh* of an exhausted sigh. "I'm sorry, Percy. Everything is going to be okay. Winston will be fine and so will the band. The album will get finished, and the world tour will go off without a hitch. I have faith in you guys," he said genuinely. Amir was always mildly stressed out, but he'd never been this panicked.

Percy pinched the bridge of his nose. "We're all on edge right now, but it'll all work out the way it's supposed to in the end. It has to."

With that, they said their goodbyes and hung up. He was afraid to look through the hundreds of notifications he'd missed, but he skimmed them anyway. Social media, emails, Amir.

Emilio...

His phone showed that his fiancé had called him three times since he'd arrived at Black Diamond. Percy intentionally ignored the first call on the night he got here. After what happened with Juney that night, he'd felt raw and guilty—not only for what he'd done. It was the thoughts he'd had. Emilio called him two times this morning, and Percy wouldn't have answered them even if his phone had been on him. He wasn't sure he'd be able to talk to Emilio for a while. Percy knew Emilio would be upset with him for that, which made him feel worse.

He tossed his phone down on the bed and pulled at the collar of his t-shirt, sweat beading above his brow. He didn't know what he was going to do.

The door swung open, and Percy nearly jumped out of his skin. His hand flew to his chest. It was just Juney who, of course, didn't bother with knocking. Percy glared at him, but his phone started vibrating on his bed. It caught their attention. He could see Emilio's contact photo on the screen.

Juney strode across the room and grabbed it. "No, no, no," Percy warned, but Juney did something he wasn't expecting. He shoved the phone at him.

"Answer your fiancé's call," he said.

Percy flinched. "No."

"This is your husband-to-be."

Juney answered the call and put it on speaker so they could both hear it. He lifted his eyebrows and pushed the phone into Percy's hands expectantly. Percy clenched his teeth.

"Hello, love... Hello?" Emilio said. The silence stretched. "Are you there?"

Percy winced at his hopeful tone. "Emilio! Hi." He stared at his phone screen intently, avoiding Juney's eyes. He didn't know what he'd find there, but he knew it couldn't be good.

"I was getting worried, love. Hadn't heard from you since you left."

"Oh, I'm sorry. I fell asleep as soon as I got here, and then I left my phone at my bungalow all day. It was dead by the time I got back, so I put it on the charger to call you this morning. I'm trying to disconnect from work while I'm here, so I want to ignore my phone," he said, making sure to keep his tone gentle and easy.

Chills shot down his spine as he felt Juney at his back.

Juney pressed against him, turning his face into Percy's neck. Percy's breath caught.

"That makes sense. You deserve to take some time off. You work so hard for that band." It was his usual thing. Percy got the feeling that Emilio didn't want Percy to work. He'd mentioned that it wasn't necessary a time or two, but Percy would never do something like that. Juney smoothed his hand up the side of Percy's thigh, and he flinched away.

"No," he mouthed silently. Everything in him protested the separation, but he knew it was the right thing to do.

Except Juney didn't care. He grabbed Percy's face with both hands and grazed his nose against Percy's. Rubbed his stubbled cheek against his smooth one. Juney's lips found a home at the corner of Percy's mouth. They were open. He just breathed. Warmth spread from the contact and radiated down his neck.

Why was he doing this? Percy held back a whine.

"Are you there, love?" Emilio asked, none the wiser.

Percy cleared his throat. "Yes. Yeah, sorry. A bit distracted right now."

Juney trailed his lips across his cheek, stopping when he got to his ear. Percy's heart thudded violently. "You were so good for me last night. So perfect, darlin'."

Percy's eyes fell shut. With the way his knees trembled, he worried he wouldn't be able to stand much longer. Juney's praise was something he'd always sought after. It was something that had always undid him most viscerally.

"Okay, love. I know you're probably very busy, and I have some work to get back to myself. Can't even have Sundays off," he grumbled.

Juney roughly held Percy's head in place, baring his neck. He brushed his lips across Percy's pulse point. He knew Juney could feel it jumping. Juney was crowding Percy at his side, and the hold he had on his head made him feel trapped by him like he loved to be. He didn't want him to ever let go. "You need to take a vacation, too, Emilio," Percy responded, trying his best to keep his tone even.

"You're right. Maybe I'll arrange something for us when you get back. Anyway, love you. Call me the next time you get a chance."

Juney's hand moved down to his throat. He gripped it tightly as he growled into his ear. "Go ahead and lie to him."

Percy squeezed his eyes shut, chest heaving. "Love you too." He hung up the phone and dropped it to the floor. Juney squeezed his neck harder for a split second before letting go. He breezed out the front door like nothing had even happened.

He stood there with his mouth agape, finding it extremely hard to steady his quivering lungs. When he finally got his shit together, he grabbed his duffel bag and rushed outside. Juney was standing there leisurely smoking a cigarette. "What the fuck was that about, Junes?"

Juney snatched the bag from his hands wordlessly and sauntered off toward his bungalow.

Percy stared after him for a while, parsing through everything. His world had flipped upside down again ever since that night. Nothing made sense anymore—not his thoughts or feelings, not Juney's actions or words. He couldn't keep up. All he knew was that he wanted Juney forever and ever. He also knew that Juney didn't want him like that. Their entire life, he'd kept his hands off of Percy. They slept together a million times and Juney never made a move on him. It had always been Percy.

So how come Juney was all over him all of a sudden?

What had changed in the last month?

He didn't understand any of it.

He watched Juney come out of his bungalow, guitar in hand, and continue down the path that led behind their little village without waiting for him. He decided he would ask him outright. Yup. That's what he would do. He marched after him to lay it all out.

His hair was still damp and sticking to his skin because of the cloying humidity. That was one of the only things he didn't love about living down south. He did his best to gather it up and put it in a ponytail. Sometimes he wanted to just chop it all off, but he'd be lying if he said he hadn't kept it this long for all of these years for Juney. Despite everything that happened over the past few years, he still liked to believe Juney loved his hair like he always had.

Juney reached a split in the path, and that's when Percy finally caught up with him. The one to the left was more dense with plants and palms. They spilled over onto the path. He decided for them and started down that one. They walked for what seemed like forever. Percy focused on the sound of Juney's steps behind him and lost track of time. He'd broken a sweat though, and his cheeks were flushed.

It was the sound of rushing water that brought him back to the present. It roared loudly, and Percy's spirits lifted almost immediately. His heart kicked up a notch as he hurried his walk.

And he was right. They were above a waterfall, directly across from it. Percy was in awe. He'd never actually seen a waterfall before. It was more magnificent than he could've fathomed. The cliff that the waterfall spilled over wasn't that tall, but the water still thundered as it pounded into the pool beneath it.

Everything else was long forgotten. Percy carefully crept down the rocky hill that led down into the basin that the water had eroded between the cliffs. His shoe slipped just barely, and Juney quickly grabbed his upper arm with a bruising grip. He still hadn't said a word to Percy, and whatever. They could exist silently. Percy didn't care as long as he knew Juney was there with him and safe.

When he got to the bottom, there was thick grass that gave way to pebbles and smooth rock at the shore. Percy's shirt and pants were off within a few seconds and he was ankle-deep, then knee-deep in crisp, cold water.

He didn't hear Juney behind him, and he didn't care. When the water got deep enough, he dove under. He cut through the water, propelling himself with his feet. When he erupted from the surface with a triumphant groan, he felt alive. His blood was pumping and his body was electric.

He scanned the shore for Juney and found him leaning against a rock with his notebook in hand. He was looking dazedly at the waterfall while tapping a beat on the paper with his pen. Percy didn't want to admit it, but he could watch him do that very thing all day long. He loved watching the gears turn behind his blank eyes when his genius was at work. Percy never understood how Juney could think up the things he did. Devastatingly beautiful lyrics and melodies that grabbed you by your soul.

No one had a mind that brimmed with as much color as Juney's did. Most people would say that Juney was dull with his drab wardrobe and apathetic disposition. Juney's sadness and pain were at the forefront of his being at all times, but Percy didn't see him that way at all. He'd never been able to.

When he looked at his Junes, he saw someone who anyone would be lucky to know. Someone soft beneath his jagged edges. He saw someone who loved his mother and father with every last drop of blood in his heart, no matter what they did to him. He knew that when Mrs. Jennings was still alive, Juney would clean up whatever he could before his dad got home from work so he wouldn't yell at her. Percy didn't know how to do dishes or laundry when they were eight years old, but Juney did.

And despite how much Juney and his father's relationship had dissolved after his mom's passing, Juney had never once uttered a bad word about him. And when Juney came to after his first suicide attempt, he'd hugged his father *hard*. Told him that he loved him.

Percy was also in charge of depositing a portion of Juney's money into Mr. Jennings' bank account every month.

Juney loved deeply and loved forever, but he didn't love often.

He plunged beneath the surface of the water again and swam in every direction. Every time he came up for air, the light spray of water from the cascade misted his skin, and *fuck*. This was euphoria. If he could live on this island forever, he would. Not only did it have the crystal-clear Pacific Ocean, but it also had a waterfall and staggering cliffs. He could get lost in all of this, and his life would be so much easier.

He floated along the surface of the water with his eyes closed. The warmth of the sun caressed his face. He wished it would take him, consume him.

Juney needed some of this—untainted by drugs and alcohol and depression.

Black Diamond was good for him.

Ten

WINSTON

Percy was ripping Juney's fucking heart out and drowning it in the pool of water he was floating in.

It was his own fault.

He knew that.

He was the one who got Percy naked and came between his sweet, sweet thighs, right behind his sac, and he knew that it would come back to bite him in the ass.

He could tell before their cum had even dried, that Percy regretted it. Then, when he saw the way Percy looked when he walked onto the porch, he knew what was going on. He was curved around himself, arms wrapped around his middle. His lips were turned down at the corners. Everything about him told a story that Winston didn't want to hear.

Percy felt guilty and disgusted. He was beating himself up.

For fucking what?

He'd wanted it. *Badly.* Winston hadn't forced any of it on

him, and when Winston separated them just a little, Percy stilled him with a leg thrown over Winston's.

He'd held Percy the way he'd been dying to for years. When his dick made contact with the swell of Percy's soft, round ass, there was no turning back. He'd ached and throbbed and Percy had pressed back against him.

Percy was right there, half submerged in the water with sunlight glinting off its surface.

Decisions needed to be made. This was it.

Percy was engaged to be married to a man.

Winston was a man, and Percy was his best friend. Winston couldn't write off what they'd done last night as anything other than sex. Percy had melted in his hands. He'd been a needy, whimpering, trembling mess.

It'd been the first time that Winston even allowed himself to consider that Percy *might* want him back. Winston didn't think Percy had sex for the hell of it like he did. It had to mean something. And most importantly, Percy wasn't innocent and naive anymore. He'd known what he was doing letting Winston touch him like that, urging him to do it.

So, it was hard to stomach that Percy regretted it. That he had a fiancé who he fully intended to marry even though Winston knew Percy didn't love that fucking suit.

He had two choices. Pursue Percy and make him realize what they'd had between them all along, or let him do what he wanted. Let him marry the guy who would be good for him. Stable and normal like Percy needed.

But Winston didn't think he could stand by and watch that. He'd fucking try—of course, he'd try, but the thought alone made him want to die.

He... no.

No.

Emilio didn't get to touch Percy. He didn't get to have him. No one did, and Winston needed to remind himself of that.

If Percy didn't want to be with him, maybe he needed to make sure he never ended up with anyone else. It wouldn't be hard considering that Percy can't speak, breathe, or think when Winston was near. Percy couldn't even resist Winston's touch when they'd been right in front of his fiancé's face.

He didn't think Ian would cosign any of that which meant it probably wasn't the right thing to do. Winston didn't care. He couldn't when it came to this.

He scribbled circles on the page he was turned to in his notebook. He might've finally channeled the energy that'd been swirling in his gut into lyrics that felt right.

His eyes danced over the words. He'd stared at them for so long that they blurred and lost their meaning. Amir swore that Winston took too much time to write a song, but this was why. There were so few words in a song. The ones that made the cut needed to be sharp.

Dream blue eyes that
Consume me from the inside, I
Couldn't stop him if I tried
And why should I?
(Why should I?)
Cause I'm in a dream state
(In a dream state)
I won't wake for you or anyone
Cause I'm in a fantasy
(In a fantasy)
I won't come down from the sun

Fall into the dark with me
You can be the light I need,
You don't mind when I bleed
And I know you can wash me clean
I can shade you from all the things that
I've done wrong
And you can keep me from drowning
Drowning
Drowning
In the ocean

The chorus was what'd been blocking him. Yeah, it was just another song about Percy. He'd written a lot of those. More than anyone even knew about. Percy had been the subject matter of most of his songs since he started writing them when they were teenagers. Some were more obvious than others.

In this one, Percy knew that he had blue eyes, but he didn't know that Winston thought they were *dream blue*. This song had the potential to make it onto the album.

Heatwave Records was bitching. Gage and Torin were bitching. And Percy was exhausted. They all thought Winston was just being lazy. They thought he wasn't trying, but they couldn't be more wrong. Winston had written a million songs, but they were all about Percy.

Telltale Dream didn't need an album filled with those, and sometimes that was all he could write about.

That was the reason they were behind on the album.

It was pathetic and sometimes made him feel like he wasn't a real musician at all. If there was only one thing that inspired him, one thing that he could create, then what was the point? He didn't deserve the spotlight he'd been given.

"Come up with anything good?" Percy asked. Winston lifted his eyes from the paper and watched as Percy rose. Water sluiced down his skin, beading here and there. His boxers were soaked and clinging to his skin, and Winston couldn't avoid the outline of Percy's soft cock, nor did he want to.

Percy sat and leaned against a different rock. The distance from Winston was intentional.

He scrutinized Percy closely, noticing how he crossed his hands right on top of his crotch as if it was something Winston hadn't seen before. He shook his head to himself. "Yep," he answered.

Percy didn't respond. He closed his eyes and tipped his head up, basking in the sun. If Winston was an artist, he would've done his best to capture that image on paper. He could only use words instead.

Winston stared at him openly which was something he'd always done. He didn't see the need to stop. He'd drink him in whenever he wanted, no matter who was around.

Eventually, Percy's lips moved around his words. "Is this what you're doing for the rest of the day? I'm sure there are other things to get into on this island."

Winston loved the sound of his voice. "This is all I've got for today. I don't wanna do shit on the weekends, but tomorrow will be more eventful."

"What's tomorrow?" Percy readjusted himself, finally looking at him with those dream blue eyes.

"Therapy after breakfast. Meditation after lunch. Dinner. Then, I'm gonna go down to the beach."

Percy's brows flew into his hairline. "Since when do you meditate?"

"I don't, but you do," he stated.

"Why are you doing this?" Percy rasped.

"Doing what?"

"You know what. Why did you... last night. You've never done anything like that to me before. Never."

Winston snorted. "Why didn't you stop me?"

Percy gaped.

Slammed his mouth shut.

"Exactly. So, do you really want to talk about it? I'm not sure that you do," Winston said.

Percy's jaw ticked. His brows were a hard line. "I'm not sleeping in bed with you tonight." Winston stared at him, much the same way Ian did. "It isn't right."

"Because of your fiancé," Winston deadpanned.

"It doesn't need to be spelled out," Percy murmured.

"We'll see."

"What? What's that supposed to mean?"

Winston replaced his notebook with the guitar and strummed an open chord. Then, he followed the rhythm that'd been making waves in his brain. It was louder for some reason, and he needed to take advantage of it.

"Juney," Percy called, trying to get his attention.

Winston didn't stop playing. The opening was starting to come together. He mumbled the lyrics he'd just written under his breath. Once he got the riff down, he repeated it over and over again until it was muscle memory. He lifted his eyes to Percy's. He was watching Winston's left hand slide up and down the fretboard. "Where do you want to sleep tonight?" he asked. Percy's lips were sealed. "It's been three years."

"I know how long it's been," he hissed. "But it isn't okay. I know that you don't date people. You just fuck them and never see them again, so you wouldn't understand."

Winston could sense something like jealousy in Percy's tone. Percy had been consistently irritated by the mere mention of anyone he'd hooked up with. He knew Percy had been jealous, but now he wondered if Percy was jealous for a different reason than he initially thought. Blood was filling his cock, and fuck. He knew there was something seriously wrong with him.

He stood up, kicked off his boots, and tossed his shirt. Then he dropped his pants and boxers in one swift motion. He felt the weight of his cock hanging stiffly between his legs.

Percy's jaw dropped. "Juney, why—"

Winston didn't feel the need to answer. He could skinny dip if he wanted to, and Percy could watch.

If he wanted to.

Winston fisted his shaft and roughly tugged on it a couple of times, hissing at the overwhelming sensation. He knew he was being watched, and one glance confirmed it. Percy's face was bright red, and he hadn't managed to close his mouth yet.

Winston left it at that. He turned around and walked into the water until he was fully submerged.

He'd planned to swim regardless, and he'd do it naked if he wanted to. Percy didn't have to look if he considered that to be cheating.

After a while, he checked.

Percy was still looking.

Winston devoured three samosas and moved on to swallowing mouthfuls of lentils in a spiced tomato sauce and rice. Percy was also eating like a starved man.

They both loved Indian food. Back in their hometown,

there wasn't an Indian restaurant. Winston and Percy weren't even sure what Indian food consisted of. It wasn't until they left that their eyes were opened to so many things they'd never had the opportunity to try, and Indian food stuck. There were tons of options when it came to vegan Indian food, and it all tasted heavenly.

This was one of those moments where Winston wasn't sure if life was real. Sometimes things happened to him that were so out of his normal, he had trouble comprehending it. Right now, he was sitting across from his lifelong best friend, the person he'd been pining after since they were just boys— the person he'd come all over last night. They were eating at a table, outside of a luxury bungalow, in the middle of a tropical island.

And he was stone-cold sober.

He was able to be in Percy's proximity without being drunk or high. It was comfortable, just like it used to be.

None of it seemed possible, but here he was.

He finished his food before Percy and lit a cigarette. They'd eaten together but hadn't said a word. That was fine by him.

Percy took his last bite at the same time as Winston put out his cigarette. He looked determined with a wrinkle between his brow as he went inside. Winston knew what he was going to do before he did it.

Percy wasted no time grabbing Eleanor.

Winston hadn't seen Percy smoke since he'd arrived at Black Diamond, so he had a feeling Percy was about to get higher than the Eiffel Tower.

Percy pulled a large mason jar from his bag and sat on the sofa. He quickly began grinding what would be an excessive amount of weed to most people. Winston sat on the bed with his notebook and pen and watched his practiced movements.

Soon, there was a small mound of weed on the table, and Percy was packing finger-fulls in the bowl of his bong.

Percy had cleared all of the smoke from the bong three times when he finally set it down on the table.

"Can't believe you brought drugs to a recovery center," Winston mused.

Percy's eyes were glassy and tinged with red. It made his blue irises even more vivid than they already were. Fuck he just wanted to look into them forever.

Percy cleared his throat a bit with a fist to his chest. "I'm not a patient. I'm your highly responsible, overly qualified and professional manager. Of course, they didn't check my bags."

Winston snorted. Right. Of course, they didn't—despite Percy having the appearance of a Woodstock '69 attendee. Winston admired his long hair. It was still damp from his swim, falling over his collarbones all the way to his stomach.

He was wearing an old band tee—one that hadn't ever belonged to Winston. He sat up, wrenched his thick sweater over his head, and tossed it at Percy. He caught it with wide eyes and somewhat slower reflexes than normal.

"Thanks, Junes, but I'm fine," he said as he folded the sweater up.

Winston's hand tightened around his pen. The image of Winston fucking Percy, while he wore nothing but Winston's tattered sweater, was frying his brain. He needed him to put it on... just so he could see.

He stood up and sat next to Percy who made a choked sound and stilled. Winston threaded his fingers through a chunk of Percy's hair and played with it. Twisted it and stroked it, feeling its softness with the roughened pad of his thumb.

Eventually, Percy leaned forward, pulling the hair from Winston's fingertips, to grab Eleanor and fire her up again.

Winston reached out to grab it when Percy tried to put it back down again. Percy leveled him with a very cute, serious look. "I don't think that's a good idea, Junes."

"I might be fucked in the head, but I'm no drug addict."

Percy blinked like he'd said something ridiculous. "You expect me to believe that you did massive amounts of cocaine, a variety of other drugs, and drank vodka like it was water because you wanted to?"

Okay. He could see where Percy was coming from. "All that was just a side effect of me not treating my mental health. Talked to Ian about that. Drugs and alcohol gave me serotonin whenever I had none, and I instinctively flirted with danger because..." He trailed off. It was best to not talk about that part.

"Because of what?"

"Don't prod," Winston said indignantly. Percy huffed a frustrated breath and took another rip from the bong that he was still holding from Winston. Percy's tolerance to weed was impressive enough to be scary.

"I thought we were... getting closer again," he said, voice muffled by his palm.

"That's why we shouldn't talk about it."

Silence stretched, and he could tell Percy was working himself up. They'd never liked keeping things from each other. Winston had always felt entitled to know every single thing about him, no matter how small or trivial it seemed. "Who is Ian?" Percy asked with a stony edge to his usually soft voice.

Winston's eyes widened, but heat spiked low in his belly. If Percy had been in charge of keeping track of his stay at Black Diamond, he figured that he'd have known the name of his therapist.

But Percy was jealous, so Winston shrugged and reached

for Eleanor again. Percy's face was pinched as he pulled it away for the second time. "You're not going to tell me?"

Winston felt the fire emanating through his chest. "He's just some guy. Can I smoke now, your highness?"

"Some guy," Percy repeated. Winston dropped his palm to Percy's inner thigh and watched as his breath caught despite his obvious frustration. "When did you have time to meet guys during your recovery in the mental health facility?"

Percy pushed Winston's hand off his thigh, and Winston had to fight the smirk threatening to curve his lips. "Why does it matter so much?"

Percy sputtered. "Well. You- you can talk to this guy about things but not me?" Winston was working out how he wanted to respond when Percy spoke again. "Of course, you'd find someone to stick your dick in—even here of all places."

Winston threaded his fingers through the roots of Percy's hair at the nape of his neck and tugged his head back. "Ian is my therapist," he said into his ear.

Percy's breaths were harsh. "Your therapist's name is Mr. Kang—"

"His last name," Winston interrupted.

Percy's teeth dug into his lower lip, and his face flushed. He was embarrassed.

Winston didn't like that, so he used his grip on Percy's hair to crush his nose to the side of Percy's face. "I missed you being possessive of me," he whispered, low and deep. Percy kept his mouth shut. "You can have all of me again if you still want it. You wouldn't have to share."

There was a strangled sound in the back of Percy's throat. "Impossible." That was all he said before turning his head to lock eyes with Winston. "I'm engaged, and you're a famous rockstar. Sounds like a whole lot of sharing to me, Juney."

Percy tried scooting away, but Winston tightened his grip on his hair. "Why are you acting like you don't want this?"

"My fiancé," he bit out. "He doesn't deserve this."

Winston's nostrils flared. He fucking hated it all. Hated the ring on Percy's finger. He hoped Emilio's face was fucked up forever after what he'd done to him.

"Your fiancé isn't here."

"That doesn't matter—"

Winston grabbed his chin roughly. "Your fiancé isn't here," he repeated. "He'd never know."

Percy's chest heaved. "It's on my conscience," he hissed. "Not yours. What if someone cheated on you? How would that feel?"

"Wouldn't happen. I'd never date anyone," he stated simply, but it was a lie. There was one person, and he was sitting right next to him. The thought of Percy doing something like that to him was... an indescribable amount of pain. He couldn't even think about something like that without feeling sick to his stomach.

But there was a difference. Emilio wasn't in love with Percy like Winston was. Emilio didn't know Percy as intimately as Winston did, and he couldn't possibly hope to. If Emilio found out what they'd done together last night, it would surely hurt him, but his pain would feel like a paper cut. Winston's would feel like a knife eviscerating his heart.

Mostly, he couldn't care less about Emilio's feelings. He wanted him to hurt.

"Exactly. You have nothing to lose," Percy said with a frown.

Winston smiled. "Neither do you, darlin'." He pressed his lips to Percy's temple and let go of his face. "You cheated on him last night. What's one more time? Two? It doesn't change anything at all."

Percy's glassy eyes were downcast. Winston grabbed Eleanor, and this time, Percy let him. Winston took as big of a hit as he could. His lungs quivered, and the sweet taste of bud coated his tongue. He wasn't going to make Percy do anything he didn't want to do, but he definitely wouldn't be the fucking morality police. "You can sleep in the bed; I'll take the couch."

Winston knew he wouldn't be getting any sleep tonight. He'd been getting less and less as the days have gone on. He spent the majority of last night watching Percy sleep, rubbing his shoulder and back, stroking his cheek. The night before that, he'd alternated between staring into the darkness and playing his guitar.

Winston could feel something electric building up inside of him. He itched to do something, but he didn't know what exactly. Had he been too forceful? Too brash?

No. Percy would've told him to shove it. He'd never had a problem doing that.

His mind was just spinning like it did sometimes.

"It's okay, Juney. I can just go back to my bungalow," he said softly.

Winston pursed his lips. "No. You can't. I want you to sleep in my bed." Percy opened his mouth, but Winston cut him off. "Non-negotiable."

With a huff of breath, Percy conceded. Winston pushed his luck. "Would you please wear my sweater?"

Percy stood up with his arms crossed in front of his chest. "I'm still... I'm still jealous."

Winston and Percy both knew how backward that was considering Percy's current relationship status. "Of what?"

"Everything," he mumbled. Winston's heart panged at how easily they'd slid back into their old dynamic. "All of it."

Winston stood and took a step forward and grabbed the hem of Percy's t-shirt, urging it up. He looked into Percy's bloodshot eyes expectantly. After a long minute, Percy sighed and lifted his arms so he could slide it off. Winston grabbed his sweater and pulled the collar around Percy's head. Percy shoved his arms through the sleeves and scowled at him.

Winston whispered, "There's no reason to be jealous." He grabbed Percy's hand and turned it palm up. He rubbed his thumb in circles over it. "You've always had me right here—since the first time that you invited me to lay under that live oak tree with you—I haven't left."

Fuck, why would he say something like that? He felt the blurred edge of panic emanating from the back of his throat, on through his chest.

He let go of Percy's hand abruptly and fled through the front door. His heart was pounding as he scrambled to pull a cigarette from his pack. There were only two left. Fuck, he'd need to find more. His hand shook like those palm fronds did in the distance as he tried lighting it. The flame flickered in and out, flagging in the near-constant breeze, and now wasn't the fucking time!

He wanted so badly to break something but there was nothing—unless he wanted to do serious damage and bust out some windows. He breathed through it, harsh and short. He eyed the table and the chairs. With the unlit cigarette still crushed between his lips, he picked up the chair he'd sat on earlier and swung it at the white picket railing that lined the perimeter of the porch. The wood cracked and gave way, but not enough. Winston kicked it with the heel of his bare foot. He knocked his head against the clay planter that hung from the roof and hissed at the blunt pain that rocked through his skull.

Didn't matter. He didn't care.

He ripped it from its hook and chucked it into the clearing. It bounced against the packed soil, spilling its contents until it landed for good and rolled to a stop.

There were only a handful of bungalows in this clearing, and most of them were vacant. He was able to explode privately until Percy swung the door open with eyes like saucers. "Juney, what the fuck are you doing?"

"Go inside, Percy." His voice was level despite the thudding of his heart and the raggedness of his breath.

"Absolutely not. You don't own this bungalow. You can't tear it up no matter how badly you want to."

Winston laughed. "I could buy every single one of these stupid huts. I don't care about Black Diamond's property."

Percy was tight-lipped, and the silence increased the roaring in his ears. It pissed him off even worse. "I'll stop, okay? Just go inside. I need some time to… think. To get my shit together."

Percy turned around. "I'm leaving the door open."

Winston didn't bother with a response. He looked down and realized he couldn't lean against the railing like he was going to, so he righted the chair and sat down. This time, he was calm enough to get the cigarette lit, and it immediately did wonders for his head. The roar quieted to a tolerable buzz.

As he stared out into the jungle on the far side of the clearing, he tried to reconcile what he'd done. What he'd admitted to. It wasn't an outright love confession, but it was far more than he'd ever planned to divulge. The last thing Percy needed to know was how long he'd been drowning in him.

With each cloud of gray smoke that plumed from his lips, his heart slowed its dangerous pace.

He pinched the orange filter and rested his forearm against his leg. He watched the cigarette smoke ribbon from the lit end. Studied it. When his fingers trembled, the smoke would dissipate.

Time passed in a haze, and he took one last drag before putting it out.

Everything was fine.

Eleven

PERCY

The door slammed shut behind Juney. He looked like nothing had even happened as he threw his shirt off —muscles bunching and extending with the long line of his arm—when just five minutes ago, he was outside silently raging. Junes had always been like that. He fought against his anger and some of it always won out.

Percy was confused. Everything had been a whirlwind, and he didn't know which way was up anymore.

Junes had never pushed this hard for Percy's affection. It was unbearable to turn him down, especially after having had a taste of what it felt like to be with him. Percy worried about things though. He wasn't entirely sure Juney was in his right mind. It was hard to tell sometimes, but a lot of the decisions he'd been making lately were on the impulsive side. There were things that Percy wondered if Juney would regret. Then there was the matter of Juney's intentions. They weren't clear and seemed so far-fetched and so sudden that Percy couldn't bring himself to fully trust them.

Percy knew all of these things in the same breath that he knew he wouldn't be able to resist Juney for long or for good.

He wanted Juney, and no matter how deluded or confused he might've been in the past, he'd always wanted him. He'd settle for scraps if he had to. He'd cheat on his fiancé.

But there were things he needed that he wasn't convinced Junes would want to give him. Percy wanted forever, and he wanted it to be stable and unwavering. He didn't want secret hook-ups or to continue the way they always had but with the same 'best friend' label. Juney hadn't even told him what he wanted from him or why. All he'd made clear was that he didn't want Percy to marry Emilio.

Juney was in his boxers now. "I'll turn off the lights for you, but I'm leaving this lamp on, so I can see my notebook."

Percy sighed and stood up. He left Juney's sweater on and stripped down to his boxers before sliding under the covers. "You can sleep in the bed, you know. I can take the couch, no problem," he reiterated. He hadn't intended to take his bed from him.

"Don't worry about it. I won't be sleeping much anyway."

That wasn't a good thing. "Do you think that's because of your meds?"

Juney flipped the light off and sat down. He was illuminated with soft, orange light from the lamp, already scratching away at his notebook, brows furrowed with focus. "I don't know," he shrugged. "You know I've never had great sleeping habits."

Percy considered him. He didn't seem the slightest bit concerned. Maybe Percy was overbearing in that way. He didn't want to helicopter him, but he also felt like the person who knew him best. Perhaps, the only person who knew him at all. "Are we going to talk about what that explosion was about?"

Junes glared at his notebook. "Nothing to talk about."

"Look at me," Percy said. He was getting frustrated.

Juney didn't move a muscle. "Go to sleep."

So just like that, Junes was back to ignoring him. He wished he could say that he wouldn't beg, but he absolutely would. It was just that there were too many things weighing on his mind, and he really did need sleep. He could feel its warmth creeping through his body. His eyelids were growing heavier. All his energy seeped from him as he curled around the thick blanket and buried his nose in Juney's pillow.

He was home.

He snapped awake and lifted his head. The lamp was still on and Juney was still sitting on the couch—paper and pen in hand. He was writing so hard that Percy heard the pen scratching against the paper, almost like he was scribbling things out. It was frantic.

"What time is it?" he mumbled. The clock on the wall showed that it was two in the morning. "It's so late. You need to get some sleep."

Juney didn't stop. He still hadn't even looked at him. "I'm fine," he responded, voice scratchy. He cleared his throat.

Percy let his head fall back to the pillow and watched Juney do whatever it was that he did in that notebook. He could follow the sharp line of his nose forever—his jaw, his collarbones. He'd never met anyone as perfect as Junes, and he knew such a thing didn't exist. Juney had always been dangerously attractive and everyone knew it, but Juney had iced everyone out for the most part. People didn't think they could get Juney to talk to them, let alone be their friend or something more.

Percy had been the opposite. He wasn't super social or outgoing, and he preferred the company of himself and Juney, of course. But he was friendly to everyone. Helpful and kind. His parents fully supported whatever he wanted to do, so he never felt much pressure. They trusted him enough that it made him feel confident in his own decisions. Percy's main concerns throughout his teens were his grades, Juney, and weed. Juney's concerns were probably a lot different.

Percy had always been painfully aware of how opposite they were. He'd waited for the day someone cooler would come around—someone who Juney didn't feel like he needed to baby. Someone who could connect with him about things Percy had no experience with—all the hardships Juney had faced.

It never happened though.

Gage and Torin were everything he'd ever been afraid of. At first, it seemed like they wouldn't be an issue. They were all casual friends, but as time went on, Gage and Torin being around Juney all the time deepened their friendship. There had been a level of understanding there that no one but them had. Percy still got to be the closest person to Juney though, and that was all he'd ever cared about. That all changed when Juney and him had their big break and it gouged a thick split into their friendship.

He tracked the thick veins that spidered around Juney's forearms. So perfect. Everything about him was—inside and out. Juney had always been larger than life in Percy's eyes. Too big for their town. Since the beginning, he'd known that Juney would be famous someday. He had all the faith in the world.

And now Juney was a full-fledged rockstar. Millions of people loved him and were obsessed with him. Percy was just an unqualified manager who got the job out of pity or something —not that he didn't take it seriously. He did, but he was nothing in comparison to Juney.

He'd always felt that way, but now it was so much worse.

Seeing him privately like this didn't feel real. All the luck in the world had been distilled into this one drop in the bucket, but luck was fleeting. He'd felt his desperation take over the minute Juney had given him his attention again.

God, he was so fucking desperate for him. He wanted to feel what it was like to be his Percy again.

He shuffled out of bed resigned to the fact that he was a liar and a cheater. This is what he'd been reduced to.

But Juney's dark eyes flitted up from his notebook and landed on him as he approached. He never tore his gaze away. Percy stopped directly in front of him. Juney had relaxed against the back of the couch with his head tilted enough to meet his eyes. They were glassy and tinged with red around the edges, and a shadow curved beneath the bottom row of his lashes.

Junes had been looking into Percy's eyes this intensely since the first day they'd met. He wasn't sure what Juney saw, but Percy knew what he saw. Juney's eyes were empty and dead, sometimes sharp and lacerating, but it was only when he looked at Percy that his eyes were gentle. That was why Percy desperately needed them on him.

His lower lip pushed out in a frown, and he knew he was pouting. It was ridiculous.

Juney's notebook was forgotten. Wordlessly, he grabbed Percy's hand which had been stiff at his side. Juney's thumb smoothed over his knuckles, melting his resolve until it was nothing but a puddle at his feet. "I can't do this," he whispered. "I need you too much."

Juney's nostrils flared one time, and his fingers tightened. He pulled Percy down and Percy unraveled. He flung his arms around Juney's lower back and hid his face in his crotch. The silky fabric of his briefs was smooth against his skin, and he was engulfed in a wave of Juney's natural musk.

He knew this wasn't normal. It was some kind of addiction, but it was only Junes. He'd never even wanted to do this with Emilio.

Juney's legs tightened on either side of him. "So you don't want to sleep alone?"

Percy nosed against Juney's stiffening shaft. It was heady. "Never wanted to. Ever. Since we were teens." His voice was muffled. Juney's hips moved a fraction of an inch, and Percy shook.

"But you want my cock now too, don't you, darlin'?"

His heart fluttered. It was too much to process. Southern accents were nothing new to Percy, but there was something about the way Juney's drawl formed that endearment—throaty and rounded out. And Percy called him exclusively by nicknames, but Juney never had one for him. That was fine until now. Until darlin'. He'd always felt special to Juney, but this was different. This was so much more.

But what had his heart racing and blood thundering was Juney's question. It made him start thinking of all the ways he wanted his cock. He whined before spreading his lips open and dragging them across Juney's shaft. His tongue danced atop the fabric as he mouthed at it. This was answer enough.

Juney groaned softly. People across the internet went crazy over the sounds he made while singing, but Percy didn't think he'd ever heard this one. This one made him want to take up permanent residence between his legs forever. He mouthed at his cockhead, soaking the fabric. He could tell Junes was trying to control his breaths, but they were tense and short.

"You gonna regret this?" Juney asked through clenched teeth.

Percy slipped his fingers beneath the waistband of Juney's underwear and quickly pulled them down. His thick cock sprung heavily from its confines. Face to face with Juney's dick, there was a hunger deep inside of him getting bigger and bigger. He kissed and licked the flared head. It set his lips on fire.

Percy's head was yanked back as Juney wrapped his hair around his fist. "Are you going to regret this?" he repeated.

"I can't regret you."

Juney's eyes narrowed, scrutinizing him. Percy knew his face was flushed and his lips were dark and wet. He hoped Juney liked what he saw. Hoped he wasn't being too much. "So, what's off limits?" he asked testily.

Percy needed to get real honest with himself. He wished it weren't true, but he'd let Juney do anything to him. "You were right. I already cheated so what difference does it make?" He wrapped his hand around Juney's throbbing shaft and tugged. Sweat beaded above his brow as he mustered up the courage to ask this question. "What do you wanna do to me, Juney?"

He tightened the hair around his fist and tugged it hard enough to sting. Percy had no idea how he expected him to answer. He was strung up by his vulnerability, right on a precipice.

Juney dropped his hair. Hands wrapped around his throat. He didn't squeeze, just applied consistent pressure that rooted him to the spot. Juney got close to his face. His breath puffed against Percy's lips. "Gonna show you who owns you."

"O-owns me?" he stuttered.

He spoke against his lips, "It sure as fuck ain't your fiancé, is it?" Shivers trembled down Percy's spine. "Do you let him pull your hair?"

Percy shook his head.

"'Cause your hair is all for me, right?"

Percy's breath hitched. Juney had always loved his long hair. "Of course, it is."

Juney brushed his thumb across Percy's lower lip. "I bet you don't wear his clothes. Bet his touch doesn't comfort you." He moved his lips to Percy's ear. "Bet his cock doesn't either."

Juney's voice was low and raspy. Percy didn't even try to hold back his moan. His dick was throbbing, and he couldn't form a complete thought. And there was guilt, but it could barely wade through his tidal wave of desire and need.

"Tell me. I want to hear that soft, sweet voice you only use on me."

He'd always talked to him that way. It was just one of the ways he showed affection. Junes always made him feel safe and warm and loved. He softened Percy like no other. Percy's teeth dug into his lip. He'd never felt like this before. His heart was in his throat, and he had no control over himself. Uninhibited.

"No. Nothing. None of that." The words tumbled from his lips. "No one can make me feel the way you do. You're the only one who can give me what I need." He didn't care how breathless he sounded—especially not when Juney's eyes were smoldering.

Juney let go of his neck and wrapped his hand around Percy's hardness. He moved it up and down his shaft, tightening the grip and quickening the pace. Percy swallowed roughly. He'd missed the weight of it in his hand. "You've always wanted me, but when did you realize you wanted my cock as well?"

Percy pushed against his hold to lap his tongue over Juney's slit. He hummed around the salty taste of precum that'd burst in his mouth. "I don't know, Junes. Everything is all mixed up in my head. I don't know what's what anymore. Just want you to keep touching me and never stop."

Juney disconnected them and they stood up. "I wouldn't have to stop if you weren't getting married," he said, words edged with stone. Fear spiked deep in Percy's gut. He didn't want to think about any of that right now. Juney grabbed his chin roughly. They were nose to nose. "I want to fuck you."

Percy felt like he might start hyperventilating. He was technically still a virgin in that aspect. Emilio was the only person he'd been with, and Percy still hadn't let him do it. He didn't know why he couldn't, but he thought it might have something to do with trust.

He trusted Emilio, but letting someone inside of him seemed like a very intimate, soul-bearing thing to him. Percy didn't feel that comfortable with him quite yet. But somehow, Percy felt like he needed Juney inside him. He didn't think he could stop it if he tried.

Juney pulled his briefs down without giving him a chance to collect himself. Instinctively, he grabbed his sweater to take it off, but Juney caught his wrists. "Keep this sweater on for me."

He nodded in response letting it fall back into place. It was a bit oversized for him, long enough that he could grip the sleeves, and it was soft against his skin. Juney grabbed two handfuls of his ass and squeezed. He dug his fingertips into the skin hard enough to bruise. Percy loved it although he was slightly self-conscious. It was a good thing the lamp was dim.

Juney had already slid his boxers the rest of the way down. Still nose to nose, he wrapped his hand around both of them. Juney's cock was burning hot against his. Percy's hips jerked forward and their shafts dragged against each other, but there was a lot of friction. Juney looked down and spit on their flared heads. "Gimme some spit too, darlin'."

Like many things, Percy hadn't ever done that, but Juney rubbing his spit into Percy's skin was driving him mad. So, he followed suit. Juney made a satisfied noise and spread their spit around until there was less friction. He jacked them with his hand, but they also inched their hips forward. "Love the way you feel against me."

"Want closer," Percy breathed.

"'Course you do," Juney said. "We'll be as close as possible soon enough. For now, bend over and put your hands on the back of that couch."

Percy's eyes widened. He was suddenly riddled with nerves, and he must not have hidden it well. "You can tell me if you don't want to do something, okay?"

"I know. It's that- um—" he trailed off, unsure of what he could say that wouldn't make him sound like a complete amateur.

Juney used his free hand to force Percy to meet his eyes. "I can tell there's something wrong."

Percy wanted to look away. "It's nothing."

After a pause, Juney furrowed his brows. "Have you done this before?"

There was no way in hell he was going to tell Juney that he was still a virgin. He didn't want to be treated with kid gloves, and he knew Junes had fucked like an animal for years now. Percy knew he wouldn't match up to all of them with his lack of experience.

"Yeah," he lied.

Juney's features hardened. "Then what is it?"

Percy didn't bother with an answer. It'd only complicate things. He steeled himself and put his knees on the couch and arms on the back. The hardest part was arching his back. As he did it, he felt more and more exposed with his hole on display.

A low groan rumbled from Juney's chest. "Fuck. You're so perfect here. Everywhere." His hands were palming his ass again, spreading his cheeks further, so it shouldn't have surprised him when he felt Juney's tongue. He gasped and accidentally pushed back.

The most he'd ever done with Emilio was different variations of handjobs and blowjobs and frotting. It'd been good enough. He'd never had any complaints, but this had his cock painfully hard and leaking. Juney slid his tongue back and forth and in circles. He sucked and blew. Percy's thighs began to shake and the moans that tumbled through his lips were getting louder and more broken. He couldn't help the way he pushed back against Juney's mouth either. "You like this, don't you?" Juney said, lips moving against his softened hole. Percy groaned and pushed back in response. "Think I want my mouth all over you. I can't get enough of your taste and the sounds you make."

Percy's high-pitched whine was embarrassing. "Why do you have to say things like that?"

Juney wrapped a hand around Percy's shaft. It'd been hanging there between his legs untouched for so long, he could've cried. "'Cause you love when I do. 'Cause I can't help it."

Percy trembled harder with every word he said. Hot breath and lips and tongue all over him, feeling Juney's face between his legs.

Nothing they'd ever done had felt this dirty.

Juney pushed his tongue past the ring of muscle and thrust inside. "Juney, oh my—fuck." His words were strangled by overwhelming sensations. Juney pulled his cheeks so far apart. His thumbs dug in, forcing his hole to stretch. "Please, please, please, Junes." His garbled moans were too loud in the silence of the room, but he had no control over them.

Juney slid his tongue back out, and Percy missed it already. "This hole is so pretty. I've never seen anything like it."

His heart skipped a beat. "Really?" he whispered.

Juney slipped two fingers inside of him. His tongue had opened him just enough for it, and Percy had definitely fingered himself before. A lot. This feeling was familiar but entirely different. It was beyond better. This was how it was meant to feel. Juney moved his fingers leisurely. "Why do you sound so surprised about that?"

He dropped his head to rest on his crossed forearms. "You've been with so many people," he said, and he wasn't proud of the admission.

Juney's other hand trailed from the base of his spine and pushed his sweater back, exposing more skin. "If you only knew. There isn't a soul on this planet with a hole as perfect as yours. Nothing even comes close. I'd wreck this ass for the rest of my life if you'd let me. Fuck, I'd never be able to stop," he groaned in that special, soft way, and Percy clenched around his fingers. Juney was just proclaiming things like it was nothing. Like it wasn't breath-stealing and life-altering.

"Do it," he said gently. "Don't ever stop."

His rim stretched around a third finger, and Juney's shaft burned the back of his thigh. It lay there, so close to where Percy wanted it to be. He couldn't help how his ass wiggled back against him. "I'm ready," he said urgently.

"I'm going to fuck you bare," Juney stated.

"But—"

"I've never had unprotected sex in my life, and they tested me when I got here. I know you get tested routinely as well."

Percy gaped. "How... how do you know that?" He asked, voice pitching up at the end.

"Doesn't matter, darlin'. Nothing was ever meant to be between us. It's *us*."

Again. He'd done it again. He'd made another claim that made Percy's heart hope for something it shouldn't. Something impossible.

His fingers left his hole quivering, and he walked away with a *whoosh* of cold air in his wake. Percy couldn't focus on how exposed he was, so he burrowed into the soft sweater. It was cozy and comforted him. He was still uncomfortable with being exposed like this despite what they'd just done.

It wasn't long before he felt Juney again. He uncapped the bottle of lotion that came with the room. He was pretty sure using lotion as lube wasn't preferable, but at least it was unscented.

Percy didn't care what he lubed with at this point. He just needed to be filled. He heard Juney smoothing the lotion over his cock and there was a drizzle of it running down his crack.

His chest heaved. Things were feeling more real now.

Juney's cock was alarmingly thick and large. It was imposing, considering he'd never taken anything more than fingers.

The blunt tip of it kissed his puckered rim. He stiffened, and Juney smoothed a hand over his ass. "You still want me in here?" he asked.

He took a few steadying breaths and pushed back. "Need you, Juney."

He nudged forward a bit, and there was pressure. It wasn't

unbearable, but then the flared head popped past the ring of muscle. He stretched wider than he ever had. It burned and stung. He gritted his teeth so as not to worry Junes.

"T-that okay?" Juney asked hoarsely while smoothing a palm over Percy's backside. The light scratch of his calloused fingers sent tingles across his skin and grounded him. "You're choking the hell out of me, darlin'." His voice was strained.

Percy focused on taking deep breaths. He relaxed his tense muscles as much as possible and bore down. See, he knew how to do this. Juney slid in a little more, and the pain evened out to something more subtle. Juney wrapped a hand around Percy's shaft and pumped it slowly, and fuck. He loved being in Juney's hands.

"There you go," Juney breathed. He bottomed out, hips pressing against Percy's ass. Percy's breath shook.

This was his best friend.

The boy he'd grown up with.

Fourteen years together.

How things had aligned for this exact moment, Percy had no clue. It was more surreal than life had any business being. His forehead creased with determination before he moved forward and slammed back against Juney again. It ached a little, but there was something else too. He felt full, and his rim was sensitive to every movement.

"Fuck," Juney groaned. "You feel like a dream." He grabbed Percy's hips firmly and made Percy meet his slow thrusts. At this rate, he'd be covered in marks by the time he left this island. He squeezed his eyes shut—he didn't want to leave. Not when things were like this.

Juney slammed to the hilt again. "How's this for close? Is this what you always wanted? What you didn't know how to ask for?"

His body flashed hotter than ever before, but it wasn't enough at all. "No," he said as Juney's thrusts punched the air from his lungs. "I need closer."

Juney made a strangled sound that was something like a disbelieving laugh. "Of course not."

He wrapped Percy's hair around his fist and pulled him so Percy's back was to his front. His other arm wound around Percy, holding him tightly as he continued fucking into him.

That was better. Juney held his hair at an angle that bared his throat to him, and Juney parted lips and teeth grazed the hard line of Percy's jaw. "I can't get much closer than this," he growled.

"On the bed," Percy breathed.

Juney didn't respond. He eased out gently and helped Percy stand and dragged him to the bed. "We have all night. We could hit the shower too."

Percy blushed. He only wanted to be in Juney's arms, but he got the impression that Juney didn't tend to do that kind of thing. He laid on his back and Juney followed. He was on his knees between Percy's legs, looking down at him. With only the lamp for light, it was dim, but he could tell that Juney was angry. There was something in the set of his brows and tight lips.

A chill rippled across Percy's skin at being naked and wide open in front of Juney while he scowled at him.

He was getting uncomfortable, wanting to cover himself. "We don't have to... you know. It's fine," he stammered.

Juney had the nerve to look taken aback, and Percy winced.

He knew this wasn't a good idea, and yet he did it anyway.

Twelve

WINSTON

Winston's chest was going to fucking explode. There were things people weren't meant to handle—things that were impossible no matter how you sliced them.

One of those things was right in front of him. Percy's head was on his pillow, his long hair fanning around him, wisping across his shoulders. He was swimming in Winston's sweater, gripping the sleeves in his fingers nervously. The hem was hiked up, so his narrow waist was visible. His feet were planted on the mattress, and his legs were spread wide open, and he was looking at Winston with these wide, doe eyes.

He'd imagined this for so long that it felt inappropriate. It felt wrong that he was going to fuck him when Percy didn't know that Winston had dreamed of this since they were teenagers. Percy didn't know about the hundreds of times Winston had jacked off while thinking of him.

Percy had no sense of the depth of Winston's hunger for him. Need that had been buzzing beneath his skin and living in his bones for long enough that it had a life of its own within him. It was a life he never thought he'd get to live, and it seemed like it was going to stay that way. Percy might've wanted this right now, but he was still engaged. He hadn't called it off.

And Winston couldn't blame him. He'd never expected Percy to want to be with someone like him. Percy had lived such a normal, perfect life. He thrived on stability thanks to his parents, and the only bumps he'd ever had in the road were on account of Winston. He'd put Percy through fucking hell and back, and he was still the same person. Nothing had changed. His thoughts... his mind was sick. He wasn't a safe bet, that was for sure.

But his life's fucking purpose was beneath him, wanting him, needing him.

A better person might've said no, but Winston wasn't fooling anyone—certainly not himself.

If he only got to have him like this, he'd take it.

If he only got to have him on this island, he'd take that too.

There was nothing he wouldn't take when it came to him.

"You having second thoughts?" he asked. Percy was getting shifty and anxious.

"No..." he hesitated, clearing his throat. "It's just that you seem... I don't know. Angry? If you'd rather fuck me from behind or something else, that's fine."

Winston's brows furrowed. "Why would I want that?"

Percy worked his lip between his teeth. He couldn't tear his gaze from it. He was well aware of the fact that they'd never kissed. After all that they'd done. Percy had even kissed Gage, but not Winston. He ground his teeth together.

"It's less personal? Unless that's how you do it with every-one. It's just that I'd be surprised, is all." Percy had always rambled with him, and it wasn't necessary. Winston got his meaning. Percy had a problem with all the people he'd slept with over the past few years, and he didn't know how to make him feel better about that. It was merely a means to an end, and Percy was right. He'd fucked a lot of people. He'd done some wild shit, but he'd never been intimate with anyone. Winston knew what intimacy felt like, and the only person he'd ever experienced that with was his best friend.

He moved closer and pushed Percy's legs up and over his thighs. He leaned over and gently threaded his fingers through Percy's hair. They were nose to nose, eye to eye. "I don't know their names. Don't remember their faces. To me, it's like they never existed." Percy blinked, looking at him through long lashes. "Do you know what I remember? I remember every single moment I've ever had with you. Every. Single. One. I know your soul, and I know every square inch of you so well that if I were an artist, I could draw a portrait with my eyes closed."

Percy swallowed roughly. "Why do you have to keep saying things like that?"

Winston dropped his forehead to Percy's and spoke against his lips. "If you want me to fuck you like an animal, I will. If you want me to take you apart slowly, I will. And if you want me to have you all night, I'll do that too. I want everything. Need to give you everything. Now, what do you want?"

Percy panted against his lips, and Winston had to refrain from licking into him. He needed to feel him on his tongue. "I just want you everywhere all at once. Do whatever you want to me."

Winston trembled. He felt so fucking weak over him, but this was *his* Percy. He belonged to Winston. No one else. He plunged his tongue between Percy's parted lips and dragged it across his. It was just a tease of sensation that lit him on fire, and that was one of the many reasons he wouldn't make it through this alive. Percy chased after his tongue as he pulled away, but Winston leveled him with a serious gaze. He hooked his thumb inside Percy's mouth, right over his teeth, and gathered all his saliva. Winston pulled Percy's jaw wider and let his spit fall directly onto his tongue.

Percy's eyes flared wide, and Winston removed his thumb to see what he'd do with the spit.

Percy slammed his mouth shut. His eyes fell closed and he hummed like a starved man. Winston's heart was beating in his throat. He was in total awe. When Percy slid his eyes back open, Winston schooled his features. It was almost embarrassing, but anyone would be rendered stupid by Percy. Anyone. And Winston didn't like the fucking thought of that. He pushed Percy's head to the side and buried his face there as he thrust his hips forward, dragging their hard cocks against each other. Percy gasped and Winston just barely held it together.

"Who do you fucking belong to, Percy? Who have you *always* belonged to?" His voice was like gravel. It was rough and demanding. Percy didn't answer right away, but Winston didn't give him a chance to. "Who did you share a bed with for years? How many people do you think I warned away from you because I refused to share you?" Percy let out a strangled whimper. "That's right. You heard me correctly. I've always been a selfish prick, and you've always let me. So, tell me, Percy. Who do you belong to?"

Percy turned his head and slammed his lips against Winston's. It knocked him back an inch and pushed his upper lip into his teeth, but he steadied himself with his forearm.

Percy's hands flew up and held Winston's face, not letting him go as he clumsily moved his lips against his. Percy was lifting off the bed to get closer to him, and Winston wrapped an arm around his back to support him.

There was lightning bursting from his chest at the feeling of Percy's soft, wet lips moving against his. Winston had him in his arms, and he was dying. Percy was making high-pitched, desperate noises in the back of his throat. He was attacking his mouth, pushing it wide, shoving his tongue as far as it will go. He held Winston's face so hard, their noses smashed together. Neither of them could breathe properly, and neither of them cared.

Percy mauled him so hard that he put Winston on his back and straddled him without breaking the kiss. He was frantically grinding his hips against Winston's crotch, and Winston dug his fingertips into Percy's smooth ass, pressing him down harder and controlling his movements.

He would never forget the feeling of Percy's lips and tongue. It was terrifying, and yet he was powerless against it. Percy was all burning hot skin and a soft cotton sweater and all of it belonged to Winston.

Percy had always been his—in every sense of the word—but he wasn't sure if Percy fully understood that or not. Over the last three years, Winston hadn't let him out of his sight. He knew everything about where Percy went and who he saw. It was how they'd always been. The only difference was that he kept his distance. He didn't involve himself at all. He didn't touch him.

Percy didn't know any of that. There was a lot he didn't know, but Winston would make some things clear tonight.

Their lips slid together, and Winston mapped the inside of

his mouth with his tongue. No one had ever experienced a kiss like this. He was sure of it.

Having Percy like this was dismantling him piece by piece. His carefully locked-up desperation was clawing its way out of him, and he couldn't help the vulnerability it revealed.

He wrapped his arms tightly around Percy's middle and pulled him down to his side. He rubbed his lips across Percy's cheek, feeling every hitch of his breath. Percy hooked a leg over him, and Winston palmed his ass, circled his slick hole with his fingers, applying pressure. Percy moaned softly, and fuck. How was that sound even real? It cut him off at the knees. "Juney," he whined. A bead of sweat rolled down Winston's temple. The onslaught of feelings inside of him threatened to boil over at the sound of *Juney* being moaned softly from Percy's lips. Pleadingly.

"What do you want, baby?" Fuck, he wanted Percy to be his baby so bad, he ached with it. They were glued together from head to toe, and he knew what Percy wanted. He pushed a finger inside Percy. He was soft enough still, so a second finger went in with no resistance.

There was a fracture splitting his chest wide open. For some incomprehensible reason, it hurt him that badly to think someone else had been inside of Percy. He knew it was hypocritical, but it would come as a surprise to no one that he didn't care. He pulled Percy's lip between his teeth, sucking on it relentlessly. Winston knew it walked the line between pleasure and pain, but he did it anyway. "I should've been the first one in here," he grunted as he shoved another finger in.

Percy's eyes shot open with the gleam of lucidity. "You... are," he whispered.

He was the first person to have Percy, and maybe he'd be the last. Either way, he'd make it fucking count.

Percy's eyes were round with apprehension. "I didn't want you to treat me any differently," he muttered.

That didn't make sense to Winston. "Of course, I'd treat you differently. I always have." He took in Percy's crestfallen expression. "If you lied about it because you didn't want me to go too easy on you, that was a waste. I wasn't ever going to do that. You aren't fragile."

Percy's eyes fluttered shut, and he dived back in, pressing his lips to the corner of Winston's mouth. Winston slid his fingers back inside of him. "I'm the only one that's ever been inside of you, so I'm sure as hell gonna get my fill."

"Have it. As much as you want. Please, Junes," he begged.

Percy was bad for his ego. "Have you been fingered before?" Winston secretly hoped he hadn't.

"By myself, yeah," he whispered back.

Winston's brain short-circuited. He was just full of fucking surprises. His not doing any type of anal penetration with his fiancé wasn't exactly uncommon. A lot of people didn't care for it, but Percy clearly did. He responded like he craved it. "Show me," he said.

Percy floundered, searching for an excuse. He hadn't expected Percy to be this shy about things considering how they'd cuddled butt-ass naked too many times to count. He'd felt Winston's boners pressed against him, he'd jacked and sucked him. He gave Percy a wet kiss before pushing him onto his back. "Show me how you do it, baby." Winston felt like he might die.

He searched quickly for the lotion he'd tossed on the bed and grabbed Percy's hand. He drizzled a lot of it into his waiting palm and sat back on his knees.

Percy's Adam's apple bobbed in his throat, but he spread his legs wide and reached between them. He wrapped one hand around his balls and the other moved further back. His long fingers circled the soft, sensitive skin around his tight fucking hole.

Blood roared in Winston's ears. "Here. Lift your hips," he said. He grabbed a pillow and positioned it under Percy's ass so he had easier access. Then, he firmly gripped Percy's ankles and pushed his legs back.

Percy squeezed his eyes shut with a pained groan. "Is all this really necessary?"

"Wanna fuckin see all of you. Wanna see you stretched wide open on your fingers while I know you're thinking of me." Winston needed it more than air.

"Juney, you're killing me. Just fuck me already!"

"No," he answered plainly. Winston's mind reeled at hearing all of those words strung together in Percy's ultra-soft voice. "Go ahead and show me how you do it."

Percy set his jaw. His fingers hadn't even stopped rubbing himself, so he slipped two in right away. Winston's cock hung heavily between his legs. It fucking wept.

Percy slowly worked them in and out. "When was the first time you fingered yourself?" Winston bent his legs further back.

"I don't remember," he hissed through his teeth.

"Put another finger in there, baby." Percy obliged with a low moan. "When was it?" Winston repeated.

Percy's abdomen was tensing beneath his strong thighs. "I-it was when we moved to Miami."

Winston was absorbed in watching Percy's ass swallow his fingers. It was a fucking filthy sight that he didn't think he'd ever get to see. Then something dawned on him. "We moved to Miami like a week after you did that bullshit with Gage. That was right after I put space between us." Percy didn't say a word, but he stroked the underside of his cock with his free hand. His pace was quickening. "So Gage really is the reason for your gay awakening then?"

Percy shoved a fourth finger in his hole, and even with the anger that was burning inside of him, he was mesmerized by the sight.

"He... no, he wasn't," Percy said breathlessly.

Winston had already suspected as much, but that didn't still the knife that was twisting in his heart. He ground his molars together, trying to control his rage. All the feelings he'd felt that night came barreling through him once more. He even considered knocking Gage's fucking teeth out as soon as he left this island. That was what he deserved. Some seriously fucking delayed retribution.

"Juney," Percy said. Winston didn't answer, and he definitely didn't meet his eyes. "I wasn't thinking of him when I did it."

"Bullshit," Winston said automatically.

"Put another finger in me. Stretch me wider." Winston had to breathe through this. He needed to stay calm. He moved one of Percy's ankles to rest on his shoulder and slid his index finger in right next to the others. They couldn't move much, but Percy was squirming around, unable to keep still.

"I was thinking of you," Percy whispered. Winston's eyes snapped up and locked on his pretty face. It was cast in shadows, but he couldn't spot a modicum of deceit. His eyes were open vulnerably. He worked his lip between his teeth like he was unsure. "I know you don't want to believe me, and I know this isn't normal. But you know how I am. It was a new house. Not just any house—a mansion big enough that you and I were in separate wings. I... missed you."

Winston swallowed around the lump in his throat. "How does that- why would that make you—"

Percy abruptly pulled his fingers out, and Winston's slipped out too. Percy's hole twitched around nothing, gaping.

His chest hurt at everything. Fucking everything.

"Get inside of me, Juney. Please, please, please." Percy was whining shamelessly, like nothing he'd ever heard before. "C'mon, Junes. I need you."

He growled, aimed the thick head of his cock at Percy's hole, and pushed. There was little resistance, and then he was sucked into heaven. Percy's ass strangled his dick, and Winston could feel himself getting too worked up. Blood was rushing. Pounding. Thrumming.

Percy threaded his fingers through Winston's hair and leaned up to meet his lips. He kissed Winston slowly but with all the intensity of being hit by a train. "I thought about you because I missed you. Missed your closeness and comfort, and I was going crazy. That was as close as you could be. In my thoughts, imagining you fucking me. Filling me with you."

Sweat rolled down Winston's face as he fought against the softening of his heart. He wasn't strong enough for this, but fuck, he wanted to be. Wanted to force his way in and steal Percy. Wanted to lock him in Winston's world and throw away the key.

Percy's nails cut into his back as Winston fucked him relentlessly. There'd be claw marks, and he wished they'd always be there. He'd go on stage shirtless, as always, and present the broken skin to all of his fans.

"What did you imagine?" he rasped through huffed breaths. His skin was on fire, and the filthy sounds coming from the meeting of their bodies echoed in his head. It was all so loud, he needed Percy to center him.

Percy's heels dug into the backs of Winston's thighs, forcing his thrusts deeper and harder. He didn't give him a break. Percy wanted him so fucking badly, it'd never been this apparent. Winston wanted to give him more than he bargained for, but he was worried it would be the other way around.

"I thought about you holding me, and I-I..." Percy turned his face away from Winston and slammed his lips shut.

Winston wouldn't have that. He wasn't going to let Percy hide from him. He supported his weight with one arm and wrapped his hand around Percy's chin, forcing him to come back. "Tell me what you thought about. I'm not going to judge you, darlin'. Never could."

Percy ran his palm all over Winston's sweat-slick chest, unfazed by it. "You held me close and fucked me whenever you wanted all night. Even if I was sleeping, you'd wake me up with it."

Winston choked and slammed his hips forward, burying himself as deep as he could go, and exploded inside of him. It bowled him over, and it wouldn't stop. He wheezed through each spurt of cum that Percy's channel squeezed out of him. His forehead fell to Percy's shoulder, and he gulped down the air. Tasted salt on his tongue that'd come from smashing his mouth into Percy's skin.

His limbs were cumbersome weights, but he reached between them and grabbed Percy's sweat-soaked, precum-soaked cock and pumped it with his fist. Immediately, a string of soft moans and high-pitched wails fell from his lips. None of it was coherent, and Winston understood that because he was in the same dream state that Percy was. "Who. Do. You. Belong. To?" he growled, each word like a punch.

Percy trembled hard enough that his voice shook with it. "Juney," he answered.

"Again," said Winston.

"I belong to you. Always have."

Percy's cock pulsed in Winston's hand as his release barreled through him. He shot thick ropes of cum between them.

Winston caught Percy's jaw with his teeth, barely able to contain the monstrous feelings eating him up inside. "Only me," he added.

Percy wrapped his arms around Winston and held him so tightly, he didn't think either of them could breathe. "Only you, Juney. There's never been anyone else."

Winston rested his full weight on top of Percy, and they held each other.

Percy whispered gently but desperately in his ear. "I miss you. Want you. Need you. Juney, I love you. Do you need me, too?"

How could he make Percy understand the magnitude of his need?

He rolled to his side and pulled Percy's leg over him. He'd had to peel their skin apart. Percy looked at him through lost and wary eyes before Winston slotted their lips together. He wanted Percy's mouth forever. His tongue could live there inside of him. "You're the only person I've ever needed. The only person I've ever loved. And I've wanted for nothing else but you since we first met."

"But you left," Percy said with a questioning lilt to his voice.

Winston shook his head and untangled himself from Percy's arms and legs. "If you only knew."

Percy's dream blue's followed him. "Where are you going?"

Winston pulled the pack of smokes from his discarded pants, slipped one between his lips, and lit it. He didn't bother going outside. What was Black Diamond going to do about it? Bill him? Go ahead. Winston had more money than he knew what to do with.

There was lightning zig-zagging through his body from his brain to his fingertips to the soles of his feet. He needed this cigarette for his sanity because he was about to lose it. Actually, he reckoned he might've already lost it.

Did he ever actually fucking have it together? You'd think after twenty-one long years, he'd be able to tell when he was well or not.

He guessed Percy had always been there to keep track of him though.

Winston took long, deep drags from the cigarette. It'd be finished in no time, and he only had one more left. He couldn't rely on chain-smoking tonight. Couldn't rely on vodka.

He considered the possibility that this was something he wasn't supposed to run from. Maybe he needed to see it through.

But despite everything they'd said to each other while rolling around in bed, a good outcome couldn't take shape in his mind. It wasn't realistic, and the only deciding factor for Winston's heart would be how selfish he chose to be.

He was riding some kind of high after what they'd just done, and he didn't want it to stop. He had to enjoy it while it lasted.

Winston put the cig out in the sink and threw it away. Then, he finally met Percy's gaze. He'd been watching him the entire time—Winston could tell. Percy's eyes were bleary. He was laying on his stomach with the covers pulled up. He looked so snug in his sweater that Winston wanted to squeeze him, crush him to his chest.

"Would you please stop thinking already? Just come lie

down." Percy said with a sleep-laden voice. "Everything is okay. More than okay."

Winston had the urge to tell him he was fucking delusional, but he would never, ever talk to Percy that way. He bit back the response and got back on the bed. He wouldn't be getting any sleep now.

He tugged the blanket down and situated himself so he was hovering over Percy's ass. Percy looked at him over his shoulder in disbelief. "More?"

"I'll never be through with you." Winston stilled Percy's hips. "Relax. Don't worry." He pressed his lips to the swell of Percy's ass, and swirled his tongue around, luxuriating in its softness. Percy's back arched in surprise, followed by a breathy sigh.

Winston was going to cover his ass in marks. He sucked his skin between his teeth long enough that he knew he'd burst the blood vessels. He dragged his lips over a couple of inches and did it again and again and again. All the while, Percy rotated his hips slowly, following Winston's mouth with his ass.

Winston devoured him. There were red and purple splotches littered across Percy's pale skin. Teeth indentations from the moments when Winston couldn't control himself. For Winston, it was always hard to remain at an even keel, but it was so, so much worse when it came to Percy.

He grabbed thick handfuls of the bruised skin and spread him wide open. Through the dimness of the room, he could tell how red Percy's hole was. "Does it hurt?" he asked.

"Nope," Percy said groggily.

Winston stretched and tugged at the skin until his hole puckered and pushed out a drop of cum that rolled down his sac. The amount of satisfaction it gave him was wrong. So wrong.

He needed to get back in there. Percy was still half awake, and based on what he'd said earlier, he wouldn't mind. Winston moved up the bed and nudged his cock into Percy's softened hole. It slipped in easily with his cum mixed with lotion lubricating the way.

Percy gasped softly and grabbed Winston's arm, pulling it around him tighter. Winston held him and fucked him slowly multiple times throughout the night, filling him with load after load. Percy never stopped him. Always opened for him.

By the time soft light shone through the windows, Winston's eyes burned. His skin was sticky with sweat and cum. He forced himself out of bed, careful not to wake Percy. His bones creaked stiffly the whole way to the shower where he soaped himself up and scrubbed thoroughly.

Percy had come to him last night, wanting him like that. He knew he hadn't coerced him, so the whole thing was a bit wonky in his mind. Percy had admitted to things though. Things like jacking off to fantasies about him for years—even if his reasoning for doing that wasn't normal. It was still more than he'd ever expected.

He got out of the shower and toweled off. There was still some time before breakfast came around, so he sat on the porch with a towel around his hips and soaked in the warmth.

The wind was especially loud. He had trouble hearing his thoughts, and his vision blurred as he watched the palm's flexible trunks sway back and forth.

Percy had always been his. He'd admitted it last night, but that didn't mean he wanted to be with Winston. Didn't want to date or marry him. Percy was too smart to do something like that, and Winston knew Percy was better off that way.

Winston had lived with a broken heart for as long as he

could remember. Since he saw his mom suffer until she took her own life. Since he first looked into Percy's eyes.

He wouldn't allow it to get worse.

Percy didn't have to be with him, but he wouldn't be with Emilio either.

Or fucking *anyone*.

He'd make sure of that.

PART THREE
Bluebird

Thirteen

PERCY

Percy sat down slowly and tried not to wince when his ass hit the seat. He could feel an ache from Juney fucking him repeatedly throughout the night. Even though he was taking it easy, his ass was covered in hickeys and bite marks. Percy wondered if this was the type of thing most people did, but he figured it wasn't. Nothing about Junes was normal.

"Are you okay?" Juney asked from across the table. There was a small smirk curving his lips, otherwise, his eyes were empty. That wasn't a good sign.

"I'm fine. Yup. Just a bit sore," he said before he took a bite of oatmeal. "Are you okay?"

Juney looked him up and down while tugging his lip ring between his teeth. His nostrils flared. "Need a fucking cigarette."

"Last night—"

"Time to go," Junes interrupted. He stood up as the golf cart approached. "Therapy time. You coming?"

Percy set his jaw. So this was how it was going to be. "I need to grab my phone first." He could catch up on some work while he waited. Something flashed in Juney's eyes, but he shrugged and boarded the vehicle. They stopped at Percy's bungalow so he could grab his phone, and then they were on their way down a path leading through a dense jungle.

Black Diamond was top-notch. They had a mental health wing, a rehab wing, and a resort. It was the perfect place for the wealthy to get away privately, which was why they were allowed so many comforts.

When they reached the building, the staff member led them down a hallway until they stopped at a door. Junes knocked as a courtesy but opened it without a response anyway. Through the entryway, Percy saw a petite man in a button-up patterned with daisies.

Mr. Kang smiled brightly at Percy, and Percy tilted his head to the side, scrutinizing him. The therapist's smile didn't waver. "You're free to wait in the garden," he said, and his voice was soothing. He guessed it came with the job description. Percy's hackles rose, but he nodded shortly and followed the staff member to exit into the garden. He was being unreasonable. Feeling jealous over a therapist.

He released a sigh. It was a little harder to be upset in a place like this. It was paradise like he'd never seen before. Tropical flowers and plants with large, leathery leaves. The earthy, floral smell was pervasive. People would bottle this up for a fragrance.

"He'll be done within an hour. Feel free to come get me at the nurse's desk if you need anything." Then the heavy door slammed shut behind him. Percy could stay here way longer than an hour. He sat on a wrought iron bench which wasn't amazing for his ass. The only other options were stone, so he moved to sit on the grass instead.

Percy wanted to close his eyes and enjoy this, but he knew there was too much to catch up on. Plus, his mind was overflowing with all things Juney right now. He needed a break.

He powered on his phone and immediately saw the notifications populate. First, he checked the group chat where Gage and Torin did a lot of talking.

> **TORIN**
> Amir told us you arrived safely. Good luck.

> **GAGE**
> Yeah, thanks for the update, jackass.

Percy snorted. Gage cared in his own way.

> **TORIN**
> Let us know if you need anything.

Percy typed out a quick response.

> **PERCY**
> Sorry. I had my phone turned off. Wanted to unplug. Thank you for checking up on me. Juney's making great progress.

They were easy enough to handle, despite the massive secret looming over his head. Percy wasn't great at lying or hiding things. It was only a matter of time before they figured it out. He didn't think they'd be upset with him, but he did feel a level of shame for what he'd done to Emilio. Gage wouldn't give a shit, but Torin might. He wouldn't castigate him for it, but it was the thought alone that made Percy uneasy.

He took a deep breath and opened his email. He wasn't surprised to see one from Lovely. She'd been busy with this debacle.

Hi Percy,

I hope you're doing well. I've been watching carefully, and only one tabloid seems to be aware of Juney's trip as of now. We paid a ridiculous amount of money to ensure that the information doesn't spread. The last thing we need is Electric Metal Magazine to get a whiff of this. On second thought, maybe it'd be a good thing. Bad publicity is certainly a way to stay relevant. Let me know what you think about leaking some information.

Kind regards,
Lovely Toussaint
Publicist
Heatwave Records

Percy pinched the bridge of his nose. What in the world was she thinking? She had to know better. It would be a cold day in hell when Juney goes public about his mental health, and Percy convinced Emilio to not press charges. He agreed as long as the altercation stayed under lock and key which Percy thought was perfectly reasonable. The whole thing was quite... embarrassing for all involved.

Hi Lovely,

I see you've lost your mind since the last time we spoke. Under no circumstance will we facilitate a leak.

Thanks,
Percy Lovell
Telltale Dream Manager
Heatwave Records

He was amazed at how much his life had changed from such small beginnings. It was surreal, and most of the time, Percy felt like an imposter even though he knew he was fully capable of excelling at his job. He might've been a shoo-in for the position, but Heatwave never once suggested replacing him.

Amir didn't bother with the formality of an email. He sent multiple text messages and did impromptu calls. Percy responded to his last text.

AMIR

Pls let me know if Winston is quitting the band so I can begin planning my funeral. Thx.

PERCY

I will update when I have concrete answers, but nothing is ever actually concrete with him. We'll see.

Percy rolled his eyes at Amir's dramatics, but it made him realize that he hadn't gotten a straight answer out of Junes yet. They'd been so busy doing... what exactly? He'd only been there for the weekend, and they hadn't established much at all. Percy figured his main goal in coming here was to offer Juney his support, but he'd been so overwhelmed with being in such close proximity to him again.

No matter what happened between them, Junes would always be his best friend. His soulmate. Percy figured those two things were one and the same more often than people realized, but soulmates weren't always meant to be together. He'd always figured that was the case with Juney, but after this weekend, he wasn't so sure of that anymore—which posed a bigger issue. What was Percy going to do? Follow through with his marriage or end it all for Juney?

Emilio was stable and treated him well. Percy could tell Emilio adored him, and if it weren't clear before, it definitely was now. Percy was convinced Emilio wouldn't want anything to do with him after what happened, but he didn't blame Percy at all. Said he wasn't responsible for his friend's actions. That was how good of a guy he was.

Percy's stomach turned. *Fuck*, he was an awful, awful person. He couldn't keep feeling this way. He would have to end things with Emilio on principle alone. If infidelity was that easy for Percy, then he had no business marrying Emilio. The thought of calling off his engagement was making him feel a bit lightheaded. He would leave this island a single man. No Emilio. No Juney.

The realization was like a lead weight in his gut.

He chewed on his lip, shredding the skin. At least he knew what was coming, but he still didn't think that would help him prepare for the inevitable end. Nothing would.

Percy needed to call him, but he wasn't sure he could even manage that. There wasn't a chance in hell he could break it off today, but he also wasn't sure he could maintain his composure enough for a simple conversation.

His thumb hovered over the green call button, but he

immediately felt sick. It was a full-body sensation that began in his gut and emanated through every limb.

Percy was about to toss the phone down when a picture of his mom popped up. His heart climbed into his throat. He never lied to his parents. They'd always been so easygoing because they trusted him, but there were some major things lately that he hadn't uttered a word to them about. He hadn't told them that he was engaged. They didn't know that Juney assaulted his fiancé. And, the worst part of all—Juney's second suicide attempt. He wasn't sure they'd ever recovered from the first one. Percy would bet that they lost a little bit of themselves just like Percy had.

He needed to talk to someone though, and he missed them something fierce. Maybe his mom would be able to ease him. He breathed a sigh of relief when he answered the call and heard her voice. "Percy, sweetheart."

Warmth suffused his chest, and he was already starting to feel lighter. He could almost smell her pecan pie just from the sound of her voice. "Yes, Mama. How have you been?"

"Oh, you know I don't do much. The marigolds and daylilies bloomed, and they're just the prettiest thing. Your baby cousin put on a show at the theatre downtown with her kindergarten class. Too precious. I'll send you a video."

His mom was vibrant in his head. She was full of love and as smart as a whip. "I want to see pictures of the flowers, too," he said. Then, he cleared his throat in order to sound more confident. "Junes and I are on a vacation at a tropical island resort. The flora is breathtaking here. I'll send you some pictures as well."

Mama hummed on the other end of the line. "Just you and Junes?" No one called Juney by his nickname other than his parents and, sometimes, Gage and Torin. She knew they'd been distant for a while. All he told her was that they grew into themselves which meant they were their own people with separate lives. It wasn't a lie, but it did gnaw at him.

"Just the two of us, yeah. We spent yesterday at a waterfall. The most crystal clear water I've ever seen. Everything here is a wonder." The words spilled from his mouth clumsily.

There was a charged silence that stretched far too long. "Are you two getting closer again? Did you find your way back to each other?" she asked tentatively.

Percy swallowed around the lump in his throat. They were, weren't they? Aside from the sex, they were teasing the line of comfort they used to have. He didn't want to get his hopes up, but it was damn near impossible. Everything in him yearned for Juney. Always. "Yea, we are," he replied, nodding his head even though she couldn't see.

"Well, I'm just so glad for you, sweetheart," she said softly. He could tell she was unsure. Percy hadn't ever been a good liar.

Percy jumped as Juney's shadow fell over him. He hadn't even heard him come outside. That's how in his head he'd been. "Talking to Mama," he said with the phone still pressed to his ear.

Juney's eyes lit up, and he grabbed the phone. "How are you doing, Mrs. Birdie? Staying cool with some iced tea, I hope."

Percy picked at a blade of grass, trying to ignore the love swelling in his chest. Juney's relationship with his parents took a long time to become what it was now. It took years for his walls to come down, little by little, and that was okay. Juney had found their unconditional love in the end.

Junes had an arm crossed in front of his chest as he slowly paced, nodding his head every now and again. "Percy told you about the waterfall already, didn't he?" He stopped pacing and locked his gaze on Percy. He couldn't decipher what he saw in Juney's eyes, but they weren't empty—that much, he knew. "Yes, ma'am," he murmured.

He crouched down next to Percy and held the phone between them. "I love you boys, and we need to arrange a visit. Maybe y'all would consider coming back home for Thanksgiving supper?"

They hadn't been back home since the day they left. It was mostly because they were always so busy, so it was easier for his parents to come stay at Percy and Juney's home in Miami. The larger reason was that Juney had wanted nothing to do with that town or his dad, but Percy wasn't so sure that was the case anymore. But Juney was as stubborn as a mule. It took him a while to come around sometimes. Percy looked at him expectantly.

Juney swallowed roughly. "We'll be there as long as you make pecan pie and peach cobbler and sweet potato casserole and fried cornbread—" He was cut off by her giddy laughter coming through the phone. Percy smiled brightly, and Juney's lips curved only a little, but it was a win nonetheless.

"Yes, of course," she replied with a sniffle. "I can't wait to see you, boys."

"Love you, Mama," Percy said.

"Love you," Junes added quickly before he hung up the phone.

Percy blinked up at him, shielding his eyes from the sun. "That'll be good. We'll be fresh off the tour."

Junes didn't respond which set Percy on edge. "You're not actually quitting the band, are you?"

He didn't expect him to answer. He didn't seem in the

mood for talking, but he did anyway. "I don't know, darlin'. Don't think so. For now, at least."

He sounded exhausted, and he looked even worse with dark crescent moons below his bloodshot eyes. "You need some rest, Junes."

He nodded and led Percy back inside. "Lunch then meditation."

"You'll fall asleep at meditation."

"Good."

They got back on the golf cart and ended up in front of another building. "The café is in there, and I'll be back to get you in an hour," the driver said.

"Thank you," they said in unison.

They walked into the building and found the café. It was somewhat busy, considering how it was lunchtime. It was optional to have your meals delivered or to dine in. He'd heard that there was a tiki restaurant too, but this was closer to them. Juney led them to a booth. They were settling in when a waiter showed up. "Who am I serving today?" she asked lightly.

"Percy Lovell and Winston Jennings," Juney stated, and wow. Their names sounded so good together—especially in Juney's voice. If they were married he was sure that Juney would want Percy's last name. *Winston Lovell.*

A blush started on his cheeks. Planning a marriage with someone who he pined after? Percy guessed he was a teenage girl now.

"Ah, yes. You're vegans, correct?"

"Yes ma'am."

"A hearty Greek salad sound okay to you?"

They both nodded, and she left.

"How was therapy with Ian?" he asked.

Juney crossed his arms in front of his chest, and his brows

were a hard line. "You don't need to be jealous of my therapist."

"I'm not," he said too fast and winced.

"Percy," Junes gave him a droll look. "My dick was in your ass damn near all night, and you're jealous over Ian?"

He hadn't forgotten. The bruises wouldn't let him—not that he wanted to. "Ian is really, *really* attractive, but it's not about that." Now Juney was the one looking jealous. "Can't you see that it's because you two are so... close. He probably knows more about you than I do."

Juney stretched, and his feet ended up on either side of Percy's, caging him in. Percy clamped his teeth down so as not to make a peep. "No one knows more about me than you do," he said like it was gospel.

Percy broke from his trance when their food was set down in front of them. His stomach growled at the sight of all of those Kalamata olives. He didn't even notice when the waitress left.

"It's also not exactly healthy to expect that of someone," Juney mused.

Percy narrowed his eyes at him, biting back a laugh. "Junes, I'm not convinced you don't have cameras in my room back home."

Juney shrugged while eating overly large mouthfuls of salad. He roughly wiped his mouth with a napkin. "So when did you realize you weren't straight? Was it with Gage?"

Percy gaped at him. His face was the picture of nonchalance, but Percy knew that wasn't the case. He didn't understand why Juney was putting on an act. "Y-you want to talk about this now?"

"As good a time as any." He couldn't possibly tell him the truth. He needed to lie, but he couldn't stomach doing that either. "From my memory, throughout everything we did, you still held onto your straightness. You wanting to be held by me and cuddled—which is somewhat normal for friends, but jacking me off isn't all that hetero."

Percy hadn't jacked him off that often over those six months. Couldn't have been more than ten times, but he was confused and naive at eighteen. Even now at twenty-one, he didn't feel super confident about his identity. "I hadn't ever felt an attraction to anyone back then, regardless of gender. For the longest time, I didn't want to have sex. Didn't want to date." He swallowed roughly. "I just wanted to be with you every moment I could. I didn't care if it was sexual, but I did need your affection more than anything."

Juney's legs tightened around his. There was a vein bulging in his temple. "When did you begin feeling sexual attraction then?"

A sweat broke out on Percy's forehead. "Shortly before we ended things," he murmured, quiet as a mouse.

"To who?"

"You."

Percy's heart felt like it was collapsing. He never intended to admit that to him because it didn't matter. It didn't change anything. Even with his newfound sexual desire at the time, he didn't know what it meant for him. He wasn't sure if it meant he should start dating or if he just wanted to hook up with people. The only thing he'd known for certain was that he wanted to be with Juney in whatever capacity he could have him, but Juney didn't want anything more than friendship with him. He didn't even want the affection anymore. It wasn't normal, and they were too codependent. The separation was probably for the best, but it never felt that way.

"You… were sexually attracted to me before you'd been with Gage?" Juney's voice sounded strangled.

Percy couldn't handle this conversation anymore, but they still had some time before their pickup. "I was."

"Why didn't you tell me?"

He scoffed. What a ridiculous question. "Juney, you already wanted me to quit clinging to you in every way possible, and you think I should've told you that you turned me on?" Percy's cheeks were on fire. "I told you we needed some distance that day because I didn't think it was right to keep on the same way we were once my feelings turned sexual. That wouldn't have been fair to you."

Juney roughly dragged a hand down his face. He looked truly bewildered. It made Percy feel worse about it than he already did. It was the thing that inadvertently dissolved their friendship.

Juney shot up from their table. "It's time to go," he mumbled. He rushed outside with Percy hot on his heels. Sure enough, there was their ride and the driver hurried to put out his cigarette. Juney waltzed up to him. "Hey, man. Never got your name."

"Victor," he replied.

Junes nodded. "Victor, can I bum a cig off of you? Tough times right now."

"No problem, dude. I can get you a couple of packs if you need them." He slid one out and handed it to Junes who promptly lit it and took a greedy drag.

"Fuck yeah. That'd be great," Juney said with so much relief.

Percy sat in the back seat and hugged himself. He'd just told Juney his deepest secret, and Juney was acting like nothing happened. There was something going on beneath the surface that he couldn't get a good read on. It made Percy uneasy.

Juney stubbed out his cigarette before sitting next to Percy without a single glance.

"Which Focus group are you going to today? Meditation, right?" Victor asked.

Percy tuned everything out the rest of the way to their destination which was the beach. Victor came to a stop at the end of the patch. "You'll have to walk the rest of the way down there. Did you want me to come back for you? Your bungalows aren't very far."

They were in the same area as the cliff that Junes fell asleep on. "Nope. We're good, but if you get those cigarettes you can leave them on the porch."

"No problem, man."

Percy watched Victor go back the way they came. What a chill guy.

Juney didn't wait up for him again and began traversing down the slope to the beach. There were about ten other people there, and some of them were definitely rehab patients. Everyone was choosing a place to sit. Percy expected Juney to sit as far away from him as possible, but he took the spot right next to him instead. Juney still hadn't even made eye contact with him since Percy's big confession.

He watched as Juney examined how everyone else was sitting so he could do it properly.

"Good afternoon, my loves. I'm Kara, and I will guide your meditation today." She wore a long, flowy paisley skirt and a crochet bralette. A couple of necklaces with crystals that had been wrapped by hand. Percy grinned despite the downfall of life as he knew it. Kara seemed awesome, and he'd love to meditate with her. Everyone here appeared to be taking it seriously, too.

Juney was quite stiff. "Loosen up a bit, Junes."

His jaw ticked.

"Okay, everyone, elongate and straighten those spines. Shoulders back. Center yourself," she said each instruction softly and patiently waited for everyone to get it right. "Now close your eyes and take a deep breath with me. In... Out..."

Percy was able to sink into it so easily. The sun's energy was powerful, and so was the ocean's. Waves crashed and sprayed their foam and light burst in flashes behind his eyelids. Sand kicked up and speckled his skin.

He peeped his eyes open to check on Juney and was surprised to find him deeply immersed.

Percy faced forward, letting his eyes fall shut once again.

This was the best thing he could have possibly done after the day he'd already had, and Juney was so thoughtful for doing this for him.

Fourteen

WINSTON

Today at approximately twelve-thirty p.m., Percy admitted that he'd wanted Winston to fuck him since they were eighteen years old. It'd been four hours now, and he was still struggling to process that information.

Winston set Eleanor on the table and blew out a thick, gray cloud of smoke. They'd smoked so much weed that the room was dense with fog.

Percy was being patient with him. He hadn't tried getting him to talk yet, but Winston could tell it was coming.

For the first time since being here–or in his life really–he wanted to talk to a therapist. He'd always known that he needed to get into therapy, but he'd never actually wanted to.

This felt like something he wasn't capable of handling properly. He didn't know what the right thing to do was. Didn't know the wrong thing, either. He'd already spent an hour with Ian today, so this would have to wait until Wednesday's session. Winston knew that would be too late because his brain was supplying him with all kinds of ideas.

Winston was stoned enough that he was couch-locked, and there was a certain softness around everything, including his thoughts. His eyes were heavy, and if he wanted to, he could probably fall asleep.

Sleep was what he desperately needed. Ian had clocked his exhaustion almost immediately and questioned him about his behavior and sleep schedule. Ian was worried that the meds were affecting his sleep or sending him into a hypomanic episode. It was hard for either of them to tell. Either way, he arranged for Winston to see Dr. Weaver again to discuss it.

The more he saw Ian, the more grateful for him he became. Winston was starting to wonder what he would do without him off-island. He didn't want a new therapist. Maybe they could have virtual appointments.

He finally looked at Percy. It was a slow perusal. He couldn't look at Percy without wanting to play with his hair, and the slope of Percy's nose was cuter than a nose had any right being. His lips were a deep shade of red from chewing on them so much. It was what Percy did when he was nervous.

Winston frowned. There was one thought on a loop in his mind. "You should've told me," he rasped. He had a bad case of cottonmouth. Percy wordlessly handed him his water.

"That's ridiculous. You must not remember how things were between us back then." Percy's voice didn't waver.

Winston reached out and grabbed Percy's hand. He stroked the pad of his thumb over his soft skin, and Percy's hitched breath didn't go unnoticed. He responded so intensely to the simplest touches. Percy's dream blue eyes looked impossibly dreamier when they were bloodshot and glazed over. "Is sex the only thing you wanted from me?"

Percy's throat bobbed. This was the most vulnerable either of them had ever been with each other which was ridiculous considering all that they'd done together. This was somehow different. He could see fear written all over Percy's face—his body was tense with it. He cracked his mouth open but shut it quickly and turned his head to look away. That was when he spoke. "I wanted everything from you. I didn't know what it meant back then—those feelings." Percy hid his face in the palm of his other hand. "You know how I was, Juney. Didn't want to share you with anyone. I needed your attention at all times. Your affection. You've been my obsession since we were seven years old."

Winston's heart galloped in his chest, and he was finding it hard to breathe.

Percy had been hanging on his arm and laying his head on Winston's shoulder since the very beginning. Winston didn't know why he'd never stopped him. It wasn't like he let anyone else touch him. No, not even close.

It was like he'd felt instinctively protective of him. He'd quickly realized that Percy was innocent and naive in the way that only a well-cared-for, sheltered kid could be, and Winston needed to make sure that he was always okay. It became his only purpose, especially after his mother had died. "Look at me," he said.

Percy dropped his hand from his face and met Winston's gaze. Winston had to look up a bit since he was slouched down on the sofa. He loved it, but he was scared. His heart hadn't stopped its painful rhythm, but he did his best to not let it show on his face. According to Percy, he looked angry when he did that. He hoped that wasn't the case now. "I was the same way, and you know it."

Percy shook his head. "It wasn't the same."

"You're right. I've always known that I was in love with you."

Percy's brows drew together. "Always?" he stammered.

Winston tugged Percy's hand a couple of times, urging him down until they were eye to eye. Percy's stilted breaths fanned over Winston's lips.

He needed to make sure Percy understood. "I have always been yours." He brushed his nose against Percy's, willing his stomach to untie itself. "I've been at your mercy since the day we met, tethered to you like a fucking guard dog. You've seen the lengths I've gone," he said raggedly. "Even over the last three years, I've known every move you made, and the interesting thing is that I know you don't mind one bit."

Percy's eyes fluttered shut. His head tipped back. Winston threaded his fingers through Percy's hair, tight enough to pull at his scalp. Winston knew he wasn't the best person in the world to be with, but if Percy was going to be with anyone, it would be him. "You know that you belong to me. We established that last night," he continued.

"I do. It might've taken me longer to understand what I was feeling, but it was always there," he said.

Winston dragged his thumb across Percy's lips, hypnotized. "I hope you know by now that you aren't going to marry him."

Percy whimpered. "I was going to call it off this morning."

Winston was overcome with warmth. "Why didn't you?"

"I chickened out," he groused.

Winston brought their lips together. Percy wasn't attacking his mouth like he'd done last night. He was kissing Winston softly and slowly like he'd realized he had all the time in the world. There was no need to rush anymore. Winston couldn't remember the last time he'd felt this way, and he was starting to feel like he never had. He couldn't even put a name to it, but it consumed him. He moaned dazedly against Percy's parted lips. "I'll break up with him for you, baby. Don't worry." It was a done deal.

Percy stiffened and pulled away. "Are you crazy?" he hissed.

Winston couldn't help but grin at the irony. "I am in a psychiatric ward as we speak."

Percy looked unimpressed. "You know that's not what I meant."

Winston was busy twisting a chunk of Percy's hair around his finger. "We'll do it however you want then. Tomorrow."

"Tomorrow?" Percy's brows climbed higher.

Winston couldn't take his eyes off of him. "Not a day later."

Percy began chewing on his lower lip again. "What does this mean, Juney? What are we doing?"

Winston understood the gravity of what they were doing. He knew that he was unequipped to be the man Percy needed, but Winston was finally working on getting himself under control. "I'm still fucked up, you know. Meds and therapy aren't magic. There are things ingrained in me that can't be changed as well as things that still need to be worked through. I'm the same Juney you've always known—the same one who introduced you to pain and stress."

Percy cupped Winston's cheeks, and it caught him off guard. "Yes, you are the same Juney I've always known. You're a creative genius with a mind that's respected around the world. You're the same Juney who I've always craved and needed, and even when you were pouring from an empty cup, you always found a drop of water for me. Your mental health struggles, your trauma—none of it defines you."

A lump swelled in Winston's throat. He wanted to look away and shield himself like Percy had, but Percy wouldn't let him. "Hope you mean all of that 'cause you're stuck with me now." Winston's low timbre was rough with gravel.

"What's new then, Junes?"

"Everything."

Nothing was the same. It never would be. Percy had only been trying to make a light joke, but Winston had never been more serious about something in his entire life.

Percy's face softened, and he dropped his forehead to Winston's. Turned his head and nuzzled Winston's cheek. "You have me any way you want me, Junes, and I'm so glad you do," Percy whispered the way he liked. The whisper that he felt in his heart.

He pulled Percy until he was on his lap. He needed to hold him because he felt like he was drifting away. Percy had to pull him back. Winston shoved his face into Percy's neck and squeezed his eyes shut. "Are you sure? Please don't do this if you aren't. Being with me won't be easy, won't be stable," he said, muffled by Percy's skin.

Percy held him so tightly. Ran his fingers through Winston's hair. Winston hadn't realized how much he needed this until now. "Have you ever heard a complaint from me? I've been at your side through everything, no matter what. You're the most stable person for me because I know you inside and out, and no one knows me like you do. Not even close."

Winston's eyes burned, and his face flooded with heat. He was overcome with such an intense feeling. It smashed right through his walls and suddenly, he felt like his heart was on full display. He didn't like this feeling.

He fisted Percy's shirt on both sides and looked up at him. Their faces were inches from each other, and Winston couldn't tear his gaze away from Percy's glassy eyes. His pupils were blown, and Winston was lost in them. No one should ever get to see Percy like this. "Is this all for me? Are you all for me?" he rasped, emotion suffusing his words.

Percy's brows knit together. "Yeah, of course," he said, brushing his fingers from Winston's temple to his jaw.

"All of you?"

Percy tightened his grip on Winston's face and grazed their lips together. "Yes."

"Forever?" He realized that he was begging, and his breaths came faster. He'd never begged.

"Forever."

"You can't leave. You can't," he murmured. "Hold me."

Percy crushed their chests together and held Winston as tightly as possible. Burrowed his face against Winston's neck. "You know I won't leave."

Winston didn't know that. He didn't know anything. "You almost married someone." He couldn't hide the pain in his tone. Even though Winston knew Percy hadn't been in love, it still ripped his fucking heart from his chest. If things hadn't gone the way they did, Winston would've had to sit back and watch the love of his life marry someone else. A hard lump swelled in his throat. He wouldn't let himself think about it. "You almost married someone," he repeated.

Percy squeezed him and shook his head against Winston's neck. "I wouldn't have. There's no way I could've gone through with it knowing how you felt about him. I was going to try, but it wouldn't have worked."

"You don't know that."

"I do," he said vehemently.

Winston felt tears welling in his eyes, but he squeezed them shut. Fought against it. "Need me," he demanded, but it sounded more like he was begging.

Percy dragged his lips across Winston's cheek and pressed them to his own. Warmth consumed him when he teased his tongue against Percy's, and the floodgates opened. He pulled back an inch and choked on a sob. A fat tear rolled down his cheek.

Percy's fingers threaded through Winston's hair. "I need you," he said quickly.

Winston's face burned. "Love me. Want me," he panted.

"I love you. I want you. I always have, even when we were just friends."

Percy sealed their lips together again and kissed him like he couldn't go another second without it. They grabbed at each other frantically.

The last three years had been a whirlwind for Winston. Drugs, alcohol, and millions of fans. Sex, money, and fights. It felt like a fever dream. Winston could be convinced none of it had ever happened because being in Percy's arms brought him back. He was in the present, and it was awash with color. It was real.

Percy was his now.

The phone in Percy's hand felt like a bomb. His stomach was twisted tightly with nerves.

What made it worse was that it didn't hurt him to leave Emilio—not even a little bit. All he felt was guilt for what he'd done. For going as far as to get engaged when he knew Emilio wasn't the right person for him. For wasting Emilio's time. He should've broken up with him way before, so it wouldn't have gotten to this point. He wasn't dumb. He knew that it wasn't normal to have to convince himself that the person he was marrying was right for him.

He didn't have to settle. Even if Juney could never be his, he still shouldn't settle. That was why he gave Emilio a chance, to begin with. He'd known no one would ever be good enough for him. No one could be better for him than Junes, so he'd spend the rest of his life alone with the bare minimum of friendship. Now he realized that would be better than stringing someone along.

After all, this was the first person he'd ever dated, and he was so blinded by the unrequited love he harbored for his best friend.

Juney was at his appointment with Dr. Weaver, and Percy was left to handle this alone. It was what he wanted to do. He still figured it was the best course of action. He would probably throw up if he had to do this in front of Juney.

His thumb shook, and he felt faint, but he pressed the call button anyway. He didn't get to feel sorry for himself when he was the one who made so many awful decisions. There were consequences to actions. Nothing happened in a vacuum.

"Hey, love," Emilio said, and Percy's heart sank to his stomach. He sounded preoccupied. Of course, he did. It was Tuesday, so he was at work—not on a tropical island being a garbage human.

"Hey, Emilio," he responded, hoping his voice held strong.

"Good to hear from you. It's been a few days. Have you been enjoying yourself?"

The question was intended to be light. A perfectly normal thing to ask, but it made Percy's hairs stand on end. "Listen, so-we- uh," he stammered, rubbing at his throat. "I'm sorry."

"Calm down, Percy. What are you sorry for, exactly?"

"I want to—I'm calling off the engagement," he croaked. A bead of sweat burned a trail down his side.

The silence on the other end of the line was charged. "This is about Winston, isn't it?" Emilio said sharply. He sounded like he'd expected this. Like he'd been proven right.

Emilio's tone bothered Percy. He wasn't sure why, but it did. "Why were you going to follow through with our engagement if you felt I may have had feelings for Winston?"

He heard Emilio's pen slam down onto his desk. "I wouldn't end an engagement over a hunch. Until today, I thought you wanted to marry me. That was all the assurance I needed to move forward."

Percy tangled his fingers in his hair, tugging at it. Emilio made their marriage seem like a business transaction, and maybe that was how Emilio looked at life. Detached and logical. He didn't lead with feelings.

Percy envied him, but he didn't want to diminish how deeply he felt for Juney. The entire history of them was etched into his heart, and every step of the way brought him to this point where he finally felt like the pain could end.

He hadn't responded because he didn't know what to say. He itched to hang up and throw his phone into the ocean and never leave this island. But that was him being a coward. This was what he deserved.

"I just need to know one thing, Percy," he said flatly, and Percy knew what was coming. "Have you been cheating on me with him? How long has this been going on?" Percy covered his mouth and held his breath for no reason other than he was too overwhelmed. He hated to lie, and even if he tried to, he knew it wouldn't be believable. He'd waited too long. "You did, didn't you?" Emilio laughed, but it was a brief, sardonic thing.

Percy had done so much wrong that he couldn't stomach any more. "We hadn't done anything until now. We rarely even spoke to each other over the past three years." His voice shook. He knew how ridiculous that sounded—that he'd ruin their engagement for someone he barely knew, but he did know Juney. Emilio wouldn't understand that, though, and he didn't have to. That fact alone didn't make it right. Nothing would.

"You cheated on me with the psycho who tried to kill me." Emilio was rapidly getting more upset. It made him realize that he hadn't ever shown Percy any real emotion. He hadn't been cold. No. He'd been dry.

But he *hated* when people talked about Juney like that—or anyone who struggled with their mental health. "Juney didn't try to kill you, Emilio, and he isn't a psycho," he seethed. It wasn't the right thing to say. He knew that he shouldn't be defending him right now, but he hadn't ever been able to bite his tongue about this. Junes wasn't proud of his actions. He never had been, and his journey to getting better has been a long, hard one. Yeah, it's inflicted damage on others but none more than on himself. Juney carried all of that on his shoulders, and it was backbreaking.

Juney was the strongest person Percy knew.

Emilio scoffed. "You know what, you're better off with him anyway. You low-life degenerates are good for each other." There was an agonizing stretch of silence that probably wasn't as long as it'd felt, and then Emilio hung up.

Percy's vision blurred as he stared at the grass. He was as disgusted with himself as he was relieved.

As he sat with his thoughts, something occurred to him. Emilio might not keep this to himself. He could leak this to a tabloid if he wanted to. Percy's heart raced, and his blood ran cold.

Oh, no. Oh, no. Oh, no.

Emilio was probably arranging something right now.

Percy swallowed roughly and dialed Lovely. She answered on the first ring. "Um. You never call me. Are you okay? What happened?" she asked frantically.

Percy pinched the bridge of his nose. It just now hit him that he'd have to admit what he'd done all over again. No one even knew they were together yet, and this is how everyone would find out? His parents? Their bandmates? Not that he minded anyone knowing, but he was excited to tell everyone himself. Despite the sick feeling in his gut, he looked forward to those moments so badly.

He figured it best to just let it all out. "I broke off my engagement, and now Winston and I are together."

Lovely choked. "I didn't hear that correctly, did I?"

"You did. And there's a strong possibility that Emilio won't keep this to himself. He's not exactly... happy, and rightfully so. But, uh, yeah," he faltered.

He heard her heels clicking as she paced her office. "Nope. The media will have a field day with this. This will be breaking fucking news. Number one trending on every social media platform there is. Oh, fuck. Fuck," she cursed repeatedly. Percy had never heard her this hysterical, and it gnawed at his gut. His decision would have a ripple effect on everyone.

The phone was grabbed from his hand, and Percy wasn't surprised to find Juney. He looked down at the screen, saw who it was, and put it on speaker. "Why does Percy look like he's been kicked in the stomach?"

A frustrated groan left Lovely's throat. "Congratulations. So happy you finally admitted your feelings for each other. But you're both about to be canceled. People *despise* cheaters. I'll do my best to buy the tabloid's secrecy, but I don't think they'll let this go. It's too big."

Juney's jaw ticked. "So be it."

Percy gasped, face twisting in shock. "What!"

"I don't think you understand, Winston. Sponsors will drop the band. The tour will have to be canceled. Hell, Heatwave might drop you guys too."

Junes didn't miss a beat. "Like I said: so be it. Telltale can replace me. I don't give a fuck. Lovely, if it's that dead in the water, don't even worry about trying to smooth it over. It would only be a waste of your time."

Lovely sighed heavily. "You don't have to give up just yet. Don't you value your career at all? People spend their entire life wanting what you have. Don't let it slip through your fingers."

"Maybe it's best someone more deserving takes my spot, 'cause the only thing I've ever wanted is Percy."

Percy was shocked by how casually Juney said that. How he was so willing to drop the band for him. Percy knew it wasn't true. Juney downplayed everything he'd accomplished. He was living his dream. He'd left Georgia, and he had something of a family between Percy, Gage, and Torin. His body of work was loved worldwide. Juney acted like none of it mattered, so it wouldn't hurt him if he failed.

Lovely was silent for a minute. "We're not going to make any hasty decisions, okay? I'll talk to Amir and plan a course of action for when one is needed. No, no. I'm sorry. I'm being negative—*if* one is needed," she rambled.

Juney pursed his lips. "Do what you do. I appreciate it no matter what."

Then, just like that, the call was over. Juney pocketed Percy's phone and helped him up. Percy threw his hair into a quick bun. Thick clumps of it'd been clinging to his sweat-slick skin. It was the temperature as well as his anxiety that was making him pour sweat.

They followed Victor all the way out to the golf cart and rode silently to Juney's bungalow. Percy wanted to hold his hand or touch him or *something*, but he couldn't help feeling like that was the wrong thing to do. He didn't know how much longer he could take this kind of guilt. Percy was not a bad person. That had always been a fact. Not anymore.

As soon as they got off the golf cart, Junes was sparking a

cigarette and taking his shirt off. "We won't be here for much longer," Juney stated.

Percy nodded. The label would want Juney to cut this stay short.

Even with the weight of all this stress, Percy couldn't help but be enamored with him. Percy wouldn't describe Juney's face as conventionally attractive. He looked just as harsh as he was. His face didn't soften—the lines of it were almost always tense and twisted, and he had a tic that caused him to blink repetitively at times, especially when he was stressed. His movements weren't fluid. He wasn't clumsy, but his limbs were jerky.

Percy loved all of him so much that he ached with it. Juney was the most attractive person he'd ever seen in his life, and he'd always thought so. He was perfect, and every time Percy looked at him, it was in admiration. He used to think it was because he wanted to be like him. When he looked back on it, he felt like it should've been obvious. It was a lot more than idolization.

Juney's skin glistened with sweat, and black jeans hung low on his hips. His Adonis belt cut deeply across his lower abdomen. A web of veins bulged from his skin there, and Percy wanted to trace them. Dark, unruly hair trailed down his stomach, and Percy wanted to feel it against his cheek.

He couldn't look at Juney and not think these things.

Junes' gaze was locked somewhere above Percy's shoulder. Percy took a step toward him, and Juney's eyes snapped to his. He clasped Percy's shoulder and pulled him to his chest. "We'll be okay, darlin'. We were okay before all this fame, and we'll be okay after. Except this time, we won't be poor." Juney had the nerve to laugh.

Percy wrapped his arms around Juney's middle and held him tightly. "The label isn't going to drop us."

Juney took a long drag from the cigarette. "I already know what's going to happen. Heatwave is probably going to spin a story that nixes the cheating claim, and the only way they can back it up is to have us keep our relationship a secret from the public—which I'm not gonna fucking do."

Percy worried his lower lip. That was probably exactly what was going to happen. "I'm sure they would only want us to lay low until the tour is over."

"We'll see."

He stubbed out the cigarette just in time for their dinner to show up. He sat across from Juney, and his appetite was so nonexistent that the food was about as good as cardboard. He had trouble with each bite and ended up with only three successful ones.

"What is it?" Junes asked, looking at him intensely.

Percy threw his fork down. "The guilt is eating me alive. It won't stop."

"What do you feel guilty about exactly?"

Percy's brows furrowed. "That's a long list. I cheated on my fiancé, and I'm ruining your career, and the entire world is going to trash me online—to name a few."

Juney threw his fork down, too. "That man was barely your fiancé, and you shouldn't be beating yourself up about that. In the grand scheme of things, it was just a drop in the bucket that led us to where we are now. Emilio was not in love with you either. I'm not sure what his motive for marrying you was, but it wasn't love, so I don't think he's drowning in heartbreak. The fucking idiot. You were the best he'll ever have—"

"The details don't matter, Juney. I still did something wrong," Percy interjected.

Junes stood up, the food long since forgotten. "They do

matter. Nothing is cut and dry. That sure would be fuckin' nice, wouldn't it?"

He understood what Juney was trying to say, but weighing how badly he'd messed up wasn't helping at all. He gulped down some water and stood up, too. He figured they would go inside, but Junes picked up his guitar and hit the path leading into the bush. Percy sighed. He wanted to lie down and sleep these feelings away.

"The beach will do you good," Junes mumbled.

Despite the inky, black pit swirling in his gut, his heart panged at Juney's thoughtfulness. It wasn't the grandest gesture, but it was more than Junes would do for just about anyone.

They trekked down to the shore and dropped to the sand. They spent a lot of time doing this when they first moved to Florida. They were within walking distance from the beach, and Percy always wanted to be there. The sun was beginning to set, and the breeze coming off the water cooled him down. Loose tendrils of hair wisped around his face. Juney was looking at him, and Percy thought he saw fear written on Juney's face.

Percy frowned. "What's wrong?"

He shook his head. "Better not get any crazy ideas," Junes said. Percy lifted a brow in question. "You're not going to be a fucking martyr for me. I wasn't able to be one for you."

"I'm not—"

"You think you're ruining my career. You said so yourself. My career is mine to decide what to do with. If there's one thing in this life that I know for fucking certain, it's that you are everything to me, and now that I know you want me back, I won't let you go. No reason is good enough. So don't go getting any ideas."

Percy's eyes widened. It would take a while for him to get used to Juney saying things like that. Maybe he wouldn't ever get used to it. The feeling it gave Percy was too big to contain—it swelled in his chest, pushing at his ribs.

He didn't want to make any promises, but he did anyway. "I'm not going anywhere," he answered, and he hoped it would be true. "I have you back, and I wouldn't be able to handle another severance. The last one killed a part of me."

Juney grabbed the back of Percy's head and brought their lips together. It was a soft kiss and a swipe of his tongue against Percy's lips. There'd always been so much restraint in the way Juney handled him. He'd figured it was because Juney thought he was fragile, but now, Percy knew that wasn't the case. It was because Juney had been holding back his feelings, and Percy hated that he'd mistaken it for anything else. There were years full of unnecessary pain for both of them.

Juney pulled back just enough to bring their foreheads together. "It's us. Nothing can split us apart, or it would've already happened by now. We will always choose each other," Juney said vehemently.

Percy knew that was true. It always would be. He nodded, brushing their noses together. "Nothing can come between us," he whispered. "Let's stay here a while."

Junes moved his guitar to the side and laid on the sand. Percy laid right next to him, shoulder to shoulder. Percy's eyes flitted from each star that shone in the pitch-black darkness. He pointed at the sky. "Isn't it gorgeous?"

Juney's head rolled to the side, and they locked eyes. "It's got nothin' on you."

Heat sprung to his cheeks, and he felt an overwhelming need to be closer, so he latched onto Juney's arm and hooked a leg around him just like he used to. "We need to go back. It's too chilly for you to be shirtless," he murmured the words against his skin.

"Not right now. It can wait."

The island produced little to no light pollution, so the sky was one of the darkest he'd ever seen. The stars were so bright in contrast, each one begging for attention, but there they were. They couldn't take their eyes off each other for even a second. They were so small next to the expansive sea, and yet Percy didn't feel that way at all. Percy felt like the love he had for Juney was greater than anything could ever hope to be, and if there was a place it did fit, it'd be here beneath the endless cloak of the night sky.

Despite the chill, they were both lulled to sleep by the water. When Percy blinked his eyes open, it wasn't pitch-black anymore. It appeared to be dawn which meant they hadn't slept very long.

Things were beginning to come back to life. Seagulls alternated between traversing the beach and flying.

He nudged Juney one time, and his eyes sprung open. He sat up quickly and looked around. After a minute, he grunted and turned toward Percy. "Let's go back to bed," Junes said. His voice was rough with sleep.

Percy yawned. "But will you play me a song before we go?" he asked gently, but it was suddenly the most important thing to him.

Juney searched his eyes for something before grabbing his guitar. "You look so pretty like that, your long hair flowing with the wind," he said and then started playing before Percy could respond. Juney strummed a song Percy hadn't heard before, but he loved it.

Percy scooted even closer to Junes than before and smiled

at him, and for the first time in a long time, Juney smiled back. Percy's heart did a flip. He loved Juney's smile.

Junes gets his attention. "Look," he said gesturing over Percy's shoulder with his chin. There was a tall, burly guy looking out at the ocean. Something about the way he carried himself reminded Percy of their bodyguards.

Percy yawned. "Okay, let's go. We can get some sleep before breakfast time."

Percy woke up to knocking at the door, and for the first time in a while, Junes was dead asleep. He wormed his way out of bed and threw on some sweats. He knew his hair was a mess since he slept with it still wet. He pulled the door open and wasn't surprised to see Victor. He knew what this was about.

"It's Winston's lucky day," he chuckled. "He's getting discharged early for some reason, so he needs to meet with a nurse to discuss treatment and whatnot. Your jet will be here in two hours. I'll be right here waiting to take you up to the facility."

"Alrighty then. Give us a minute, please."

Victor was already walking back to his golf cart. Percy shut the door, and his eyes locked on his phone that was on top of the nightstand. The hair on the back of his neck stood on end. He was afraid of what he'd see if he opened it and wished they could just disappear and miss the rapidly approaching storm. He released a heavy sigh and walked back to the bed where Juney looked the calmest he possibly could. Percy hated that he had to cut it short and wake him up to the harsh reality they faced.

Juney startled awake after only a couple of nudges to his shoulder. "Gotta wake up, Juney."

His eyes popped wide open as he took a second to reacquaint himself with life. Percy watched understanding trickle through him until he sat up, scrubbing a hand down his face. "What's up, darlin'?" Juney's drawl was thick with sleep, and Percy felt his insides melt.

He floundered for a second before regaining his composure. "We're going home."

Juney groaned. "When?'"

Percy stood up and looked around. They didn't have much to pack. "Two hours. But you gotta see the nurse first." He grabbed the clear bag that Juney's belongings had come in and began packing the stuff he'd put away for him.

Strong arms wrapped around him, caging him against Juney's warm, solid chest. Percy held onto Juney's forearms and relaxed against him. Juney wound Percy's hair around his fist and used it to bring their lips together. It put Percy's neck at an awkward angle, but he found it hard to care when Juney was sliding his tongue over every square inch of his mouth, eating him from the inside out. Juney kissed Percy like he wanted to consume him, and Percy was pliant and took it all. Opened his mouth wider. Matched his movements.

When Juney pulled away, they were breathless. "Nothing can come between us," Juney repeated the words Percy had said last night. Percy hated that Junes felt the need to remind him of that as if it wasn't a sure thing, but a lot was on the line here. There were forces working against them, and he knew that Juney didn't want him to have doubts.

Juney let go of him, and Percy frowned. He felt so... lost and vulnerable without Juney. Keeping distance from him for three years was brutal, and maybe even traumatizing. Percy did feel a low simmer of anxiety surrounding the security of their relationship. They were both afraid.

Percy turned around quickly. "Just hold me a little longer," he said, and he knew he was pouting.

Junes pulled him back into his arms, but this time they were chest to chest. Percy was able to shove his face into Juney's neck and inhale him. "Missed you so bad. I always miss you," Percy whispered. Anyone would think he was crazy with the way he needed Juney in every way possible.

"Things are better now. Fuck whatever anyone has to say. We have each other."

Percy nodded and regained the strength to continue functioning like a normal person who didn't need a human crutch. They were packed and out the door in a matter of minutes.

As they drove off, Percy couldn't help but feel sentimental. This place changed their lives forever. They'd think back on this place for the rest of their lives. Juney placed his palm firmly on Percy's inner thigh and didn't move it the entire way there.

Percy waited in the golf cart when they got to the main building. There wasn't any reason for him to go wait in the garden. Juney was gone for no longer than fifteen minutes. When he came back, his face was set with determination. "I'm going to continue seeing Ian virtually, and I'm going to keep taking my meds," he said.

Percy nodded. "Good. I'm glad you're taking your mental health seriously." He really, really was. Juney had struggled his entire life, and it was about time he started taking care of himself. They both knew that the meds wouldn't magically make him better, but the check-ins with Ian would go a long way toward helping Juney get things out and in teaching him coping mechanisms. He knew Juney had already learned so much. There was a noticeable difference in him.

"Alright let's fucking go. The only reason I'll ever step foot on this island again is to stay at the resort," Junes grumbled.

"This has to be the nicest psychiatric stay available. Couldn't have been too bad."

Juney lit a cigarette. "There's no such thing as a nice psychiatric stay, darlin'. Most of it was hell." He swung his gaze to Victor. "Thanks for everything, Victor. Percy, will you take down his phone number, please?"

Percy's eyes widened. "I have to stay off my phone," he said, trying to communicate how terrified he was.

Junes understood right away and rooted around in his bag until he found his notebook and pen. He took down Victor's phone number. "We'll hook you up with tickets and merch and shit, no problem."

Victor's jaw dropped. "Dude, that's so not necessary. I've just been doing my job."

Junes folded the notebook closed and blew out a stream of smoke. "Cool. Consider it a bonus then."

Juney liked to joke around about Percy's perfect southern hospitality, but Junes had a way of his own too. It was how they were raised. Not just by parents but by school staff too.

They'd become pretty far removed from their upbringing since moving to a place that was the polar opposite of where they'd grown up, but some things stuck.

Percy grinned to himself. When they went back home for Thanksgiving, they'd go as a couple. Boyfriends. Partners.

He knew his parents would be happy for them. They'd always loved Juney like he was family, so it won't be much of an adjustment for anyone.

Things were going to be okay. He just had to keep reminding himself of that.

Sixteen

WINSTON

Winston rarely showed up to meetings, but there was no way in hell he would miss this one. He wouldn't let anyone decide for him when it came to Percy.

Lovely and Amir were sitting in the band's living room. Lovely was tense, and Amir wrung his hands anxiously. Winston sat down on one of their black couches, giving Percy not even an inch of space. Apparently, it wasn't close enough for Percy because he nudged closer. Winston wrapped an arm around his shoulders and tried not to dwell on the somber look on Percy's face.

"Out with it," Winston said.

Amir snatched the manila envelope from the table and opened it. He looked up at the ceiling and sighed heavily before reading aloud.

WINSTON JENNINGS: A VIOLENT
HOMEWRECKER?

According to trusted sources, the lead singer of the chart-topping
band Telltale Dream was admitted into a psychiatric facility, a
little over a month ago, in the aftermath of an aggravated
assault that landed the other party in the hospital.
It's also alleged that, more recently, Winston had been having an
affair with the band's engaged-to-be-married manager, Percy
Lovell. Sources say that the engagement has ended.
Winston has a history of this kind of behavior, but this scandal
might be the tipping point for the rockstar.

"Oh my God," Percy said under his breath. His face fell into his open palms.

"No mention of Emilio?" Winston questioned.

"He probably didn't want the world to know any of it had anything to do with him. I mean, you put him in the hospital and stole his fiancé. Not a great look for a CEO with an ego the size of his high rise," said Lovely.

Winston's face twisted into a scowl. "It's not like no one knows that he was dating Percy. Anyone could come forward with that information."

"Maybe he cares more about wanting to keep the assault a secret. I'm sure he paid off the medical team that treated his injuries," Amir said exasperatedly.

Winston grabbed his cigarettes from the table and lit one in a matter of seconds. "Emilio Alvarez is a fucking pussy," he stated.

"Oh my God," Percy repeated with a groan.

Amir stood up and slapped the folder back on the table. "None of that matters. The only saving grace we have is that there's no photo evidence of either claim," he said. Lovely was nodding emphatically, eyes wide with desperation. "We will deny everything, and you two will keep *this* out of the public eye."

Winston found it ironic that Amir wouldn't even look him in the eye when he said it. Winston had known this was coming, but that didn't prepare him like it should've. His stomach turned with fear. Percy would leave him over this. He just knew it. He was too good of a person for any of this, and Percy didn't know what it felt like to be hated by anyone, let alone thousands of people.

If Winston were a better person, he'd let him go. But he'd come to terms with the fact that when it came to Percy, he would never let him go again. All he could do was hope Percy was on the same page.

Percy finally lifted his head from his hand and pushed back his hair. "And I'm guessing we need to keep up the act until the end of the tour?"

Lovely grimaced. "Well, yes."

"It shouldn't be very difficult considering Winston will be too busy in the studio to go out. There's only a week until the tour kicks off," Amir said.

Percy's brows furrowed. "And what then? They get increased publicity when they're on tour."

Lovely and Amir shot each other a look that was too nervous for Winston's liking.

It was Lovely who had the balls to speak. "Percy will need to sit out this tour. Heatwave will appoint a temporary manager for the band."

Percy blanched, and his mouth fell open. Winston took deep breaths. Percy and Winston hadn't spent more than a couple of days apart for as long as they'd known each other, so the mere idea that they would was so far from plausible that it had to have been a joke.

A long silence descended, and Winston considered that maybe his treatment at Black Diamond had helped him in some ways. He hadn't rampaged through the room or went for the vodka. He wasn't yelling.

"Have you spoken to Gage and Torin?" Percy asked.

Amir pursed his lips. "Yes."

"And?"

"Gage told us that we were out of our fucking minds, and Torin insisted that we shouldn't present the plan to Winston," he grumbled.

They hadn't even gotten the chance to talk to Gage and Torin yet. They were ambushed as soon as they walked through the door.

Winston was the picture of calm. "I won't be leaving Percy anywhere. We're a package deal, so tell your boss he can shove our contract up his stiff ass. I will walk right now," he threatened, and it wasn't an empty one.

"Juney," Percy hissed, begging him with his eyes to stop.

"#WinstonScandal is already trending online, followed closely by #PercyNoMercy. If you two don't lay low until this storm blows over, all of the band's sponsors and affiliates will drop you. Things can ramp up quicker than you think," said Lovely as she fidgeted nervously with one of her braids. She sounded resigned like she wasn't confident any of this would work.

Winston didn't have anything more to say. He'd made his point known. "We're done then?" he asked, but it sounded more like a statement. He wanted to tell them to leave and never come back.

Lovely and Amir rose from the couch, and Amir opened

the front door before Lovely even grabbed her purse. Lovely took a few tentative steps toward Winston. She reached out a hand to touch his forearm, a comforting gesture, but she flinched back before it connected with his skin. "Oops, sorry," she laughed. "I know you don't like being touched, but I just wanted to remind you to not make any hasty decisions. Think about it this way, whether you go on tour alone or not, you won't lose Percy. If you go, you'll realize quickly if you can continue to do it. If you can't, you'll make it known."

Then she was gone.

Percy was still sitting on the couch. Winston could see the anxious thoughts pinging between Percy's ears. He crossed the room and held his hand out. Percy sighed and let Winston pull him up. "Let's go lay down," he said.

"But it's noon," Percy said without any conviction.

Winston led him toward the hallway. "You're coming to my bed."

"Are you sure—"

"I'm going to keep you there forever. You won't be allowed to leave," Winston stated. He opened the door and ushered them inside. He didn't think Percy had ever been in here unless he was a stalkerish weirdo like Winston.

Percy looked at him. "It's cool to see what you did with your bedroom now that you have the ability to do whatever you want. It feels like you," he mused. Winston had a four-poster bed that was draped with a black canopy. The dark mahogany was ornately carved, and all of the furniture in his room was done the same way.

Just about everything else in his room was black. The vaulted ceiling and the walls. The heavy velvety curtains that he got to keep his room dark when he wanted it to be.

He didn't have many personal effects, but he did have some

pictures. The dresser he had was older, just like the rest of the furniture, so it had a large mirror mounted to it. He had three photographs in total, and he had them wedged along the perimeter where the mirror met wood.

Percy spotted them almost immediately. "I didn't know you had a picture with her," Percy indicated the picture of him and his mom in front of a Christmas tree. It'd been taken three years before she died.

Winston sidled up next to him. Most of the things Winston treasured, he kept to himself. These pictures. The guitar the Lovell's had gotten him. The glass figurine of a blue-bird his mom had kept on her nightstand.

Percy gasped. "Did you take this from my photo album?"

Winston toyed with his lip ring, looking at the picture. It was a picture Percy's dad had taken of them during their vacation to St. Simon's Island. They were sitting side by side on the sand at the beach. Percy was as close as physically possible, and when his dad walked toward them with a disposable camera, Percy planted his hand in the sand behind Winson's back and smiled brightly. It was ridiculously intimate for two best friends, especially with parents around, but Percy's parents never raised the topic.

He smirked. "Yes."

"You could've just asked," Percy groused, but Winston could hear the smile in his voice.

"Or I could just take," he shrugged. He moved to stand behind Percy, wrapped his arms around his middle, and rested his chin on Percy's shoulder. Percy's breath hitched, and he swallowed dryly.

He pointed at the third picture. It was a photo of his parents at their wedding before things took a nosedive. Winston wasn't sure if he'd ever seen them look at each other the way they were in the picture. "Have you talked to him?" Percy asked, barely a whisper.

Winston didn't want to talk about it, but he was trying to open up more. Talking to Ian had given him the courage he needed to be vulnerable with people, specifically the man he was holding right now. "No. I don't see the point."

Percy met his eyes in the mirror. "Did you know he still lives in that house despite all of the money you've given him?"

Winston did not know about this. All he knew was that he had a certain amount of money deposited into his dad's bank account every month. He didn't care what his dad did with it, but he had thought he'd buy a nice, new house. Ditch the old rust bucket for a new truck. "Wonder if he's touched the money at all then," Winston responded. He hoped his dad would at least quit his job.

"Why do you give him money if you won't even talk to him?" Percy asked.

Winston wasn't sure he even knew the answer to that question, but he knew one thing for certain. "It's the right thing to do."

"Since when do you care about right and wrong?" Percy sounded exasperated, but he had a point.

"I don't..." he trailed off. He hadn't ever put much thought into it, which he tended to do more often than not. "I don't hate my dad. I guess I understand why he lost himself the way he did, even though it wasn't right. 'Cause if something ever happened to you—if you died, I don't know what I'd do. Over a decade of grief, depression, bipolar disorder—you fucking name it— wouldn't come close to the pain that would cause me."

Percy's eyes softened, and he turned in Winston's arms to

cup his cheeks. "I know, Junes. I'm sure your dad felt something like that, but he had a kid to take care of."

Winston gazed into those dream-blue eyes. "Well, he didn't off himself. Didn't stop working. Didn't abandon me. I can't say that I'd be able to manage any of that if I was in his shoes." The thought alone sliced at his heart. He tightened his hold on Percy. "He leaned on alcohol to get through it, and that was the worst thing he could've possibly done. I'd know," he said sardonically.

Now that he was saying these things aloud, parsing through his thoughts in real-time, he hurt. It cracked something open inside of him. He would talk about his mother with no problem, but his father? He never said a word about him. Not to Percy or anyone. He'd just busted the stitches on one of his deepest wounds.

He retreated, letting Percy's hands fall from his face. He undressed and slid into bed. Percy did the same thing, and immediately molded himself to Winston's side.

Winston's eyes could've rolled back into his head at the relief of Percy being in his bed for the first time. He'd thought about it daily since they moved into this house. He hugged Percy close, feeling every inch of his skin and knowing that it made Percy feel just as crazy as he did. Although, Winston secretly thought that what he felt for Percy was far more intense than Percy could ever fully understand.

"It's okay, you know. That you don't hate your dad. That you care enough about him to see things from his perspective. That's a hard thing to do when it's someone who's hurt you," Percy whispered the words into Winston's chest. He wondered if Percy could feel how erratic his heart was beating. "Maybe you could help him."

Winston's brows pulled together. "Help him?"

"Send him to Black Diamond's rehab facility."

The idea of Hunter Boone Jennings meditating on the beach at Black Diamond was as outrageous as the idea that Winston would ever end up being a rock star. "There's no way. I don't think he even wants to stop drinking." Winston scratched Percy's scalp just the way he liked it.

"Maybe if he worked through all of his trauma, he wouldn't need to drink to live with it. That's all I'm saying. If you're not gonna give up on him, you could offer him help, but that's ultimately up to you. He sure as shit didn't get you help when you needed it."

Winston turned the thought over in his head.

His dad might not want anything to do with him now that he was openly gay. Winston hadn't told him, but it wouldn't be hard for him to find out if he paid even a little bit of attention to the news surrounding the band. He had no clue what his dad thought about the LGBTQ+ community, but the general consensus in that town wasn't great. His dad probably didn't even know what the acronym stood for, but one thing Winston wasn't going to do was try to convince his dad to accept their relationship. In that case, he could fuck off.

Maybe he would attempt a conversation with his dad during their Thanksgiving visit. If it went to shit, so be it.

The silence stretched comfortably, and Winston could go for an afternoon nap. When he saw his psychiatrist about Ian's concerns with his sleep and behavior, Dr. Weaver ultimately decided that they would get rid of the antidepressant he was on and stick with the mood stabilizer. He knew it was too soon to tell if his sleep benefited from it, but maybe this had to do with Percy. Percy wasn't a magic sleep aid, but there was something about finally having him, in every sense of the word, that brought a certain level of calm to his soul.

"What are we gonna do about all of this?" Percy mumbled.

Winston wished he had all the answers, but he didn't "For one, you need to stay off of social media for good. It's not like content will be created when we're supposed to be laying low, so you have no reason to be on there. It won't do you any good to see how nasty people on the internet can be."

He really fucking hoped Percy would take his advice on this. Thousands of people telling you how awful you are, that you should kill yourself, and even threatening your family can cut down the strongest person. Percy hadn't built any immunity for it, and he shouldn't have to. Percy is perfect, and anyone who thinks otherwise is flat-out wrong. Simple as that, and Winston would knock their teeth out if need be, but unfortunately, that can't be done through a computer screen.

"Okay. I won't," Percy agreed.

"We'll take it day by day. I need to record these last three songs. No matter what happens, they need to be heard. Then, we'll go from there. If it comes down to it, I will leave the band. It's not worth it. Nothing has ever been more important to me than you, and that includes music."

Percy sighed deeply. His breath fanned across Winston's chest. He knew Percy didn't think that was the best thing to do, but like he'd told Winston, he didn't get to decide for Percy, so Percy doesn't get to decide for him on this either then.

Percy raised up on his hands and leaned over Winston's face. His long hair hung around Winston's head, grazing his cheeks as he brought their lips together. Percy's kiss quickly turned needy. He sucked on Winston's lips, held his face tightly, and tugged at his hair. All the while, he rutted against Winston's thigh.

God, he loved Percy.

His lips were so soft, and he kissed Winston like he wanted

to make a home in there—he never wanted to stop. He would keep going forever, and Winston didn't mind at all. Loved Percy's lips on his. Percy's tongue on his.

The weight of Percy on top of him and the slide of their warm bodies, while Percy devoured his mouth, was undoing him. His heart beat so hard that it ached, and at some points, he felt like he couldn't fill his lungs with enough air.

Then there were his moans. Soft and sweet or high and desperate, either way, they made Winston want to give Percy the world.

He didn't know if he'd ever be able to handle Percy.

Winston rolled them over so Percy was on his back and positioned himself between Percy's legs without breaking the kiss, but when he wrapped his hand around Percy's burning shaft, Percy gasped. Winston stroked him slowly and licked a stripe across his neck while Percy grabbed his shoulders, but Winston had plans. He hadn't sucked Percy yet, and he needed it desperately.

Slowly, he moved back. Percy tried to follow him but stopped once he realized what was happening. He squeezed his eyes shut. "Oh, fuck," he rasped.

Winston grinned, feeling very pleased with himself, but sobered quickly because suddenly, Percy's legs were on his shoulders. His hips were lifting off the bed. Winston didn't waste time. He sealed his lips around the dark, flared head, and Percy made an indecipherable, strangled sound as he jolted forward. He loved how responsive Percy was.

As he slid his mouth down further, he swirled his tongue around the shaft, stopping sometimes to tongue the underside of his cock head. Percy was a writhing, whimpering mess, and Winston had to secure his hips. He wanted Percy's sac in his mouth, so he unsealed his lips and moved down. He sucked one ball into his mouth, tonguing the soft skin. Percy's blunt nails dug into his back hard enough that Winston knew they'd leave marks, and Winston had waited so many—too many— years to be marked by Percy. In the back of his mind and the pit of his stomach, he felt like they should always be marked by each other in some way. Maybe Winston would get a tattoo.

He finished mouthing at Percy's sac and fisted Percy's cock, hard and deliberate, twisting his palm around the head. "I want my name on your body," he said through clenched teeth. Percy squeezed his eyes shut, and his body convulsed once, twice, then ropes of cum shot exploded from him.

"Juney," he whined, and Winston gritted his teeth against the monstrous feeling that rose within him.

"Need inside you, baby," he grunted. Percy's legs fell from his shoulders, and he was wrung dry. Winston reached over to the nightstand, moving further away from Percy than he wanted to, and grabbed the lube he kept there.

He was moved quickly, and the blood throbbing in his cock intensified as he got a look at Percy. He was dazed and limp and still grabbing for Winston, so he drizzled a healthy amount of lube on his hand and began massaging Percy's entrance. He dragged the flat of his tongue across one of Percy's hard nipples as he pushed two fingers inside of him. "That okay?" he asked, knowing Percy might be sore still.

Percy hummed, "So good."

So, Winston moved his fingers with the sole purpose of getting him soft enough to take his cock. When he was ready to add a third, he scooped Percy's cum from his abdomen and pushed it inside of him. He watched Percy's rim stretch around his cum covered fingers and bit back a moan himself. Fuck, he was done for. He would blow as soon as he got in there.

He withdrew his fingers and grabbed the lube again. He

slicked up his cock with it, and Percy watched with what Winston could only describe as hunger. It did things to Winston's stomach. It flipped or fluttered or some shit. He tried to regain his composure, but his hands shook as he nudged the head of his cock against Percy's softened hole. He used a little force to push his leaking head past the tight ring of muscle, and Percy gasped.

Blood roared in Winston's ears and his mouth hung open as Percy's hole sucked him in. He trailed a palm over Percy's narrow waist and down his side. He gave a test thrust, and Percy still looked lost in a haze, so he picked up the pace. He watched a drop of sweat fall from his face and land on Percy's neck. Their bodies were overheated and sweaty. They moved against each other like a dream. Winston dragged his palm over Percy's nipple and then wrapped it around his throat. When he dipped down to kiss him, Percy met him halfway.

As their lips moved together like they'd been doing it for years, Winston trembled. Percy's hole was choking his dick, but Winston wanted to get Percy to come again. He clumsily reached for a pillow. His cock slipped out of Percy, and he whined, "Juney, what—"

Winston got the pillow beneath Percy's hips and nudged his cock at Percy's entrance again. It was soft and fucked open enough that Winston's cock slipped inside with little resistance, and Percy sighed in relief. He thrust slowly, trying to find that sensitive spot inside of him. It didn't take long. Winston wrapped a hand around Percy's cock again and pumped it while sliding the head of his dick against Percy's sweet spot over and over again. Percy trembled just as fiercely as Winston did, and a string of moans fell from Percy's swollen lips.

He was flushed red from his chest to his cheeks.

"Are you gonna come for me again?"

Percy's breaths were ragged. His throat was dry from all the panting, but nodded his head emphatically. Percy's body tensed and his mouth fell open. Winston watched him closely as he came. His long dark hair was stuck to his neck and forehead and his mouth fell open, releasing a harsh breath as each wave of his orgasm hit him. Winston punched into Percy's ass harder than ever before, and his head moved up the pillow with each thrust.

Percy's heels dug into him, and he wrapped his arms around Winston's middle, holding him as close as he could, forcing him as deep as possible. "Please come inside of me," Percy begged. "I need it so badly."

Winston groaned. Percy had somehow managed to render him speechless, so he didn't get an answer, but his balls tightened on Percy's command and Percy's ass milked his load right out of him. Winston sealed his teeth around the sharp line of Percy's jaw, moaning and panting against his skin.

His forehead fell to Percy's shoulder as he tried to calm his racing heart. "Fuck, you're so sweet, Percy. So good. I'll fuck you forever. Love you forever."

Percy rubbed Winston's back. "Mmm, yeah. You can live inside of me for good. I need that from you. All of you."

Winston never felt closer to tears than the moments after Percy makes him come. No one else has done this to him, but of course, they hadn't. No one could ever be Percy. He slotted their lips together, and they kissed languorously as Winston's softened cock slid out of Percy's ass.

Winston broke the kiss and sat back on his haunches. He helped Percy roll to his side and pushed one of his knees up, so his hole was on full display. Percy looked away. Winston could tell he was shy about Winston seeing his hole like this. "You have nothing to worry about, baby. The prettiest hole I've ever seen, remember? Especially right now. Red and puffy with my cum leaking out of it."

Fuck, Winston's chest hurt.

He gathered up the stream of cum with his fingers and pushed it right back inside Percy. He rubbed circles around Percy's ass cheeks, over all the marks he'd left there. He gripped and pulled and watched Percy's hole stretched, and damn. Winston was hypnotized. He still hadn't grasped that Percy was truly his, and there was a hefty amount of fear lingering in the recesses of his brain. Winston did not want to lose Percy again.

He left Percy's ass alone and crawled back up the bed to hold him. Percy latched onto his arm, holding it against his chest and pushing his butt back. Winston groaned hoarsely and buried his nose in Percy's hair.

"You and me, we're gonna be okay. As long as we have each other, nothing can touch us."

Percy pulled Winston's hand up and peppered kisses across his knuckles. "I believe you," he whispered.

Seventeen

PERCY

P ercy pulled on one of Juney's sweaters and watched him get dressed through the mirror. They'd been back in Miami for a week now, and there was something he'd been wanting to ask Juney. He'd finally built up the courage.

"Will you brush my hair?" he asked.

When he was ten, he'd told his mom that he wanted to stop getting haircuts, and she'd allowed it—no questions asked. The longer it got, the more time she'd spend brushing it. And so what if his mother brushed his hair when he was a middle schooler and even sometimes in high school too? If anyone at school had known that, he would've never lived it down.

But Juney knew. He'd watched her do it many times, and Percy had always wondered if seeing that kind of thing hurt him.

Juney froze. "You want me to? Like how your mom did it?"

Percy nodded. "If you want to," he said quietly.

"Of course, I do, darlin'. You know how much I love your hair." Juney ran his fingers through Percy's hair reverently. It was so endearing that Percy could've died right there on the spot, but he only handed Junes the brush instead.

Junes grabbed his desk chair and beckoned Percy to sit. Once Percy sat down, Juney leaned around him and kissed his cheek. Then, he split Percy's hair down the middle and did it *exactly* how his mom had always done it. Percy couldn't believe he remembered.

Juney surprised him like that often now.

They'd been best friends their entire lives, so of course, they were comfortable around each other, but there was a noticeable difference now. Percy always had some amount of focus being used solely on keeping his hands off of Juney for as long as possible. That'd been an invisible wedge, and he realized that Juney seemed a little... lighter.

He didn't know if it was a result of the meds or their new relationship, but Percy figured it was a little bit of both. Junes just seemed like there was happiness inside of him. It was just a tiny wellspring, but it was there and seemed to get a little bigger all the time. Junes was not enthusiastic or anything like that, but around Percy especially, he was lighter than Percy had ever seen him. Less calculated and stiff.

Percy wished they hadn't spent so long unaware. It felt like time wasted.

"Looks like you might be ready for a trim," Juney mused, pulling a chunk of hair through his fingers to show him the split ends. "I can do it for you later if you want."

Percy grinned. They weren't supposed to leave the house

for anything, and it wasn't worth it to risk having a stylist come. But he had a feeling Juney offered because he wanted to. It was the hesitancy to his words when he had always been incredibly blunt. Hesitant was not a word he'd use to describe Junes in a million years. "Totally. I'd love it if you did," he responded.

Juney smoothed his fingers through Percy's fully detangled hair one more time before he put the brush down. Junes threw on a backward cap and ushered them out of the room. The door to their studio was on the far wall of their living area. Gage and Torin were already in. Gage was messing around with his drumsticks, spinning them from finger to finger effortlessly. Torin had his bass, but he was doing something on the laptop.

They only had one more song to record, and Junes was ready to lay the vocals down today. Two weeks to record three songs didn't seem like enough time, but not for Telltale Dream. When Juney writes, he composes everything. By the time he presents it to the band, he already knows every detail about the song. And Gage and Torin are almost always on the same page. Gage gets a bit snippy sometimes, but he's mostly level in the studio. As long as he gets drum solos, he's happy.

"I'm ready," Junes said without preamble. He went straight to the isolation booth, let himself in, and grabbed the headphones. He put them on and adjusted the mic—no messing around.

Percy sat on the couch next to Gage.

The studio was ambiently lit, and Percy always loved being here with them, even if he was working at the same time. There was just a certain level of calm. It took him back to the beginning when they'd squeeze in Gage and Torin's small bedroom and smoke ridiculous amounts of weed while Torin and Junes played guitar and Gage drummed on the table. In this studio, it was easy to forget they were inside a mansion in Miami.

Torin pressed a button and spoke through the intercom into the booth. "The final track. Dream Blue. Think you can do it in one take?"

Of course, he could. That went without saying.

Percy watched Winston nod once through the thick glass, and Torin did something on his laptop. He actually produced and mixed all of their music, then he'd hand it off to someone at Heatwave to polish it, but it was important to the band that they have the final say in everything.

"First verse," Torin told Winston.

Torin pressed a button, Percy watched Winston's eyes fall shut and his lips begin to move. It was hard for him to believe there was ever a time when Winston didn't want to sing in front of anyone other than Percy. Now he sang for the world.

A million things had changed since they were seven, and yet, Winston still felt the same about Percy. He would always be Percy's constant.

Percy hadn't heard this song yet which wasn't surprising considering how busy they'd been, but Winston looked almost anguished while singing it. He'd always sung so passionately. It was an intimate experience for anyone listening.

There was a knock at the door, and he jumped. Gage stood up. "Who the fuck—" he trailed off as he opened it. Amir stood on the other side with wide, nervous eyes. Percy looked back and saw that Torin wasn't paying them any attention.

"The big boss wants to speak to you," he said through his teeth as he wrung his hands.

They hadn't spoken to Mr. Marshall since they signed their contract. He had other things to worry about, so this really couldn't be good. "Okay... we'll be out in a minute," he said.

Amir shook his head gravely. "He wants to speak to you. Alone."

Percy swallowed roughly but shrugged and followed him out. There wasn't anything he could do to stop his impending doom. Percy was sure Mr. Marshall would've held this little meeting in his office at Heatwave if it weren't for the fact that Percy was America's Most Wanted.

Amir led Percy all the way to the back patio and left him there. Mr. Marshall was kicked back on one of their chairs wearing a linen button up, jean shorts, and sandals. His sunglasses were pushed back on top of his head, holding back his shoulder length brown hair.

Percy sat down, and Mr. Marshall gave him a smile that wasn't unkind. He was a very handsome guy, and most people seemed to cower around him despite the fact that he was only in his thirties and dressed like this.

Percy locked his gaze on the oversized, gold swordfish pendant that hung from a thick, gold chain Mr. Marshall wore. It was the same one he was wearing when they'd met him. "Mr. Marshall," he said by way of greeting.

"Call me Max," he responded lightly.

Percy gave him a short nod. "Max." It was short for Maximus.

"In your words, what has transpired over the last two months?" Max asked.

Percy swiped a hand over his eyes. He figured it best to get this over with. "I got engaged to Emilio Alvarez. That same day, Winston met him and... He beat Emilio up, badly enough that he needed to be admitted to the hospital. Then, Winston attempted suicide," he paused and closed his eyes against the images that were carved into his brain. "Winston was sent to Black Diamond's mental health facility where he was supposed to spend sixty days. I was sent to keep an eye on him."

"And then what?" Max pushed.

"I had an affair with Winston and called off the engagement with Emilio." Percy's face burned.

"Look at me, please," Max said. Percy set his jaw and obeyed. "That story sounded pretty bad when you described it, didn't it?" Percy didn't need to respond. "If it sounded that bad coming straight from the horse's mouth, how do you think it sounds after being passed around thousands of strangers online?"

Max had a great point. He pulled out his phone and pulled something up before sliding it across the table to Percy. "Flip through those screenshots."

Percy looked at the screen, and his heart immediately dropped. It was a social media post that read, "Percy's nothing but a stupid whore. Pitting two men against each other? He's gonna cheat on Winston, too. Mark my words."

It had fifty thousand likes.

No matter how hard he tried to fight it, his chin wobbled. "I get the point. I don't need to read anymore," he said flatly.

"Some of the band's sponsors and brand deals have dropped them. That's not only to do with you, of course. People aren't happy with Winston's alleged aggravated assault either. People are stepping forward claiming a wide range of injuries Winston gave them. The tabloids are having a field day."

The salty breeze rushed through the patio, rippling across their infinity pool. It was a beautiful, sunny day, and Percy felt a bone-deep chill.

"Magically, there's an upside to this. There's zero evidence that Winston ever touched Emilio because Emilio wouldn't dare let the world know about what happened. That leaves only one issue."

Percy swung his eyes back to him. "Me," he answered with no inflection.

Max pierced him with crystal-blue eyes. "Winston will release a statement claiming the allegations are false, and in order to back that up, you will need to disappear until the tour's over at least. When you come back, we can slowly introduce your relationship to the public in a way that feels organic."

Max said it as airily as a person who'd never been in love might. Percy's heart was splintering down the middle. He knew it was supposed to be the right thing to do. The easy thing. "Winston will quit the band if I leave."

"Sounds like you need to convince him otherwise." Max stood and left that final statement looming above Percy's head.

Percy slouched in the chair and tilted his head up to the sky. Nothing about this was easy or right. Max was two bricks short of a load if he thought Juney could be convinced of that. There was only a week until the tour started.

One. Week.

Percy would need to wait until the last minute. If it was possible to convince him, that'd be the only way.

The door opened, and then, his first and only love was in front of him.

"What's the look for?" Juney asked before lighting a cigarette.

Percy wasn't a great liar in general, but he definitely couldn't get anything past Juney. His lips twitched into a tentative smile. "You were in the studio for so long. I missed you," he mumbled and grabbed Juney's free hand to trace his knuckles.

"Let's get tattoos," Juney said. His brows were set in a hard line, and his nose was scrunched in thought.

Percy worked his lower lip between his teeth the same way Junes was doing with his lip ring. "Of what?"

He shrugged. "You'll see when the artist gets here."

Percy rolled his eyes. "You arranged it already."

Junes nodded with the slightest smirk.

Percy sighed fondly. "Did you get the vocals laid down?"

"All done. I think the fans are gonna love this one. It's big and anthemic with a heavy breakdown."

It was so refreshing to see Junes happy about their music again. "What's the song about?"

"You," he said.

Percy's heart panged. "Really?"

"You're in a lot of Telltale's songs."

Juney was saying these things so offhandedly. Ever since they... got honest with each other about their feelings, Junes had been dropping bombs left and right. Percy was on top of the world. "Maybe you'll have to show me sometime." This was only their second album, so there couldn't be too many. "Did you guys seal the deal on the album's title?"

Juney's eyes brightened almost imperceptibly. "Bluebird."

The door swung open again, and Gage called out to them, "Tattoo artist is here."

Percy stood up with a nervous, churning feeling deep in his gut. He hadn't ever gotten a tattoo. He followed Junes. They had an entire room for getting tattooed since everyone in the band got them often. Junes walked in and went straight for his artist.

"Hey, Zep," Percy said. Zep was short for Zephyr. He owned a shop named Thanatos Tattoo and Art Collective back downtown where they used to live. That was how Junes befriended him.

"Nice to see you, Percy. Haven't tattooed you yet," he said.

Percy laughed a bit. "Yeah, total tattoo virgin."

Zep's eyes pinged back to Junes who was already looking at him.

"You trust me, right?" Juney looked at Percy intently.

Percy's heart started to race. "Of course."

"We're getting matching tattoos, and don't ask. It's a secret. You gotta trust me. I wouldn't mess up your perfect skin."

Percy believed him easily. There wasn't a doubt in his mind. He pursed his lips. "Okay. I'm down."

Zep was setting up his equipment, observing both of them quietly. His hair was tied up in a bun just like Percy's, but Zep's was jet black.

"I'll go first," Junes said. "I'm getting two tattoos though, so it'll take a little longer. You should go eat something while you wait."

Percy nodded. There was already sweat breaking out on the back of his neck. He wasn't worried about the tattoo itself; he was more concerned with the pain. Juney appeared in front of him and cupped the side of his face, bringing his lips to Percy's. He shuddered. It was a slow kiss that had the same intensity as it did the first time. Percy had a feeling it would always be that way.

"You don't have to get one, darlin'," he whispered. He didn't sound angry or upset at all. It was genuine.

Percy pulled back, scratching his jaw. "How much is it gonna hurt?"

Junes snorted. "That's what you're worried about?"

"Well, yeah."

It was Zep who answered, "Everyone's pain tolerance is

different, and some spots hurt worse than others. The tattoo is fairly small and simple, so it shouldn't be too bad at all."

Zep had a certain level of calm that Percy resonated with. It helped ease his nerves. "Sounds good to me."

Junes began taking his shirt off, and Percy stole a glance before he left. He walked to the kitchen and took out one of their premade meals. It was another one of those uncanny things. Neither of them had ever even considered that they would have a private chef someday, but it did make the most sense for them. It helped him and Juney to have nutritious vegan meals to eat. Neither of them were creative enough to come up with more than a handful of basic, go-to dishes.

He pulled off the lid and heated it up in the microwave. Then he sat at the bar and tucked in. It didn't take long for Torin and Gage to show up. They also pulled out their premade food which wasn't vegan.

Torin leaned against the counter that faced Percy and cut right to the chase. "What did Mr. Marshall have to say?"

Percy chewed longer than necessary. "I have to leave until the tour is over."

Torin's brows nearly jumped off his face, and Gage bellowed a laugh. "Our first world tour is as good as dead," Gage said.

Torin didn't need to say anything for Percy to know that he agreed with Gage. "You're probably right, but I'm going to try like hell to convince him. It's only two months," Percy said, hoping his voice didn't shake. Two months that far away from Juney was sickening. They'd never been apart longer than a couple of days, but they were adults now. They needed to live separate lives. They'd done it for the past three years... sort of.

"We're here if you need our help. We don't want Junes to quit the band, but ultimately, we'd support him in whatever decision he makes," Torin said. Percy had known from the beginning that they would be good friends, but it still caught him off guard that they would be so supportive. "It had always been obvious to us and everyone else that you and Winston were gone for each other. It was plain to see from the outside, and yet, it still took this long for you and him to recognize it. I understand why he would put you above the band."

Looking back, he knew that they both had been so obvious, but Percy had been blind to it. "It'll be fine. Everything will go how it's supposed to," he said with no confidence whatsoever.

They both sat down at the bar with him and began eating. "So, are y'all happy with the album as a whole?"

"Winston put so much heart into these songs. Amazing lyricism, as always," Torin responded.

Gage pushed his container away, somehow already finished, and grabbed his beer. "I love the album. It has Winston's signature lyrics, but it also has lengthy drum and guitar solos. Brutal breakdowns. It's just really some of our best work yet," he added.

Percy grinned. "Juney sounded happy with it, too. I have a feeling this will be even bigger than the last one."

Gage lit a joint and that sweet, sweet smell filtered through his nose. He took two puffs and passed it to Percy.

They took their conversation to the living room and smoked a lot of weed over the course of the next two hours before Juney called for him. Percy jolted from surprise and got up quickly. His stomach shouldn't be tying itself in knots when he was this stoned. The anxiety was supposed to go away.

When he entered the room, his eyes found Juney first. His hand had a translucent adhesive bandage over it, and there appeared to be one peeking out of his collar, too.

"No looking," Junes said.

Percy sighed. "Where am I getting this tattoo?"

Juney lifted the hem of Percy's shirt and used his knuckles to brush against the skin on the right side of Percy's lower abdomen. Then, he moved them lower, pulling down the waistband of his pants. Junes indicated the spot to the right of where his happy trail met his pubes.

Percy gave him a droll look. "Really?"

"Yeah. It'll be hot. Promise," Junes said.

Percy took his word for it and met Zep by the tattoo chair. Junes sat in a chair and watched intently. "First, I need to shave the area where the tattoo will be. Then, I'll put on the stencil, and since it's a surprise, Winston can okay it or not."

"Right," Percy confirmed.

There wasn't much hair in that spot to begin with, but Zep shaved it anyway. He placed the stencil slowly and deliberately, and when Junes saw it, his lips curved into something close to a smile. His eyes were soft when they met Percy's. "Perfect," he told Zep.

If it made Junes look like that, Percy knew he wouldn't regret it. So, he got situated in the tattoo chair, and Zep began. It felt like he pulled one long line. "That okay? Not so bad, right?"

It stung in a way that felt more uncomfortable than painful. "Yeah, I think it'll be fine," Percy responded.

That was all Zep needed. He sunk into a deeply focused state and didn't waiver for the duration of the tattoo.

Percy's skin was on fire by the time Zep was finished. Zep removed his gloves and stepped back. Junes set his notebook down. "I'll show you mine first," he said as he pulled his shirt off. "This isn't the matching one. It's just something extra that I wanted."

Percy got closer and gasped at what he saw. "You didn't," he said, covering his mouth. "It's so big." He stared at the new ink with dismay. Between all of the tattoos Juney had, there was only a narrow space at the base of his throat that had been untouched. But now Percy's name was tattooed there in large traditional-style letters.

"Heard that a time or two," Junes said, and Percy glared at him, but his heart was tripping over itself.

He knew this wasn't normal and had heard the superstition surrounding couple tattoos, but he found that he didn't care. "I love it," Percy said.

"You'll love our matching ones then," he responded with a devious smirk, even though his eyes shined with something else.

Juney held his hand out, and Percy grabbed it. Beneath the transparent bandage was an American traditional-style bluebird. It looked like it was in flight, and there was a banner caught around it. "P.L.L.," he breathed. "My initials?" *Percy Linus Lovell.*

Percy walked over to the mirror and looked at his. Sure enough, it was the same bluebird but with a banner that read W.J.J. *Winston June Jennings.*

"Why a bluebird?" Percy knew it wasn't because of the title of their new album. He'd have a deeper meaning for something like this.

Junes cleared his throat. "My mother's favorite."

Percy had to blink away tears that threatened to spill. Of course, it was.

Juney stood behind him and wrapped an arm around his waist. His fingers on his tattooed hand curved around Percy's bluebird. Percy watched Juney through the mirror and saw longing in Juney's eyes.

Percy was having trouble breathing properly. He wasn't surprised by this at all. "I have always wanted to live in your skin," he whispered quietly enough that only Juney would hear.

Juney turned his head so his lips were at Percy's ear. "And I've always wanted everyone to know that you are mine."

He couldn't believe any of this was real, but he had an ache, deep in his chest.

They'd belonged together since the moment they met. Percy would've gotten this tattoo way before he realized that he was in love with his best friend. He snorted.

"Something funny?" Juney mused.

"I just can't believe I'd ever thought of you as just a friend. I would've let you tattoo your name right on my neck for anyone to see."

Junes stepped back, and as usual, Percy missed his presence. His hard body. Junes ignored what he'd said and turned his attention to Zep. He was getting the last of his things packed up. "Thanks so much, man."

"Of course. Thanks for being such an awesome client," Zep said with a genuine tone. He hadn't mentioned their scandal at all. Percy felt like there wasn't a person left who didn't hate him, so it was a relief to know there was at least one.

But as they walked Zep to the front door, Junes didn't acknowledge Percy at all. His jaw was set. Percy must have said the wrong thing. He knew what he said wasn't normal but nothing about them was. Percy's mouth had dried by the time Zep was out and on his way.

He didn't have time to think before Juney grabbed his wrist and slammed him against the wall. Percy's eyes widened. Juney grabbed Percy's throat, just firm enough to keep his attention, and smashed their lips together. He kissed Percy wildly. Sucked his lower lip into his mouth. Sucked on his tongue. Licked across his mouth. Percy couldn't keep his hips still.

Juney dragged his lips across Percy's cheek, and Percy panted for air as goosebumps caused his hair to stand on end.

"You would've gotten my name on your throat when we were in high school?" he grunted.

Percy's hips wouldn't stop moving, seeking friction. He nodded quickly. "So platonic and straight of me, I know."

Juney's eyes were dark. "You always wanted to be mine," he said roughly.

Percy slid his hands down his back and felt his muscles bunching beneath his skin. "That much I did know. I wanted to be the most important person in your world."

Junes growled and lowered himself to his knees. He pulled Percy's pants down, and his hard cock sprung forward. Percy's words were strangled. "What about Gage and Torin?"

He wrapped his hand at the base of Percy's shaft. "They'll hear us. See us," he stammered.

"Maybe." Junes shrugged, and then, he lapped his tongue across Percy's leaking cockhead. Junes swallowed him to the hilt in one swift movement, and any and all words died in Percy's throat. Lightning zipped all the way down to his toes. His knees began to buckle, but Juney steadied him with the death grip he had on Percy's hips.

He carded his fingers through Juney's messy hair, feeling his head bob beneath them. Juney broke the suction and pulled back, still jacking him in his hand. "Go ahead and fuck my face, baby."

Percy's eyes widened. He wasn't going to last long. His thighs were already trembling at the sight of Juney on his knees deep throating his dick like that. It was something out of his fantasies.

He sealed his dark, puffy lips around Percy again, reminding himself to be quiet. He started with a shallow thrust and watched Juney's cheeks hollow. Junes slid his hands around to Percy's ass, grabbed handfuls, and used them to push Percy's dick further into his mouth. A breathy whimper escaped him.

He held the sides of his face and thrust deeper until he hit the back of Juney's throat. It was tighter back there. Juney tipped his head at an angle. Now Percy was fucking his throat. It gripped his dick, and Percy was going to explode.

Filthy, wet sounds came from Juney's lips as saliva flew from his mouth, and his eyes watered. But he didn't want Percy to stop—urged him to keep going. Percy's abdomen tensed, and his movements became erratic. He panted hoarsely as his balls drew up and filled Juney's mouth with his cum.

Darkness was clouding the edge of his vision when Juney came face to face with him again. Junes grabbed his jaw and brought their lips together. He tasted his cum. It coated his mouth as Percy licked it into him. Percy whimpered. It felt so dirty to have Juney feed him his own cum, but it also made him hotter than anything ever had.

Junes pulled back, licking his lips. "You can tattoo my name on your throat whenever you want. It would be another matching tattoo."

Percy wanted to marry this man.

No. Percy *would* marry this man.

Eighteen

WINSTON

The past month had been the greatest of his life.

He hadn't been too far down or too far high. Hadn't been dull either. He felt evened out and present. The medication change seemed to work since he didn't have trouble sleeping anymore.

That meant he was fully present for all of the moments he'd had with Percy, and there had been so fucking many. Basically every second of every day.

Percy rolled off of the float he'd been laying on and landed in the water with a splash. Winston watched Percy's long, dark hair fan out underwater as he swam toward him. His head popped from the surface a couple of feet from him. Percy smoothed his hair back and droplets of water rolled down his body like some shit out of a movie.

Percy huffed a breath. "Needed to cool off. Wow, that felt good."

Winston dunked his head into the water to cool down as well. The temperature was damn near in the triple digits today, so they really shouldn't be in the pool to begin with. Not to mention, their tattoos were still fresh. But Percy insisted on a quick dip. "Alright, time to get out before the sunburn gets worse than it already is."

They trudged out of the water, and Winston was finding it hard to focus on anything other than Percy's toned abs and long legs. He was a fucking picture.

Percy couldn't keep his eyes off of him either. Winston loved it. Shot his ego all the way into the sky. He sat down, and Percy didn't even look at any of the other chairs. He sat on Winston's lap instead. It was a tight fit but neither of them seemed to mind.

He tilted his head back so he could see Percy's eyes. They both were sunburnt on their faces and shoulders. Percy's cheeks were a little red but not enough to be painful. It was hardly a burn.

Percy dropped a chlorine-soaked kiss to his lips and held Winston close.

The silence stretched on for a long time, and Winston didn't feel the need to end it. But Percy had other ideas. He knew what was coming.

"I'm leaving tomorrow. Going back home for a couple of months, and you can't stop me. This is what I *want* to do," Percy said.

There was a twinge in Winston's chest at the thought of being that far away from Percy for two months—especially over something as ridiculous as this. "You aren't going anywhere," he stated.

"Juney, I won't let you leave the band. You deserve—"

"Percy," he interrupted. "I have a plan."

Percy floundered for a second but landed on, "No."

Winston snorted. "Yes."

"Fill me in on this magical plan then."

"All you need to know is that I'm getting on that tour bus tomorrow, and I will be performing at our first show. You'll stay here." Winston saw the wheels spinning behind Percy's eyes, but this was so out of left field. He wouldn't be able to figure it out. "Just trust me."

"This is a big deal, Junes. There are real repercussions," Percy warned.

Winston knew what the repercussions were, and he was ready to accept all of them. His cause was more important than Heatwave's money. "It will be okay in the end."

Percy chewed on his lower lip. "Well, I know you can't be swayed. I'll support you no matter what."

Winston nudged Percy to stand so they could go back inside. It was way too cold after being outside for that long, especially considering his trunks were still damp. Percy immediately started shivering, and goosebumps rippled across Winston's skin.

They rushed to Winston's room and dropped their shorts. They both pulled on sweats and Percy wore one of Winston's sweaters. No matter how many times he did that, it still made something warm curl around Winston's heart. Percy gave him those kinds of feelings a lot lately. Being in love was fucking overwhelming.

Percy slid into bed and wrapped up in the blankets before Winston could even turn the TV on. He joined him in bed. "Warm me up," he said. It was a joke. They both knew Percy would be glued to him anyway. Percy obliged and fit himself to Winston's side while he picked a movie to watch.

He didn't think it was possible to love Percy anymore than

he already did, but the trust he'd been putting into Winston was lifting him to new heights. He worried that he'd let Percy down since that was what happened more often than not. But he was equally as confident, if not more, that he would do the right thing.

He'd already told Gage and Torin and they basically said, "Why the hell not?"

The only people that mattered to him were the only ones supporting him in this—for now.

They stood in the shadow that the tour bus cast. Percy wouldn't let go of him. They were hugging, but it felt more like they were strangling each other to death. "It'll only be one day max," Winston said. "The first show is in Orlando tonight. That's it."

Percy slowly let go of him. "Fine," he sighed. "I know I'm being dramatic. I'm just worried. You won't even tell me what's happening."

Winston ran his fingers through Percy's perfect hair. He brushed Percy's hair every day now. "You'll know soon enough."

"Let's go, loverboy," Gage yelled from the entrance of the bus.

Winston pressed a quick kiss to Percy's lips and walked away without another word. He knew they would stay there for another hour if he didn't cut it short.

Once Winston was on the bus, it all hit him at once. All of the memories he'd had from their last tour. They'd drink to get loose before a show, and then they'd get hammered afterward, usually with a couple of groupies. Percy would kick it too, but all he did was smoke copious amounts of weed—no alcohol for him.

"Back on the fucking road," Gage said.

Torin passed him a joint. Winston hadn't drunk since before Black Diamond, and he reckoned he shouldn't start now. Who knew what kind of crazy shit his meds would do when mixed with alcohol.

He hadn't been tempted to drink at all, so this should be easy. He'd always known that the alcohol and drug abuse were symptoms of his mental health.

The drive to Orlando took about four hours, but it felt way faster. Gage and Torin had done most of the talking. Winston had paid attention, but his mind was floating around somewhere else. Another life for him and Percy. One where they were both happy. He would make it fucking happen.

They were getting close to it. Winston couldn't remember the last time he had thoughts of suicide or self-harm. He didn't wake up with a head full of negative thoughts that would bog him down all day until he couldn't take it anymore and crawled back into bed. Everything wasn't a fucking drag, he was actually capable of feeling joy without being manic.

He usually felt damn near sick to his stomach with anxiety before their shows, but as they walked through the back entrance into the amphitheater, Winston felt fine.

Their temporary manager, Rhonda, appeared and led them down a crowded hallway. She had traveled separately and arrived before them to get things set up properly. That was what Percy did, but he also traveled with the band. There was no way in hell he'd have Percy out sleeping in shady motels in random cities every other night, and regardless of what had happened between them, Percy was still their friend.

They were all dressed and ready for the show in their normal, everyday clothes. Winston wore black jeans that were ripped to shreds and a t-shirt. Usually, he'd go shirtless, but now he had Percy's name plastered on his chest.

"The tattoo on your hand will be a dead giveaway. You hold your mic with that one," Torin pointed out.

Winston smirked. "Oh, I know." That was intentional on his part.

Torin shook his head fondly.

"Crazy bastard," Gage said before tipping back a shot of vodka. Winston watched him take two more in rapid succession. Winston's stomach turned. He used to drink vodka like water just like that.

Gage was one of the few people he cared about, so maybe Winston should at least try talking with him. See what was going on inside of his head because it probably wasn't pretty. He just wanted to make sure Gage was alright. Now wasn't the time for that though.

They were getting hyped up for their first show on the tour which might even be their last, but Winston knew everything would be okay.

This was a big one. A sold-out show in an arena that holds twenty-thousand people. They could hear the rumble of their voices through the concrete walls. Their final opener had just finished, so Telltale Dream was up in thirty. "Which new song should we surprise them with?"

"Dream Blue," they said in unison.

"We'll play it after you handle your shit," Gage said.

Their first song was one of their most popular ones. It would get the crowd's energy up. He would do it right after that song finished.

Rhonda swung the door open and beckoned them out. She

was a nice lady and all. Did the job. But she wasn't Percy. That was all it took for Winston to have it out for her.

Torin put out a joint, and Gage downed another shot. Winston patted his pocket and was ready to go. They followed Rhonda through a hallway and up some stairs until they were stage right.

Feel-good music was playing for the crowd. Thousands of voices sang the lyrics, and the sheer force of it had Winston's hair standing on end. It was a feeling he wasn't sure he would ever get used to.

They were affixed with their earpieces so they could hear themselves over the noise.

Their intro music came on, the lights went out, and the crowd got louder. Gage and Torin were the first onstage—Gage was behind his drum set and Torin was in the front with his bass in hand.

Winston was handed his guitar and ushered onstage. Bright, blue lights lit up the stage.

Winston grabbed the mic and the crowd fucking roared. Their intro music led straight into the first song on their setlist. It had a catchy chorus that everyone loved, but Gage was a monster on the drums and Torin's solo made the crowd melt. Winston shredded. His fingers moved lightning-fast with the right amount of precision. Their music wasn't meant to sound perfectly polished. It had distortion and grit.

People were shoved against the rail, white-knuckling it for dear life so they wouldn't lose their front-row spot. Winston tried to make eye contact with as many of them as he could. Winston knew what it felt like to have your favorite band only a few feet away and wanted to make it worthwhile.

Winston had to scream the last verse of the song. It was a

guttural, harsh vocal. A circle pit opened up in the crowd, and Winston encouraged it.

As the song came to an end, the lights shifted, and Winston grabbed a bottle of water for his throat. There was high-octane adrenaline pulsing through his veins, and the plastic bottle got crushed without even meaning to. His hands were stiff from gripping the fretboard of his guitar.

Gage did a slow drum roll to get the crowd's attention again since they were gushing to each other about how amazing Telltale was. Winston wasn't sucking his own dick. It was just a fact that he'd come to expect.

He scanned the arena, trying his best to take it all in, but it was unfathomable. Even when it was right in front of his face, he found it hard to believe. But their energy was palpable from the stage, and they fed off of it.

Torin threw his guitar pick into the sea of people, pulled out another from his pocket, and smiled when he saw a girl brandishing it in the air. Winston sauntered paced with the mic in hand. When he brought it up to speak, it was clear as day on the big screen.

He heard what sounded like people whispering to each other about *his* private business, but Winston wasn't deserving of privacy anymore. That was one of the many costs of their fame.

Heatwave Records expected him to release a statement that denied all of the allegations. Winston thought they were endlessly fucking stupid, and if people were going to speak on his life, he'd give them the story straight from his mouth.

"Make some noise if this is your first time seeing us live," he said, and the crowd roared back at him. "Now, make some noise if you've seen us before." Their response was loud but not louder than the first lot. "It sounds like we have some new

Telltale Dream fans. We appreciate you no matter how long you've been around."

Torin looked at him expectantly, and Winston figured it was time. "I want to share something personal with y'all tonight.

"I've struggled with my mental health for as long as I can remember, but I'd never wanted to admit it. It seemed to be passed down to me from my mother who I loved dearly.

"I left my mental health unchecked for so long that I turned to alcohol and drugs to help me make it through each day for the people I cared about. But sometimes, my mental illnesses were stronger than me. They won out. Earlier this summer, I sank too low to be retrieved and attempted suicide for the second time in my life."

Winston gave the crowd—and himself—a minute to process it. He never thought that someday he would tell the world about his deepest insecurity. Winston had run from it his entire life, but now he had to wear it on his sleeve for millions to see.

Looking into the crowd, he didn't see any ridicule. He saw glistening eyes, tears, and soft frowns.

He also saw smartphones held up in the air, recording the event. That was exactly what he wanted them to do, but he wasn't finished.

"Gage and Torin have been two of my closest friends since I met them at a house party nearly four years ago," he said, smirking at his bandmates. Torin held his hand over his heart dramatically and Gage blew him a kiss.

"I have one more friend. He's even closer to me than them. We've been friends since we were seven years old after we met under a live oak tree back home in Georgia. We've been insepa-rable ever since. His name is Percy." Mumbles and gasps rippled through the sea of people like a wave that crashed at his feet, threatening to pull him under. He could see their mouths moving, probably coming up with lies.

"While I was working on my mental health, I wrote a letter that was never intended to see the light of day. It was just an exercise to help me free up space in my mind." Winston reached into his pocket and procured a folded-up piece of lined notebook paper. The crowd gasped. They were wide-eyed with disbelief, but he cleared his throat and began.

Percy,

Knowing that you won't ever see this note makes writing it a lot easier. I never had a fucking diary, but I do write song lyrics—mostly about you. I've been writing songs about you since we were sixteen. That was when I first started to explore songwriting, and the only thing I could think to write about was you. It hasn't changed yet, and that's why it takes me so long to write a song. My brain always circles back to you.

I was possessive of you from the moment we met. I'm not sure when it shifted to more, but fuck did it shift. You became my world, my obsession, my purpose. And I don't care how unhealthy that sounds. It wasn't ever a choice on my part. It was more like things slid into place, where they were always meant to be.

You saved me before I knew that I needed saving, and you never gave up on me. I made it so hard for you, but you stayed through everything. No matter how deep I sink, you're always there with your tether. Your light.

My mother had a glass figurine of a bluebird that she kept on her nightstand. It's the only thing I have of hers. She told me that it symbolized happiness. I didn't understand at the time because she didn't seem happy at all, but she watched sunlight refract through the glass every day. It made her smile.

You've always been the only reason I've ever felt anything other than half-dead.

You've always been my bluebird.

He folded the paper up and shoved it back into his pocket. The tears he'd been ignoring were sliding down his face. Torin was looking at him like he could see directly into Winston's soul. Gage roughly rubbed at his eyes.

When Winston dared to look at the thousands of people that had witnessed whatever the hell that was, what he saw nearly bowled him over. He realized that he'd never heard a crowd be this silent. That paired with the way they were looking at him with too much empathy to bear let him know that he'd made the right decision.

Their true fans would stick around, and Winston was willing to bet that there were far more people in support of them than not. It's just that negativity was always the loudest.

Videos of what he'd just done were almost definitely spreading through the internet like wildfire.

Heatwave has no choice in the matter anymore. The fans made it for them.

Winston took his shirt off, and the crowd collectively gasped at the tattoo. "This next song is from our upcoming album, and you all get to hear it first. It's called Dream Blue."

Everyone in the arena went crazy, and they still had the same energy an hour later when the show was over.

Winston, Gage, and Torin exited the stage the same way they came in. Rhonda watched them leave wordlessly. Winston couldn't blame her. There wasn't anything she could say because she'd felt the same way the crowd did.

As soon as they were on the tour bus, Winston's brain caught up to his fucking mouth. He felt raw and carved up. The space around him might've been too sensitive to touch. It was a comforting thing that Gage and Torin knew how he could be, and yet they still always had his back.

"That was perfectly done. Incredibly brave of you, Junes," Torin said.

All three of them were drenched in sweat, and Winston's chest was still heaving from the exertion of performing for that long. It was their first time in a couple of years, and it showed.

There was a soft knock on the door, and Winston let Rhonda inside. She stood in the middle of the room, fidgety and timid. "Mr. Marshall called. He said you did a great job, and that it didn't matter how you got to the finish line as long as you got there," she cleared her throat. "He also said that you'll talk to him before doing anything like this again, or he won't be so forgiving."

Gage snorted and Torin shielded the smile on his face with his hand. "Maybe you should relay to him that his balls are in our pockets, so he shouldn't throw around threats," Winston said calmly.

Torin shook his head quickly. "Nope. No. Rhonda, that isn't necessary."

"I need to get ahold of Percy," Winston said.

"Oh, he should be here any minute now. Apparently, he left sometime after we did," Rhonda replied.

Winston set his jaw. He should've known Percy wouldn't stay put, but it wasn't that unreasonable. Winston had left him without answers. If the roles were switched, Winston would've done worse.

The door slammed open. Percy rushed in, and Rhonda slipped out behind him.

Percy's cheeks flushed when Winston pinned him with his gaze. He grabbed Percy's hand and led him back to the only bedroom on their bus. It had a queen-sized bed, otherwise, there were four large bunks. They'd always rotated who got to sleep in the bedroom to keep things fair between them. None of them were more important than the other.

Once they were inside, Percy launched himself at Winston. For several long minutes, Winston breathed in Percy's smell. It did wonders at soothing his mind. Percy had always centered Winston. "So, you saw?"

Percy nodded.

"How did you see if you were driving?" Winston asked. His brows were a hard line, and Percy better not say he'd watched it while driving.

Percy hugged him tighter. "Amir called me, losing his mind, so I pulled over. I still haven't been on social media, but Amir texted me a video of your entire speech. He said that a million people saw it before the show had even ended."

Winston moved them over to the bed. He needed to hold Percy, especially after the day he had. His heart would be sore for weeks.

Percy glued himself to Winston's side and hooked his leg around Winston's. It was just like he'd always done, and it still felt the same, if not better. Winston couldn't ever get Percy close enough. It drove him crazy that no matter what they did, he always felt like he needed more of him. After tamping those feelings down for so many years, it was a relief that he didn't have to anymore.

Percy hummed softly into his skin, and Winston threaded his fingers through the hair at Percy's nape.

Winston's eyelids were getting heavier by the second until Percy spoke. "You never told me that about your mom."

It was gentle. Not accusatory—Percy would never. "I felt like I had to keep it to myself, just like the feelings I had for you."

Percy stroked Winston's bicep. "Now the whole world knows."

Winston tightened his grip on Percy's hair and used it to bring their lips together. Winston had full control and kissed him hard. The way he devoured Percy was violent, but Percy didn't seem to mind. Percy's eyes were dazed when he blinked them open.

"Now the whole world knows that you're mine and always have been," he corrected. "My Percy. My bluebird. No one else can have you."

Percy brushed his lips against Winston's, featherlight. "You're the only person I've ever wanted. You've always been my Juney."

Winston wasted no time. He walked swiftly across the yard past his favorite live oak tree.

Their small town felt different from Miami in every way. There was a whole lot *less* here. Less cars. Less concrete. Less people. But there was also a whole lot more. More fresh air, more trees, and more stars in the sky.

He found the overgrown path he'd worn in the dirt years ago. He moved through it, branches smacking his face and grazing his arms. His skin crawled by the time he made it to the other side. He wiped his hands all over his body in case any spiders had hitched a ride.

When he finally let his eyes travel from the weeds up to his dad's house, his face flushed hot. It... hadn't changed at all.

He passed the same broken-down car on his way to the porch. His truck was there, so Winston was sure he would be home. The dilapidated porch creaked beneath his weight. He took heavy footsteps in hopes that it would give his dad some kind of warning.

The door swung open before he had a chance to knock, and he met his dad's wild-eyed gaze. It was the same look on Winston's face.

It'd only been five years, but the man was noticeably older looking. His wrinkles were deeper, and he just looked haggard in general.

Winston watched him closely and saw no signs of anger. "Dad," he said by way of greeting.

"Son," he replied, barely a grunt.

Winston's mouth was suddenly very dry. "Happy Thanksgiving."

His dad frowned. "What are you doing here?"

Winston hadn't exactly expected a warm welcome, but his

heart still panged. "It isn't uncommon for people to visit their parents on holidays."

His dad leaned against the doorframe. "No shit, Winston. Never once expected it though. Reckoned I'd be waiting 'til the cows come home."

Winston cocked his head to the side. "And would you blame me? You haven't even invited me in yet."

His dad stepped back, pulling the door wide open.

The living room was just the same except beer cans weren't decorating every surface. He didn't see any trash either. He saw the kitchen behind his dad, and there weren't even dishes piled up in the sink. His face twisted in confusion. "Did you get a roommate?" he asked.

His dad took a seat in his recliner, and Winston hesitantly sat on the couch. There was sunshine beaming through the open windows. His dad never pulled the curtains back when he'd lived there.

He heard the flick of a lighter. His dad lit a cigarette and placed the ashtray on the old coffee table. He was inviting Winston to smoke a cigarette with him.

Winston narrowed his eyes as he lit a cigarette of his own.

What the fuck was going on?

"I don't have a roommate," he grumbled. Winston looked at him expectantly. "I quit drinking."

Winston blinked. "You expect me to believe that line of bullshit?"

His dad didn't even flinch. Didn't retaliate. He said, "I don't *expect* anything from you."

A sweat broke out on the back of Winston's neck. He couldn't make sense of any of this. He shot to his feet and rushed to the kitchen. When he swung the door open, there wasn't a beer in sight. Winston's face was set in stone when he sat back down. "When? Why now? Why did I have to endure all of those years with a drunk for a father?"

The damage had already been done, so Winston wasn't sure he needed an answer to that. It didn't matter anymore.

But his dad spoke anyway. "Percy gave me a call after you tried taking your life again," his voice broke, but otherwise, his expression remained hardened.

Winston clenched his teeth behind thinned lips. Percy was so fucking lucky Winston was in love with him. "That's why you quit?" Winston deadpanned.

The smoke from their cigarettes curled in the air, opaque in the sunlight. A conversation with his dad wouldn't have even gotten this far back then. Despite his better judgment, he found himself hanging on to every word. He didn't have a choice in the matter.

"It was my goal to quit this year. I stayed away from the bar and slowly tapered down the amount I drank. Very, very slowly. Until I got that call," he trailed off and put out his cigarette. His elbows hit his knees, and he roughly scrubbed his face with his hands. "I've been praying. Asking God for guidance."

Winston ignored the religious part like he always had, but he was confused about the first thing he'd said. "If that's the case, why didn't you quit the first time I tried to off myself?"

"Don't be so crude," he snapped. His father looked at him with a deep crease between his brows. Winston stiffened. It was the first sign of anger he'd seen from him so far, but he wouldn't even call it that. His dad was upset. "I didn't stop drinking because I was weak. I drank because your mother left, and then I had to drink even more after you attempted to do the same."

Winston's heart raced. "All you did was ruin what relationship we had left which wasn't much to begin with. It was easier to feel like you wanted me to go."

His father flinched and covered his mouth. "I know. I don't expect you to forgive me. Once again, I don't expect anything from you. You're my son. I was supposed to do good by you, not the other way around."

Too little, too late, Winston thought, even though his chest ached.

His father hadn't said anything wrong. It was the exact opposite, and it was throwing him off. His dad didn't just say insightful shit like that. "Why are you talking like that?" he asked, and he knew his dad would know what he meant.

"I've been going into town for AA meetings every week," he mumbled. "Helped me to understand things that I couldn't before."

Winston slouched back into the couch, overwhelmed by having a full conversation with his dad. A normal, healthy conversation. It was something he'd never thought possible.

His father's jaw was covered in salt and pepper stubble, and his hair covered his ears. He might've gotten sober, but he still didn't put much effort into taking care of himself. That went down the drain after his wife died. Winston knew that if they wanted to unpack everything they both carried on their shoulders, it would take forever and a day. And seeing as how his dad was... tolerable now, he suspected they would talk again. They had time.

But there was still one thing he needed to be answered. "Why haven't you touched the money?"

His father knew what money he was talking about and shook his head. "That's your money, Winston. You've earned it. You deserve it."

"You don't think you deserve it?" His father looked at him

like he was dumb. Winston scoffed. "I don't deserve it either, so pot meet kettle. You might as well use it. Accept it, and move on. Build a new home, so you don't have to worry about a leaky roof and sagging foundation. You own all of this land. You can do whatever you want with it. Build a car garage like you've always wanted to."

Winston understood his father's mentality, but the money would never go away. But his childhood home would continue falling apart and his dad would continue living half of a life.

Winston knew what that was like and didn't necessarily think anyone deserved it. He looked around and wondered how alone his dad must feel. It was the bed that he made for himself, but that didn't make it any easier to get through.

Maybe therapy was doing something for him because he couldn't stomach the thought of his father sitting here alone on Thanksgiving.

Winston stood up and spotted the narrow basket his dad kept next to his recliner. It was one of Telltale Dream's covers with *Electric Metal Magazine*. There were numerous magazines and newspaper articles. Winston could see enough to know they were all about his band.

He straightened his spine. This would be the make-or-break moment for his dad. "Have you heard the news about me lately?"

"'Bout your relationship with the Lovell boy?" he asked as if he didn't know Percy's name.

Winston pinched the bridge of his nose. He'd walk away and never return if need be. "Yes. I'm dating Percy," he said easily.

His dad's thick brows lifted. "Okay?"

Winston's eyes narrowed to slits. *"Okay?"* he repeated. "You don't care?"

"Am I supposed to be upset? You've been gay as long as I've known you."

Winston gaped at him. "You never even liked Percy."

His father leveled him with a tired gaze. "I didn't like anyone. Not even myself. I've got nothing against the boy."

That was another thing he could relate to, except he had one person that he liked. "Come to the Lovell's for dinner," Winston said.

"No," he said without even taking a second to think about it.

"They invited you to come. What's the hold-up?"

Judging by what he knew about the man sitting in front of him, this had to be about pride. He was embarrassed by all that he'd done, and the Lovell's were his witnesses.

"I'd rather sit here and watch my program," he said, grabbing the TV remote, and effectively ignoring Winston's presence.

His stomach sank—only a little. That was answer enough. He pulled open the front door, but his dad's words stopped him. "I love you," he said evenly.

Winston froze with his back to his dad, thankful that he couldn't see Winston's face.

"I don't expect anything from you," his dad repeated. It was the third time.

His dad hadn't said those three words since his hospital stay after his first suicide attempt. Winston knew in his soul that he loved his dad, but it didn't feel like the kind of love that deserved to be said aloud, yet.

'Yet' hadn't ever been an option until today. With that thought, he nodded and closed the door behind himself.

Winston made it into the Lovell's front yard and passed Mrs. Birdie's marigolds and daylilies. They were as beautiful as

Winston thought they'd be. Her garden always was. He hit the steps to the wraparound porch and let himself inside.

Immediately, Percy's extended family's voices reached his ears. They were talking over each other and laughing. Percy's household was usually quiet enough to hear a pin drop when it was only the immediate family. The noise was jarring at first, but Winston had spent enough time at Percy's family's holiday gatherings over the years to tune them out quickly. There were arched entryways on either side of him and a large staircase straight ahead. Framed pictures adorned the walls. Percy's home had always felt warm to him. There was soft lighting and thick rugs that cushioned your feet against the hardwood flooring. Even with all the competing voices, Winston felt like he was home.

He got his boots off and stumbled over one of the dozen pairs of shoes at the door. He righted himself then went left toward the kitchen. Percy usually liked helping his mom, and Winston appreciated it since it gave him an excuse to escape the crowd. All the family stuff became overwhelming pretty quickly.

It was no surprise when he happened upon Mrs. Birdie washing dishes and Percy hefting a large, golden turkey from the oven.

Shit. It was nearly time to eat.

Percy looked up, locked eyes with Winston, and a smile lit up his face. He put the turkey down, rushed over, and wrapped Winston in a hug. Winston realized how much he needed it after the hug went on for too long by conventional standards.

Eventually, Percy backed up a step. "Did it go okay?"

Winston winced. "Went way better than I expected it to. We might start talking to each other."

Percy grinned. "That's a great start."

Mrs. Birdie quickly put him and Percy to work—putting out serving spoons, carving the turkey and the like— and, before long, people were starting to file in to load up their plates. Winston realized he was starving. He pulled Percy by the baggy sleeve of his sweater, which actually belonged to Winston. It was the same sweater he'd worn the first time Winston had fucked him, so he guessed that counted for sentimental value. He also felt a little smug, knowing Percy chose that perfectly inappropriate thing to wear to Thanksgiving dinner.

As they waited in line for the food, Mrs. Birdie gave him a one-armed hug. She knew that was about as much he could handle. "I'm so happy you both made it, sweetheart. We'll talk later, okay?"

"Yes ma'am," Winston responded.

Winston and Percy grabbed their plates, and she pointed out which dishes were vegan. There was a wide variety of roasted vegetables among other things, but those and her homemade vegan mac and cheese were his favorite.

Once Winston filled up his plate, he followed Percy through all of his family members until they emerged in the living room. Winston sighed. He hadn't realized how hot it'd been in the kitchen. They ate while standing up since they were younger than most of the people who gathered here today.

Once everyone had a plate, Mrs. Birdie got everyone's attention. She was sweaty, and her cheeks were flushed red, but she looked so incredibly happy.

"Thank you, everyone, for being here. There are some new faces and some old, and my amazing son and his partner were finally able to make it back home for a holiday," she said. Everyone's heads swiveled to look at Percy and Winston. Percy elbowed him in the side. So, he waved at everyone with something very close to a smile and began shoveling mac and cheese into his mouth so they would stop staring. "Okay! Would anyone like to say something they're thankful for?"

Percy stepped forward. "I will! I'm thankful for Juney," he said, and Winston choked on a roasted potato in his surprise. As he was clearing his throat, he blinked his eyes open and found Percy down on one knee in the middle of his entire family. Time seemed to slow down.

There were gasps and Mrs. Birdie's hand flew to her mouth.

Winston's heart was in his throat. Percy looked more confident than Winston had ever seen him. He was perfectly calm.

Someone took Winston's plate, and he wished they hadn't. Now what was he supposed to do with his hands? They trembled.

"Juney. I'm not as perfect with words as you are, so hopefully this is okay. You found me fourteen years ago, and I've been clinging to you ever since. I needed you then, I need you now, and I always will. Somehow, you don't mind, and somehow, you need me just as badly.

"I know in my heart that we'll always have each other, but I want rings to signify it too," he said with a smile. Winston heard quiet laughs from the people around them.

Mr. Lovell handed Percy a small black box, and Percy opened it, revealing a silver wedding band. He met Percy's watery eyes.

"Will you marry me?" he asked, sounding unsure for the first time.

Winston couldn't believe it. Couldn't believe any of it, but he leaned over and pulled Percy to stand in front of him. He did what he'd been wanting to do since they got here. He slammed his lips against Percy's and kissed him. It was big and wet and definitely not appropriate, but Winston didn't care. It settled him. Steadied his heart, so when he broke the kiss and held out his hand, it didn't shake.

Percy grabbed it and slid the band onto Winston's finger. Then he brought Winston's hand to his lips and kissed the bluebird tattoo. Winston saw the scar running the length of his forearm and frowned. If it had worked, he wouldn't have gotten to experience this. But if it hadn't happened, he wasn't sure they would've made it to this point. He liked to believe they would've. That no matter what, they were always supposed to end up together. He needed to believe that.

Winston pulled him back into his arms and squeezed. He allowed himself to scan the crowd. They'd started to eat again. Some were wiping their eyes. Winston was about to pull away when his eyes landed on... his dad.

His body jolted against Percy's, and he looked up to see what was wrong. His dad stood in the very back with tears streaming down his face.

A lump swelled in his throat. Maybe he and his dad would be alright.

All he knew was that he was better than he'd ever been, and he was going to marry his bluebird.

ACKNOWLEDGMENTS

This book couldn't have been completed without my AMAZING alpha reader Anna. She deals with my bullshit (*a lot* of bullshit) like it's nothing.

My best friend for being my pillar through everything always.

My amazing editor, Heather. I'm endlessly grateful for her eyes and her willingness to work with me because <u>I am a mess</u>.

My beta readers: Sam, Amy, and Rosy. They did magic, and this book wouldn't be what it is without them. And another thanks to Sam for sensitivity reading this one.

As always, my street team. They've been here, rooting for me, since the beginning.

A huge thanks to Nicole for coming up with this shared world series idea and to all the other authors who came together and brought this thing to life.

Of course, I want to shout out my readers. I don't fully understand why y'all are here but, damn, am I grateful. I love all of you.

Last but not least, I want to thank the surgeon who removed my appendix when I was almost done writing this book. It might not have ever been completed if it weren't for her.

Redbull. That's all.

ABOUT THE AUTHOR

Bailey is an author who loves writing LGBTQ+ romance books.
They'd much rather write about fictional worlds and characters than themself, but they love interacting with readers.

You can stalk them here:

f facebook.com/authorbaileynicole
📷 instagram.com/authorbaileynicole

ALSO BY BAILEY NICOLE

Worthless Boys

Cruel and Careless

High and Hopeless

Lone and Lifeless

Standalones

The Weight of Your Wishes

His Revelry: A Dark MM Romance Novella

Consumed: A Black Diamond Novel

Made in United States
North Haven, CT
08 September 2023

41292376R20221